DOUBLE CONTACT

BOOKS BY JAMES WHITE

The Secret Visitor (1957)
Second Ending (1962)
Deadly Litter (1964)
Escape Orbit (1965)
The Watch Below (1966)
All Judgement Fled (1968)
The Aliens Among Us (1969)
Tomorrow Is Too Far (1971)
Dark Inferno (1972)
The Dream Millennium (1974)
Monsters and Medics (1977)
Underkill (1979)
Future Past (1982)
Federation World (1988)
The Silent Stars Go By (1991)
The White Papers (1996)

THE SECTOR GENERAL SERIES

Hospital Station (1962)
Star Surgeon (1963)
Major Operation (1971)
Ambulance Ship (1979)
Sector General (1983)
Star Healer (1985)
Code Blue—Emergency (1987)
The Genocidal Healer (1992)
The Galactic Gourmet (Tor, 1996)
Final Diagnosis (Tor, 1997)
Mind Changer (Tor, 1998)
Double Contact (Tor, 1999)

DOUBLE CONTACT

A SECTOR GENERAL NOVEL

JAMES WHITE

TOR®

A TOM DOHERTY ASSOCIATES BOOK
NEW YORK

DOUBLE CONTACT

Edited by Teresa Nielsen Hayden

A Tor Book
Published by Tom Doherty Associates, LLC
175 Fifth Avenue
New York, NY 10010

www.tor.com

Tor® is a registered trademark of Tom Doherty Associates, LLC.

Library of Congress Cataloging-in-Publication Data
White, James, 1928–
    Double contact : a Sector General novel / James White.—1st ed.
        p.   cm.—(Tor fantasy) (The Sector General series)
    ISBN 0-312-87041-8 (alk. paper)
    I. Title. II. Series: White, James, 1928–   Sector General series.
  PR6073.H494D6   1999
  823'.914—dc21   99-37459
                                                     CIP

First Edition: November 1999

Printed in the United States of America

0 9 8 7 6 5 4 3 2 1

DOUBLE CONTACT

CHAPTER 1

The late afternoon sun, its outlines shredded by ground-heat distortion and the continuous toxic gales that swept the planet, wavered in and out of visibility in the brown sky like a dull red and ragged-edged flag. When it set in a few hours' time there would be total darkness. The moon was too dim to be seen through the turbulent and nearly opaque atmosphere, and the stars had not been visible from the surface for close on three centuries.

The world that was Trolann raged and stormed and stank all around them as they paused for a moment outside the first of the series of detoxification chambers that gave access to their underground home, because they wanted to look at the familiar and abhorrent scenery for what would be the last time.

Their lifesuit sensors told of a film of insects and windblown spores that were trying vainly to penetrate the superfine joints in the mechanisms that provided ground mobility, and kept their visors clean so that they could see virtually nothing with more clarity.

"Not a druul in sight," said Jasam. "It's safe to go in."

He pressed the activator on the first entry seal with the suit's forward manipulator, then swept it around to indicate the dull, wavering sun, the driving, poisonous fog and the blurred outlines of the surface extensions of their neighbors' homes. He looked at Keet and sighed.

"We had a good life together here," he said, "and for the next few days"—he made an attempt to lighten their mood as he went on—"this hi-tech hole in the ground will be a very happy home."

"Until we find a new one," said Keet, impatient as always when he stated the obvious. "I'm hungry and I want us out of these things."

"Me, too," said Jasam with enthusiasm; then, in a more reasonable voice he went on. "But there's no need to be hungry. The suit food is no worse than the stuff in the larder. Since our final selection it's been the best available. So go ahead and eat; that's as good a way as any of passing the decontamination time."

"No," said Keet firmly. "I want us to eat together, every chance we get while we still can, and not separately like a couple of working colleagues. Sometimes, Jasam, you display the romantic sensitivity of, of a druul in heat."

He did not have to answer this grossest of all personal insults because they both knew that she was joking, and that people only joked about that particular form of hellish Trolanni life in an attempt to hide their utter fear and loathing for it. Besides, his answer would come later in actions rather than words.

Neither of them made use of their built-in food supply while their suits went through the slow, tedious, but absolutely necessary stages of surface cleansing with disinfectant sprays, surface irradiation, and flash heating. Many of the microorganic and insect life-forms that had recently evolved on the surface, when given the chance to penetrate the defenses of a Trolanni household, had proved themselves capable of wiping out the occupants in a few minutes. But when they both finally emerged into the core living quarters, they were as sure as it was possible to be that they were free of unwanted organic company.

Jasam stood for a moment looking at Keet, or rather at the delicately contoured head, shapely body, and short, tapering limbs of her lifesuit, while she stared back at the taller, more ruggedly handsome, and well-muscled shape that he wore. Protective suits were invariably as well-formed and lifelike as their owners could afford. While still young adults, Keet and himself had progressed to a level of excellence in their field where they could afford the best. But the people inside those realistic lifesuits were much smaller, more sickly, and, regrettably, not nearly as beautiful as their handsome body coverings.

Outside them, however, they could touch each other without a cybernetic interface diluting or crudely enhancing every tactile sensation.

With intense but controlled impatience he detached himself from the suit's visual, aural, and tactile relays, its food and water spigots, and, even more cautiously, from the deeply implanted waste-elimination systems. He had extricated himself before she did, and watched her lovingly as she opened the long, abdominal seal and struggled free like an adult newborn climbing slowly out of its mother's womb.

Her body, as did his own, showed the areas of rash, the skin discoloration, the pocking and scars of past skin eruptions that were the visible inheritance of living in an environment that no longer supported their kind of life. But she looked little different from the time he had seen her like this on their first night of mating, and she was beautiful. When she freed herself, their beautiful and handsomely proportioned lifesuits were left lying lifelessly on the floor as they crawled eagerly towards each other.

When they had to pause for a necessary rest, they ate a meal to which Keet had added various decorative and olfactory touches to disguise the taste of their standard, aseptic, and machine-processed food. But the searchsuit project chief had told them that their unsuited time together would be limited to the next three days, and eating and resting was not what they most wanted to do together. They tried not to talk about the project, but there were times when their physical and emotional resistance was so low that the subject sneaked up on them.

"I'm not complaining, mind," said Keet, "but after three days of this we won't be at our best for the surgeons. We'll be, well, very tired."

"They won't mind that," Jasam replied reassuringly. "You weren't listening between the lines during our last interview. Suit-insertion surgery, especially into an experimental one of this complexity, will be a lengthy, unpleasant procedure that requires conscious, cooperative, and relaxed subjects. Don't worry, about it. At least we'll be in a physically relaxed condition before they go to work on us."

Even though they were already pressed together so tightly that such a thing was physically impossible, Keet tried to snuggle even closer. She said softly, "This is how babies are made."

"Not for us," he replied sharply, and tried without much success for a gentler tone as he went on. "If that had been possible, if either of us had been healthy enough and fertile, we would never have been allowed to volunteer, much less be accepted for *Searchsuit Three*. Instead we would have been buried more deeply and protected behind even more detoxification chambers than we have here, and given every comfort a mortal Trolanni could desire while teams of doctors tried to provide the medical and psychological support that might enable the sickly members of our poisoned species to procreate and our civilization to survive beyond the next few generations. The emotional feelings or otherwise of the couples concerned for each other would not have been the prime consideration. Survival would have been a necessity, an artificially-supported evolutionary imperative rather than a pleasure."

Once again Keet's expression was reflecting her impatience at being reminded of things she had not forgotten, and he was anxious not to spoil even a moment of their remaining touching time together.

"We would be even more debilitated than we are now," he added quickly, "but without having as much fun."

Even though the honor of being chosen to wear a searchsuit

was greater than that previously accorded to any two members of their race, the pride they both felt was intense, so much so that there was little room in their minds for personal fear. But they did not speak of the project again, and neither did they look at the container that housed the tiny, hermetically-sealed, and triple-protected sphere with its short-duration life support into which they would climb when the project engineers signaled that they were ready for the crew insertion. The few hours spent in that sphere, while it was being transported under maximum protection from their home to the project surgery, would be the last they could ever spend in physical contact with each other.

The first searchsuit had been intercepted and destroyed by the druul while it was still in atmosphere, and the second, if it had succeeded in finding anything, had not returned to report. *Searchsuit Three* was the most advanced and technologically sophisticated fabrication to be produced by Trolanni science and, considering their planet's deteriorating environment and diminished resources, it would almost certainly be the last. On its success rested the hopes of their species.

It was a suit built for the two of them and designed to cater to their physical needs for a period far beyond their most optimistic projected lifetimes on Trolanni. In it they would be in constant communication for as long as they lived. But the suit was huge—bigger by far, and with more complex and wide-ranging control and sensory systems, than either of its predecessors. So large was it that when they wore it, they would never in their remaining lifetimes be able to touch each other again. In spite of the greatly increased anti-druul defenses and the supporting treatments provided by the project's engineers and psychologists, he wondered if the dangers facing them would be mental rather than physical.

"At least," said Keet, as if reading her mind, "we'll be able to play with our dolls."

CHAPTER 2

The inner office of Sector General's new administrator and chief psychologist resembled a medieval torture chamber from the history of Earth, according to the memories of the current DBDG mind donor he was carrying. But the resemblance was not close—partly because a collection of tastefully-chosen views of non-terrestrial land and seascapes hung on the walls, and partly because the torture devices were actually weirdly shaped and deeply upholstered furniture. On these, the other-species staff that had business with Administrator Braithwaite could sit, squat, hang, or otherwise take their ease—assuming that whatever they had been doing had not warranted the criticism of the most powerful being in the hospital.

On this occasion Prilicla's own conscience was clear, and as an empath he knew that the same condition applied to his smartly uniformed companion, Captain Fletcher, who was standing before the big desk beside him. The emotional radiation emanating from the similarly Earth-human Administrator Braithwaite, composed as it was of a strange combination of concern with a strong undercurrent of urgency, was such that Prilicla knew they would not be invited to make use of the office furniture. Even so, the other was for some reason feeling hesitant about speaking.

"Sir," said the captain, glancing at Prilicla, who was hovering close to its shoulder and stirring a few strands of its brown head-fur, "I was told that you wanted to see me urgently. I met Senior Physician Prilicla on the way here, and it had received the same message. We only work together on ambulance-ship rescue missions, so presumably you have another job for *Rhabwar*?"

Braithwaite inclined its head without speaking. Before its recent promotion to administrator it had been a Monitor Corps officer like Fletcher, the principal assistant to the then–Chief Psychologist O'Mara, and an outwardly imperturbable individual who wore its uniform as if it had been born with it as a well-fitting and wrinkle-free second skin. Now that it had resigned its commission, its impeccably-tailored civilian clothing still gave the impression that it was completely in control of itself and, in all physical and mental respects, ready for inspection.

"Possibly," it said finally.

Prilicla was beginning to share the captain's growing feeling of puzzlement. He said, "The administrator feels hesitancy, friend Fletcher. I can read emotions but not thoughts, as you know, but I feel sure that friend Braithwaite would prefer that we volunteered for this particular mission."

"I understand," said Fletcher. Still looking at the administrator, he went on. "We appreciate the politeness, sir, but you must be pretty sure what our response will be, so you would save time by simply telling us to volunteer. *Rhabwar* is maintained in constant flight-readiness, as you well know. The technical and medical crew haven't had any exercise with her for close on six months, and if the mission is urgent . . . well, we can't hurry in hyperspace, so the only response time we can save will be between this office and the dock and, of course, our ship's speed in getting us out to jump distance." It hesitated and glanced quickly towards Prilicla, radiating a degree of uncertainty so mild that it was highly complimentary before it went on. "We volunteer."

Prilicla, who was far from being physically robust, belonged to a species which considered cowardice, moral or otherwise, to be its prime survival characteristic. The possession of a highly developed empathic faculty forced him to be agreeable to everyone in order to keep the emotional radiation in his immediate surroundings as pleasant as possible. He spoke with greater hesitation.

"Friend Braithwaite," he said cautiously, "what precisely are we volunteering for?"

"Thank you both," said the administrator, radiating relief. It pressed a key on its desk console and went on. "I've transferred all the available information to your ship's computer for later study. It isn't much, and all we know for sure is that three distress beacons have been detonated within a standard day of each other from the same location in Sector Eighteen. As we would expect from one of the incompletely explored areas, the first two bore radiation signatures that were new to us as well as being significantly different from each other in signal strength and duration. The third was a Federation standard-issue beacon belonging, we presume, to the Monitor Corps survey cruiser *Terragar*, which was engaged in mapping that sector, and which must have responded to the earlier two distress beacons. Our communications people don't know what to make of those first two beacons, if they were in fact distress beacons. That's why I hesitated about ordering *Rhabwar* to take this one."

Captain Fletcher's voice and emotional radiation still reflected the puzzlement they were both feeling, but Prilicla remained silent because he could feel that the other was about to ask the questions he himself wanted answered.

"Sir," Fletcher said respectfully, "your background is in other-species psychology, so you may not be aware of the technical background. But if this potted lecture is unnecessary, please tell me to shut up.

"Just as we know of only one method of traveling in hyperspace," it went on, "there is only one way of sending a distress signal if a major malfunction occurs and a vessel is stranded in normal space between the stars. Tight-beam subspace radio is not a dependable means of interstellar communication from a ship, subject as it is to interference and distortion from intervening stellar bodies as well as requiring inordinate amounts of power to send, power which a distressed ship is unlikely to have available. But a distress beacon doesn't have to carry intelligence. It is simply a nuclear-powered single-use device which broadcasts a location signal. It is a subspace cry for help which, in a matter of a few minutes or hours, burns itself out.

"Answering such calls for help from regions where the distressed vessel is almost certain to belong to a new, star-traveling species," it concluded, "is the reason why *Rhabwar* was built. I don't understand why you are hesitating, sir."

"Thank you, Captain," said the administrator, showing its teeth briefly in the peculiarly Earth-human snarl that denoted amusement. "Your explanation was clear, concise, and unnecessary. My hesitancy is due to the fact that three seperate distress beacons, two of them with radiation signatures that reveal a low order of design sophistication, were released in the same area. There may be three different and closely positioned ships out there, two of them belonging to a new intelligent species and all of them in trouble. But my communications specialists tell me that the first two appear to be crude devices which might not be distress beacons at all. Instead the signals may have been the radiation byproduct of a hyperspatial weapon of some kind. In short, they may not be cries for help, but shouts of anger. You could find yourselves rescuing other-species casualties who have been involved in an armed conflict. So be careful, with our special ambulance ship as well as your own lives. That is presupposing that Prilicla still intends to take part."

Its two recessed, Earth-human eyes were fixed on Prilicla and it was radiating feelings characteristic of a mind that is concealing something as it continued. "More important matters may require your attention here. The chief medical officer's position on *Rhabwar* is one for which you are overqualified. This would be a good time to nominate a replacement."

Prilicla had been given a legitimate, face-saving excuse for refusing a potentially very dangerous mission, for which he was grateful; but he had also been asked a question which, in an emergency situation like this one, required an immediate answer.

He said, "My principal assistant, Pathologist Murchison, has much prior experience in ship rescue operations and is entirely capable of replacing me—but, if you will pardon me discussing your present emotional radiation in front of friend Fletcher here, you are feeling unusually high levels of concern over this mission. That being the case, I think that you would prefer me to accept it, which I do . . . Ah, I feel your relief, friend Braithwaite."

The administrator exhaled slowly, showed its teeth again, pressed a stud on the desk's communicator, and said briskly, "Thank you. *Rhabwar*'s crew members have now been alerted and are on their way to the ship, so I need detain you no longer. Good luck, gentlemen."

Prilicla wasn't sure that he liked being called a gentleman when he wasn't even an Earth-human, but he knew that the term was intended as a courtesy and that friend Braithwaite's feelings of concern for him were strong and sincere. He executed a steep, banking turn and flew rapidly towards the office entrance, knowing from long experience that no matter how fast he flew it would open in time to let him through.

He knew that the captain would not take offense at him using his natural advantages while traversing the six levels and intervening corridor network to reach the ambulance ship's dock before it did, because by now all of *Rhabwar*'s personnel were engaged on a similar race against time rather than against each other. Fletcher had to use his large but nimble Earth-human feet and occasionally his voice and elbows to negotiate the crowded corridors, while Prilicla either flew above everyone's head or scampered along the ceilings on his six sucker-tipped legs as he met, overtook, and passed above a constant succession of creatures who looked visually horrendous, beautiful, repugnant, or terrifying in their obvious physical strength and frightening variety of natural weapons which, being civilized members of the medical fraternity, they were rarely called on to use. Besides, all of them were his colleagues and, in most cases, his friends.

Not for the first time Prilicla asked himself why a fragile, delicately structured, insectile Cinrusskin empath had decided to spend his professional life in Sector General, surely one of the most dangerous working environments in the Galaxy for one of the GLNO classification, but the answer was always the same.

Despite the fact that his every waking moment was spent in a condition of perpetual vigilance verging on terror that would have driven the majority of his species mad, he had discovered that this was the only place and type of work that he wanted to be and do. Doubtless a Healer of the Mind would have talked learnedly about deeply buried death wishes, professional masochism, and the pathological need for constant danger, and would have pronounced him psychologically abnormal if not downright insane. But then, that diagnosis would have applied to the majority of beings who had aspired to permanent positions in the multispecies medical menagerie that was Sector Twelve General Hospital.

Considering his ability to fly unobstructed above everyone else's heads, it was no surprise that he was the first to board *Rhabwar*, where he logged his presence before moving quickly to his tiny, deeply upholstered quarters, checking that both backup sets of his gravity nullifiers were in operation. His cabin closely resembled the cocoonlike living quarters of his home world, and its artificial gravity was already set to Cinruss normal, which was slightly less than one-quarter of a standard Earth G. He stretched his wings and limbs to full extension, then distributed them into their most comfortable position for sleeping. Cinrusskins, fragile but physically active, needed a lot of sleep; and he knew that nothing important would be said or done until they were many hours into hyperspace.

A few minutes later he heard the captain coming along the

boarding-tube and climbing the central well to the control deck, closely followed by the other three Monitor Corps officers and the members of the medical team who collected on the casualty deck. They were complaining loudly and bitterly at the sudden interruption to their work or recreation, but all of the emotional radiation they emitted was of controlled excitement rather than bitterness.

For a few moments he eavesdropped on the emotional radiation filtering through to him from the casualty and control decks. They all knew that he couldn't help doing that because it was impossible to switch off his empathic faculty, so their emotional radiation was subdued, well-controlled, and, at this range, restful. They knew better than to radiate unpleasant feelings when their boss was trying to sleep.

CHAPTER 3

The briefing tape provided by Administrator Braithwaite had been played but not yet discussed, and their feelings of curiosity, caution, and growing impatience filled the casualty deck around him like a thick, emotional fog.

Captain Fletcher was sitting on a padded Kelgian treatment frame, flanked by Lieutenants Dodds and Chen, the communications and engineering officers respectively, while the astrogator and current watch-keeping officer, Lieutenant Haslam, viewed the proceedings through the control deck's vision link. Pathologist Murchison occupied the swivel seat of the diagnostic console with its back turned to the screen; Charge Nurse Naydrad had curled itself into a furry question mark on the nearest bed; and the polymorphic Dr. Danalta sat in the middle of the deck like a small green haystack from which it had extruded an ear and a single stalked eye. In order to avoid even the slightest risk of injury from sudden, unthinking movements of the others' limbs, Prilicla maintained a stable hover close to the ceiling while they all stared at the wall screen below him.

"As we have just seen," Prilicla said, "we will be entering what may be a unique situation for us, and we will have to be very careful . . ."

"We're always careful," Naydrad broke in, its mobile fur

rippling into waves of impatience and anxiety. "How careful is 'very'?"

Kelgians always said exactly what they felt—because their mobile fur made their feelings plain, at least to another member of their species—or they said nothing at all. He was aware of all of Naydrad's feelings, spoken and otherwise, and ignored the question because he intended to answer it anyway.

He went on. "The information available is sparse and speculative. We will be faced with the possible recovery of survivors from two distressed ships. One should be a normal, straightforward rescue and should pose no problems because it is the Corps' survey vessel *Terragar*, whose crew are Earth-human DBDGs. The second vessel has a crew whose physiological classification is as yet unknown. With survivors of two different species involved, one of which is . . ."

"We assess the position at the disaster site and rescue the casualties, of whichever species, who are in the most urgent need of attention first," Pathologist Murchison broke in quietly, its mind radiating the emotions of expectation, curiosity, and confidence characteristic of one who is accustomed to meeting professional challenges. "I don't see the problem, sir. This is what we do."

". . . is possibly responsible for causing the casualties on the first ship," Prilicla went on firmly. "Or perhaps another, undistressed vessel or vessels in the area have caused both sets of casualties. We must prepare and organize now for that eventuality, beginning with a clarification of the chain of command."

For several minutes nobody spoke. The level of their emotional radiation increased in strength and complexity, but not to a stage where it was affecting him physically. The three Monitor Corps officers were reacting with controlled restraint in the face of possible danger, the feelings characteristic of the military mind. Murchison's radiation was complex and negative, as was Naydrad's, but neither of them were feeling strongly enough to vocalize their objections. Unlike the others who were feeling minor non-specific anxiety and uncertainty, Danalta projected the calm self-assurance of a shape-changer who felt itself to be impervious to all forms of physical injury.

"Normally," Prilicla went on, "friend Fletcher here is in operational command of *Rhabwar* until it arrives at a disaster site, after which it is the senior medical officer, myself, who has the rank. But on this mission it may well be that, initially at least, military tactics will be of more benefit to us than medical expertise. I feel your agreement, friend Fletcher, and also that you are wanting to speak. Please do so."

The captain nodded. "Have you and the other medics considered the full implications of what you are saying? I realize that at present all this is pure speculation, but in the event of our being faced with a situation of armed conflict, difficult—and to all you medics, disagreeable decisions will have to be taken, and orders issued by myself. If I am called on to make those decisions, my orders will have to be obeyed without question or argument, no matter how objectionable they will seem. This must be fully understood and accepted by everyone right now—before, and not during or after, the event. Is it?"

"At any space accident or surface disaster scene, that is how we obey Dr. Prilicla," Naydrad said, its fur and feelings projecting puzzlement. "This is normal procedure for us. Why are you stressing the obvious? Or am I missing something?"

"You are," said the captain, its emotional radiation as well as its voice quiet and under control, as it spoke words it was feeling an intense reluctance to say. "This ship is unarmed, but not without weapons of defense and offense. Lieutenant Chen."

The engineering officer cleared its breathing passages noisily and said, "For a limited duration, no more than a few hours, our meteorite shield can be stiffened sufficiently to give protection against shrapnel from missiles tipped with chemical-explosive warheads. But if one was tipped with a nuclear device, we wouldn't have a prayer."

Lieutenant Haslam, whose astrogation speciality included long- and short-range ship handling, joined in without being asked. It said, "My tractor-pressor beam array, which is normally used on wide focus for docking or pulling in space wreckage for closer examination, can be modified to serve as a weapon, although not a very destructive one. Providing we can control the distance of the object and precisely match its speed, the pressor focus can be narrowed to within a diameter of a few feet to punch a hole in the opposition's hull plating. The catch is that it would increase the already heavy meteorite-shield drain on our power reserves, the shields would go down, and we'd be defenseless against whatever form of nastiness the opposition wanted to throw at us."

"Thank you, Lieutenant," said the captain. To the others it went on, "So you can see that we are poorly equipped for a military operation. The point I am making is that, should we encounter a situation of armed conflict or its aftermath, I shall assess the tactical picture and the decisions thereafter will be mine. These will include an immediate withdrawal to the safety of hyperspace if the action is still in progress. If not, and if there are damaged vessels in the area which I consider incapable of threatening our ship, I shall take, but not necessarily follow, the advice of the senior medical officer regarding the choice of which set of survivors, if any, is to be recovered first. These should be the Monitor Corps Earth-humans rather than the new, other-species casualties because—"

"Captain Fletcher!" Murchison broke in, its words accompanied by an explosion of shock and outrage that made Prilicla feel as if he had flown into a solid wall, an effect reinforced by the emotional reactions of the other medics. "That is not what we do here!"

The captain paused for a moment to order its own thoughts and feelings, which closely resembled those of its listeners, then continued quietly. "Normally, it is not, ma'am. I was about to say that there are sound tactical and psychological reasons for rescuing our own people first. They at least know who and what we represent and can furnish us with current intelligence regarding the situation, while the other people will be confused, frightened, and probably injured aliens who will take one look at us" —he glanced quickly at the medical menagerie around him— "and feel sure that we mean them harm. You must agree that it would be better to know something about the strangers, however little, before attempting to rescue and treat them.

"In the event," it went on, looking up at the hovering Prilicla, "the decision and choice may not be necessary. But if it is, the med team must be prepared to treat the casualties in the order I designate. Is this clearly understood?"

It was, Prilicla knew, because there were no strong feelings of negation coming from anyone, and the surrounding emotional radiation was settling down to a level which enabled him to maintain a stable hover. It was Naydrad, their specialist in heavy rescue, who broke the lengthening silence.

"If nobody has anything else to add," it said with an impatient ripple of its fur, "I for one want to review the medical log and space-rescue techniques. After six months in the hospital where all the patients are neatly stretched out in beds or whatever, one gets a little rusty."

Without saying anything else, the captain left the casualty deck, closely followed by the two junior officers. Naydrad began running a visual summary of *Rhabwar*'s early missions and the often unorthodox rescue techniques involved while recovering casualties. Murchison and Danalta joined it before the screen, probably because it was the only thing that was moving, apart from Prilicla's wings. Their emotional radiation was complex but firmly controlled as if they might be holding back the urge to say something. Prilicla excused himself and flew up the central well to his quarters so as to have the opportunity of thinking without the close proximity of outside emotional interference—and, of course, to give them the chance to relieve their feelings verbally.

"This is not what we do here," Murchison had said.

He did not need Naydrad's viewscreen to remind him of all the things they *had* done on *Rhabwar*, including the rules they had broken or seriously deformed, because the memories were returning as sharp, clear, and almost tactile overlays on the flickering grey blur of hyperspace outside his cabin's viewport. Prilicla had an outstandingly good memory.

He began with the briefing on operational philosophy before the first and supposedly routine shakedown cruise. It had been explained that over the past century the Monitor Corps, as the Federation's executive and law-enforcement arm, had been charged with the maintenance of the Pax Galactica, but because the peace they guarded required minimum maintenance, they had been given additional responsibilities and an obscenely large budget for stellar survey and exploration. In the very rare event that they turned up a planet with intelligent life, they were also given responsibility for the delicate, complex, and lengthy first-contact procedures. Since its formation, the Corps' other-species communications and cultural-contact specialists had found three such worlds and established successful relations with them, to the point where they had become member species of the Federation.

But there is a tendency for travelers to meet other travelers, often in distress and far from home. The advantage of meetings with other space travelers was that both species were already open to the idea that intelligent and possibly visually horrendous beings inhabited the stars—as opposed to contacting less advanced, planetbound cultures, who would be much more suspicious and fearful of the terrifying strangers who had dropped from their skies.

The trouble where the travelers were concerned was that there was only one known system for traveling in hyperspace, and one method—the nuclear-powered distress beacon—of calling for help if a catastrophe occurred that marooned the distressed ship between the stars. The result had been that many other highly intelligent and technologically advanced species had been discovered with whom they could not make contact because they were nothing but dead or dying organic debris lying tangled inside the wreckage of their starships. With the rescue ships' medical officers unable to provide the required assistance to completely alien life-forms, the casualties had been rushed to Sector General, where a few of them had been successfully treated, while the rest ended up in the pathology department as specimens whose worlds of origin were unknown.

That was the reason why the special ambulance ship *Rhabwar* had been constructed. Not only was it commanded by an officer skilled in unraveling the puzzles presented by unique alien technology, its crew included a medical team specialized both in ship-rescue techniques and multi-species alien physiology. The result had been that since their ship had been commissioned, seven new species had been contacted, and subsequently became members of the Federation.

In every case this had been accomplished—not by a slow, patient buildup and widening of communications until the exchange of complex philosophical and sociological concepts became possible, but by demonstrating the Federation's goodwill towards newly discovered species by rescuing and giving medical or other assistance to ailing, injured, or space-wrecked aliens.

The memories and images were returning, sharp and clear. In many of them, unlike this time, he had not borne the clinical responsibility for rescue and treatment because the then–Senior Physician Conway had been in charge of the medical team, with himself assisting as a kind of empathic bloodhound whose job was to smell out and separate the dead from the barely living casualties. There had been the recovery of the utterly savage and non-sapient Protectors of the Unborn whose wombs contained their telepathic and highly intelligent offspring; and the Blind Ones, whose hearing and touch had been so sensitive that they had learned to build devices that enables them to feel the radiation that filtered down to their world from the stars they would never see, even though they had traveled between them; and there had been the Duwetti, the Dwerlans, the Gogleskans, and the others. All had presented their particular clinical problems and associated physical dangers, especially to a fragile life-form like himself who could literally be blown away by a strong wind.

He wondered how the present-day Diagnostician Conway would have handled the current situation, where its beloved special ambulance was in danger of becoming a ship of war. Certainly not by flying away to hide in its room.

CHAPTER 4

It was four days later. Beyond the direct-vision panel and on the main screen that was relaying the control deck image, the flickering grey motion of hyperspace gave a final, eye-twisting heave before dissolving into a view of normal space. Within a few moments the relayed voice of Lieutenant Dodds on the sensors was telling them and the ship's mission recorders what they were already seeing.

"We have emerged close to a planet, Captain," it reported crisply. "The coloration and cloud cover suggests an atmosphere capable of sustaining warm-blooded, oxygen-breathing life and the vegetation to support it. Two ships are in close orbit around the planet within fifty miles of each other. One is *Terragar*; the other has a configuration that is new to us. Neither is showing serious structural damage."

"Split the screen," said the captain. "Give me maximum magnification on both. Haslam, contact *Terragar*."

The casualty-deck screen blurred suddenly, then showed images of the two ships that expanded rapidly until they touched the edges of their display areas.

"*Terragar* is not obviously damaged," said Dodds, continuing to describe what they were seeing. "But it is tumbling slowly with a pronounced lateral spin, and there is no light from the flight-deck canopy or the viewports. Sir, it looks like they have no power, certainly not for attitude control. . . ."

"Or communication," Haslam broke in. "They aren't responding to our signal."

"The other ship also appears to be unlit," Dodds continued, straying, "although that could be explained by visual hypersensitivity on the part of the crew. The outer hull is intact apart from two areas amidships about three and four meters in diameter. They are deeply cratered, which suggests the recent presence of intense heat accompanied by explosions. There is no evidence of the fogging that would indicate escaping air or whatever it is that they breathe. Either their safety bulkhead seals worked very fast, or the hits they sustained were lethal and the ship is airless and probably lifeless.

"The outer hull," it added, "shows no evidence of anything recognizable as external weapons launchers, or of the protective covers that would conceal such weapons. First indications, sir, are that this vessel was a victim rather than an attacker."

Even though half the length of *Rhabwar* stretched between them and the emotional radiation was attenuated, Prilicla could feel the captain coming to a decision.

"Very well," it said. "Move in. Continue trying to raise *Terragar*. I want to know what happened here. . . . Power room. Chen, we're now too close to the planet to jump, so stand by for maximum thrust on the main drive. Haslam, be ready to pull out at the first sign of anything resembling a hostile action. I'll need the fastest possible reaction time on this."

"Understood," said Haslam.

Around them the casualty deck gave an almost imperceptible lurch as the artificial-gravity system compensated for the sudden application of thrust. The repeater screen returned to showing a single, unmagnified picture of the two ships as they grew larger with diminishing distance.

Prilicla dropped lightly to the deck, where he folded his wings and legs tightly before pulling on his spacesuit. Murchison,

Naydrad, and Danalta were already climbing into theirs, all radiating minor levels of excitement, expectation, and caution. When he had checked his own air supply, antigravity system, and suit thrusters, he looked around at the others in turn.

"The medical team and powered litters are standing by, friend Fletcher," he reported.

"Thank you, Doctor," the other replied. "We are closing with *Terragar* now."

Prilicla began to worry. Although it was completely without weaponry, in overall structure *Rhabwar* had been modeled on the Monitor Corps' heavy cruiser, a class of vessel whose broad delta-wing configuration enabled it to be areodynamically maneuvered within a planetary atmosphere. But he was afraid that it was much too massive for it to be capable of the small and precise movements in three dimensions that were needed to bring it to within two hundred meters of the distressed ship. Bearing in mind its tremendous mass and inertia, if *Rhabwar* were to collide with *Terragar* it would sustain only superficial damage, while the other vessel would have its hull caved in, with consequent disastrous injuries to its crew.

An ambulance wasn't supposed to *make* medical work for itself.

But there was no sign of worry or even uncertainty in the emotional radiation that was filtering down from the control deck, so he moved to the direct-vision panel to watch the approaching planet and the two orbiting ships that were being lit by the bright, tattered carpet of clouds, consoling himself with the thought that his specialty was other-spieces medicine and not ship-handling, and wondering what new physiological challenges awaited them.

"Still no sign of life or movement from the alien," Haslam reported. Its voice was calm and unemotional but it and everyone else on the control deck was radiating intense relief. "The sensors indicate low levels of residual power from two areas amidships, but in my opinion, not nearly enough for a weapons power-up, and the ship appears to have been radiating its internal heat into space for several days without any attempt to maintain living temperature levels, whatever they are for these people. I'd say that the alien ship is a problem that can wait, sir."

"I agree," said the captain, "but keep your eyes on it, just in case. Casualty deck?"

"Yes, friend Fletcher," said Prilicla.

"We will be at one hundred meters and motionless with respect to *Terragar*'s position in eleven minutes," said the captain. "I realize that we will be at extreme range for your empathic faculty, but please do your best to detect the crew's emotional radiation, if there is any."

"Of course, friend Fletcher."

The quality of the captain's own emotional radiation belied the calmness in its voice, otherwise it would not have wasted time and breath asking him to do the job that he was here expressly to perform. But the crew of the distressed ship were all Earth-human DBDGs. Perhaps it had friends among them.

He watched with the other members of the team at the direct-vision panel as their ship closed with the Monitor Corps survey vessel. *Terragar* was rolling, as well as slowly pitching end over end. The canopy of the unlit control deck was moving past them at an awkward angle which did not allow a clear view of the interior. But for one brief moment the angle was right, and Prilicla was able to see movement.

"Friend Fletcher," he said urgently. "I think I detected motion behind the control canopy. Nobody else down here saw anything or they would be emoting about it by now. It was just a glimpse, of faces, hands, and upper bodies of at least three Earth-humans. They are alive, but the distance is extreme for an empathic reading."

"We didn't see anything, either," the captain replied, "but compared with your GLNO sensorium, ours makes us feel as if we're wearing mittens and blindfolds. Haslam, deploy the tractor beams and kill the spin on that ship. Position it for a clear view into the control canopy. Then push across a cable with a communicator fitted with a two-way sound-conduction pad. Land it, but gently, on the canopy. We badly need information on this situation, and, of course, to know if anyone needs medical attention."

The misty-blue light of two of *Rhabwar*'s tractor beams flickered out to focus on the bows and stern of the Monitor ship, gradually reducing its spin. A moment later a thinner beam lifted out the communicator, but held it midway between the two ships to wait for its target to come to rest. Prilicla had a slightly longer and clearer view of the people inside the canopy before they rolled out of sight.

"Friend Fletcher," he said urgently, responding to feelings that zhe felt sure were not all his own. "I saw four officers, that's the entire complement of a survey vessel. They were waving at us, shaking their heads vigorously in your DBDG non-verbal signal of negation, and showing the palms of their hands. One was pointing repeatedly in the direction of the alien ship and our communicator. The empathic range is extreme but they are radiating high levels of agitation."

"I saw them, too," said the captain. "They don't appear to be seriously injured; they're about to be rescued and have little to feel agitated about. Still . . . Haslam, is the alien ship doing anything to worry us?"

"No, sir," the lieutenant replied. "It's still dead in the water, so to speak."

Prilicla paused for a moment, nerving himself for the effort of saying something argumentative if not disagreeable to another person whose irritated or angry reaction would bounce back and hit him hard.

"It was their feelings I read," he said carefully. "Because of the interference from the emotional radiation around me, theirs were difficult to define. There was agitation, however, and it had to be intense to reach me at this distance. May I make a suggestion and ask a favor?"

The captain was feeling the irritation characteristic of an entity whose ideas and authority were being questioned, but it was quickly brought under control. It said, "Go ahead, Doctor."

"Thank you," he said, looking around the casualty deck to indicate that his words were for them as well. "It is this. Would you please instruct your officers, as much as they are able, to relax mentally and avoid intensive thinking or associated feelings? I would like to get a clearer idea of what is bothering the *Terragar* crew. I am having a bad feeling about this situation, friend Fletcher."

"And since when," said Murchison in a quiet voice that was just loud enough for the captain to overhear it, "has a feeling of Prilicla's been wrong?"

"Do as the Doctor says, gentlemen," the captain replied promptly, pretending that it hadn't heard. "All of you make your minds blank"—it gave a soft Earth-human bark—"or at least blanker than usual."

All over the ship, from the control deck forward and the power room aft and from the medical team around him, they were staring at blank walls and deck surfaces or the backs of closed eyelids, those who had them, or were using whatever other means they had of reducing cerebration and feeling. Nobody knew better than himself how difficult it was to switch the mind to low alert and think of absolutely nothing, but they were all trying.

Terragar's control canopy had rolled out of sight, but that had no effect on the crew's emotional radiation, which was still tenuous, confused, and at a strength that was barely readable. But without the local empathic interference the individual feelings were gradually becoming clearer and easier to define, and they were anything but pleasant.

"Friend Fletcher," said Prilicla urgently, "I feel fear and, intense negation. For me to be able to detect them at this range, those feelings must be extreme. The fear seems to be both personal and impersonal, the latter emotion characteristic of a being who fears a threat to others besides itself. I'm an empath, not a telepath, but I'd say . . . Look, they're coming into sight again. . . ."

He could see no details of the four faces other than that their mouths were opening and closing. Their hands were gesticulating wildly, sometimes pointing at the alien ship but more often towards *Rhabwar* and the communicator floating at the end of its sensor cable midway between their two vessels. Their pale, Earth-human palms were showing as they pressed them repeatedly against the inside of the canopy.

What were they trying to say?

". . . They're pointing at the alien ship and at us," he went on quickly, "but mostly at the communicator you're sending over. And they're making pushing movements with their hands. Their fear and agitation is increasing. I feel sure they want us to go away."

"But *why*, dammit?" said the captain. "Have they lost their senses? I'm just trying to stabilize their ship and establish a communicator link."

"Whatever you're doing," said Prilicla firmly, "it is making them fearful and they badly want you to stop doing it."

One of the four gesticulating crew members had moved quickly out of sight. Before he could mention it to the captain, Fletcher spoke again. Its voice and the feelings that accompanied it were calm and confident with the habit of command.

"With respect, Doctor," it said, "the feelings you read from them make no sense, and won't until we talk to them and they explain themselves and this whole damn situation. We need that information before we can risk boarding the alien ship. Haslam, move the communicator close and be ready to attach it when you've killed the spin."

"Please wait," said Prilicla urgently, "and consider. The other crew aren't injured, they emote no feelings of pain or physical distress, only agitation at our close approach. So the matter isn't clinically urgent. It will do no harm if you move back a short distance, temporarily, just to reassure them if nothing else. Friend Fletcher, I have a very bad feeling about this."

He felt the captain's continuing intransigence as well as the beginnings of hesitation as it spoke.

"I'm sorry, Doctor," it said firmly. "My first requirement is to talk to them as soon as—"

"Sir!" Haslam broke in. "They're pulling free of our tractor beam, on their main thrusters, for God's sake, at over three Gs. They've no attitude control—otherwise they'd have checked their own spin by now. That's stupid, suicidal! They're diving into atmosphere, and when they move farther ahead and their ion stream hits us, we'll be toasted like a . . ."

It broke off as the hot, blue spear streaming from the other ship's main drive flickered and died, immediately reducing the fear feelings coming from *Rhabwar*'s control deck.

"Friend Fletcher," said Prilicla gently, "I told you that they didn't want us to close with them, but neither do they want to kill us."

The captain used an Earth-human expression that his translator refused to accept.

"You were right, Doctor," it went on, "but we'll need to get very close to them indeed, unless we want to watch them burn up in atmosphere."

CHAPTER 5

Terragar belonged to a class of vessel that had been designed to operate in the weightless and airless conditions of space, and to dock only with other ships or orbiting supply and maintenance facilities. It was not an aerodynamically clean object and the structural projections supporting its complex of long-range sensors and mapping cameras made it resemble a cross between a falling brick and a stick insect. The congenitally tactless Naydrad observed that physically it bore a close resemblance to their chief.

Even though he knew that his Cinrusskin body was unusually well-formed and beautiful, Prilicla had neither responded nor taken offense. Kelgians always said exactly what they felt; telling a lie was for them a complete waste of time. It was the strong, unspoken emotions of Naydrad and the others, the feelings of loyalty, admiration, concern, and deep personal regard, that were important. Besides, the crucial words and feelings were coming from the people on the control deck.

"Catch up to them and kill that spin," the captain was saying urgently. "There's no need to be so gentle, dammit! Check all motion, refocus to full strength, and drag them back. We have the power."

"Yes, but no, sir," Haslam replied, its voice hurried but respectful. "The tractor acts on the nearest surface. If we drag them back too suddenly we'll peel off most of their outer skin and external hull structures. I have to be gentle to avoid pulling the whole ship apart."

"Very well," said the captain. "Be gentle, then, but faster."

"We're picking up atmospheric heating," Dodd's voice reported; "so are they."

In the direct-vision panel Prilicla could see the ponderously spinning shape of *Terragar* as the tractor beam enclosed it in a pale blue mist and drew it closer. The tumbling action was gradually slowing to a stop, but both ships were entering the upper atmosphere much too quickly for the safety of the vessel ahead. Through the confusion of emotional radiation coming from *Rhabwar* he could still feel the intense fear mixed with dogged determination emanating from the other crew. His empathic reading just did not make sense. Not for the first time, he wished he could know what others were thinking instead of feeling.

"You're getting there," said the captain. "Once you kill the rest of that spin, try to position them so they'll go in tail-first. The stern structure is stronger than the forward section and will burn away slower than the control canopy. Can't you slow them down faster than that?"

"In order," said Haslam. "Yes, sir. No, sir. I'm trying, sir."

The other ship was stable and directly ahead of them, with its control canopy continuously in view. The crew had donned heavy-duty spacesuits with the helmets thrown back. Their mouths were opening and closing widely as if they were shouting, and they were still making pushing motions with their hands. From his present viewpoint Prilicla could not see the heating of the ship's stern, but the peripheral sensor arrays and their spidery support structures were turning bright red and being bent backwards by the tenuous gale of near-vacuum that was blowing past them. Suddenly one of them tore free and there was a loud, metallic clang as it glanced harmlessly off *Rhabwar*'s superstructure.

"Why don't they use their main thrusters again?" said Dodds, radiating anger and impatience. "That would help us to slow them down."

"I don't know," said the captain. A moment later it went on. "Doctor, do you have any answers?"

"Yes, friend Fletcher," said Prilicla. "In spite of their fear and certainty of imminent termination, they won't help you because they don't want us to come near them. I don't know why they are doing this, either, but their reasons must be very strong."

For a moment he felt the emotional gale raging on the control deck, with the captain's mind its storm center, then it became still with the calmness characteristic of a decision taken and a mind made up.

"I don't know why they seem intent on suicide, Doctor," it said quietly, "but the fact that they've put on their spacesuits suggests that they still retain some of their will to survive. Whether they want to or not, I'm going to do my damnedest to save them. Or are you suggesting otherwise?"

"I was not suggesting otherwise, friend Fletcher," said Prilicla, "just warning you about the way they are feeling. No rational person fully understands why another intelligent being wants to commit suicide, but in every civilized culture we have ever found, it is considered a person's bounden duty, regardless of personal risk, to stop it from doing so."

The captain did not reply, but he felt its gratitude as it said, "Haslam, slow them down. Be less gentle."

From the ambulance ship's position slightly above and behind the distressed ship. Prilicla could see *Terragar*'s stern section changing gradually from metallic grey through dull red to glowing orange. The lattice support structure carrying the mapping sensors were like bright yellow spiders' webs that sagged, melted, and were blown away by the slipstream. With a dreadful certainty, Prilicla waited for *Terragar* to explode into a disintegrating fireball. But incredibly, someone in Control was radiating feelings of optimism.

"Sir," said Haslam, "I think we may have done it. In a few more seconds their speed will be slowed to the point where there will be no more atmospheric heating beyond what they've already picked up. But they're not out of trouble yet. . . ."

The red-hot particles of metallic fog were no longer streaming back from the other ship's superheated stern, but to Prilicla, nothing else seemed to have changed.

". . . Because," the lieutenant went on, "I estimate that in about twenty minutes the heat from their stern will be conducted along the structure until it is evenly distributed throughout the ship. By then the survivors will be in a bad way."

"Then lift us out of atmosphere," said the captain. "Let the heat dissipate into space. You're able to do that now without causing their hull to break up?"

The voices in Control were calm but the feelings behind them, as were those of the medical team around him, were not. The emotional radiation coming from the people on the other ship was even worse.

"Yes, sir," Haslam replied. "But it will take an hour or more for all that heat to radiate into space and until then it would be too hot, as well as too late, for the rescue team to go in for them. By then they would be cooked in their own juices if they aren't that way already."

"Please ignore the lieutenant, Doctor," said the captain quickly. "Sometimes he has about as much tact as a drunken Kelgian. How are the survivors?"

For a moment Prilicla was silent as he watched the hot, red stain that was creeping inexorably forwards along *Terragar*'s hull, its progress clearly visible in spite of the bright carpet of clouds and sunlit ocean unrolling rapidly below it. Suddenly the despair he was feeling began to be diluted by excitement and hope.

"They are alive," he said, "but the emotional radiation is characteristic of beings who are fearful and in intense discomfort. I am not a ship handler, friend Fletcher, but may I make a suggestion?"

"You want to try to recover them anyway," said the captain incredulously, "from a ship that is nearly red-hot? You and your team would die in the attempt. The answer is no."

"Friend Fletcher," said Prilicla, "I am not emotionally capable of doing, or even of thinking of doing, such a brave and stupid thing. Instead, I was about to ask you to take both ships to the planetary surface as quickly as possible. Our altitude is less than fifty miles above an equatorial ocean and there are many islands, one with what looks like a sandy coastline coming over the horizon. If we had enough time we might cool *Terragar* by immersion."

Lieutenant Haslam swore out loud, something Prilicla had rarely heard it do in the presence of its captain and never while the recorders were running, and said, "My God, it wants us to dunk them in the ocean!"

"Can we do that, Lieutenant?" said Fletcher. "Is there time?"

"There might be," Haslam replied, "but it will be close."

"Then do it," said the captain. "We'll need to reduce our rate of descent to zero by the time we reach the surface, but to save time, hold off the deceleration until we're a few miles above sea level. The sudden braking will put a strain on the tractor beam, not to mention the other ship. Use your judgment, and try not to pull it apart at this late stage. Nice idea, Doctor. Thank you. How are the casualties?"

Friend Fletcher's gratitude, hope, and excitement were clear for Prilicla to feel, so there had been no need for the other to express them verbally. But when their ship was involved in a situation where anything might happen and every incident, instrument reading, and word were being recorded in case of an unforeseen calamity, he knew that the captain's tidy mind would want the credit for the idea and its gratitude to go on record.

"Still alive, friend Fletcher," he replied formally: "Their emotional radiation indicates deep personal fear and despair but not panic, and increasing physical discomfort. They are not visible to me, but the indications are that three of them are positioned closely together on the control deck, which is probably the coolest place in the ship, and a fourth one is farther aft. The rescue team is ready to go, on your signal."

Around him he could feel a combination of anxiety, impatience, and excitement as his team checked equipment that had already been checked many times. He remained silent because there was nothing useful he could say, and kept his eyes on *Terragar* and the dull red tide of color that was creeping slowly towards its bow. He was startled when it disappeared suddenly as both ships plunged through the dark interior of a tropical storm. A few moments later it reappeared with a brief, overall puff of steam as the rainwater boiled off its overheated hull. Ahead of and below them, the smooth expanse of sunlit water was expanding and showing the first wrinkling of the larger waves. There was no feeling of deceleration because *Rhabwar*'s artificial gravity system was maintaining the customary one-G, but *Terragar* was feeling it. Two small areas of the other ship's hull plating bulged outwards suddenly under the double pull of deceleration and the tractor beam, but they didn't peel away. By now their speed was being measured in tens rather than hundreds of miles per hour.

"This hasn't been what I'd call a covert approach to a newly discovered planet," said the captain, radiating sudden anxiety, "but we had no other choice. Did you scan for intelligent-life signs?"

"Briefly, sir, on the way down," said Haslam, "but the sensors are on record for later study. They report zero atmospheric industrial pollutants, no traffic on the audio or visual radio frequencies, and no indications of intelligent life. Altitude, five hundred meters and descending. The coastline of the island ahead is coming up."

"Right," said the captain. "Check forward velocity to put us down no more than three hundred meters offshore, and it will save a few minutes if there's a nice, even seabed under us."

"There is," said Haslam. "The sensors indicate hard-packed sand with no reefs or rock outcroppings."

"Good," said Fletcher. "Power room, in five minutes we'll be supporting two ships. I'll need maximum power for the stilts."

"You'll have it," said Lieutenant Chen.

Their forward motion ceased as they dropped slowly to within five hundred meters of the waves, which were high and smooth and rounded so that each one seemed to throw back reflections of the sun. Against that continually moving dazzle, the red coloration of *Terragar*'s hull had darkened almost to a normal, metallic grey, but the emotional radiation from its officers belied the appearance of normality.

The medical team, already suited-up and sealed, were watching him and the tremor that was shaking his limbs. He felt Pathologist Murchison's sympathy. It was wanting to talk and to help him—probably by trying to take his mind off the casualties by giving it something more cerebral to think about—but when it spoke, the subject remained the same.

"Sir," Murchison said, "earlier you said that their emotional radiation indicated that they were physically unharmed. Was there evidence of any psychological abnormality present? Why would they try deliberately to commit suicide rather than let us near them? By now they will have sustained overall burns or, if they kept their suits sealed and their cooling units at maximum, massive dehydration and heat prostration. But with respect, sir, there has to be something more wrong with them. What else can we expect?"

"I don't know, friend Murchison," Prilicla replied. "Remember, there was no suicidal intent, just extreme determination not to let us approach their ship. They tried very hard to get away from us, but it was the attitude of their ship which took them into atmosphere, and that was accidental."

It was a guess rather than anything as definite as a feeling, but he was wondering if there might be something, or perhaps someone, on their ship who was no longer living, that they had not wanted *Rhabwar*'s crew to go near. He kept that thought to himself, and the pathologist rejoined the general silence until it was broken by the captain.

"Deploy the stilts," it said. "Drop them in, but gently. Immerse them for five minutes."

Rhabwar was now positioned directly above the other ship and holding it horizontally above the ocean with a single tractor beam. Suddenly four more speared out in pressor mode, widely angled so that the ship was supported by a pyramid of misty-blue stilts that penetrated and pushed aside the water to rest solidly on the seabed. *Terragar* dropped gently towards the waves.

There was a tremendous explosion of steam and outflowing streamers of boiling water as it touched and then slipped below the surface. Everything was obliterated by a dazzling white fog for the few minutes it took for the strong, onshore breeze to blow it clear. But there was nothing to see except a large circle of boiling and bubbling ocean.

"Pull them up," said the captain.

The ship that rose into view was barely recognizable as *Terragar*. Steam and furiously boiling water were streaming out of the large gaps in the hull plating and where the entire control canopy had burst open. It looked as if the tractor beam was holding the ship not only up, but in one piece. Prilicla answered the question before the captain could ask it.

"They are still inside, friend Fletcher," he said, "but deeply unconscious and close to termination. We need to get to them, now."

"Sorry, Doctor," said the captain, "but not right now. Our sensors say that their hull interior is still too hot for your people to survive it, much less recover casualties. Haslam, submerge them again, this time for ten minutes."

Once again the other ship was immersed, but this time it seemed the sea above it was steaming rather than boiling. The emotional radiation of the casualties remained unchanged. When

Terragar reappeared this time, the water running down its sides and pouring from the gaps in its hull was, according to the sensors, very warm rather than hot, and no longer a threat to the rescue team.

"Instructions, Doctor?" said the captain.

Plainly the other was feeling that their situation no longer contained a military threat and was immediately passing the operational responsibility back to the senior medical officer on site.

"Friend Fletcher," he said briskly, "please move the wreck towards the beach and place it in the shallows at a depth that will not inconvenience us but where the wave action will continue to cool it. We'll board with four antigravity litters while friend Murchison remains with you to supervise the transfer and erection of our field dressing station and the special equipment we may need. The casualty deck will be reserved for the recovery of the possible other-species survivors in orbit. As quickly as possible, use your tractor beam to position the unit's structures, friend Murchison, and its equipment onshore within one hundred meters of the wreck. Land *Rhabwar* farther inland at a minimum distance of three hundred meters. Should you need to take off or change position for operational reasons, you must not approach the medical station or the wreck any closer than that from any direction until instructed otherwise."

The captain was radiating puzzlement, feelings shared by everyone else on the ship, as it said, "This is ridiculous, Doctor. Surely you are being unnecessarily cautious about an unpowered and helpless wreck."

Prilicla paused for a moment. When he spoke, he tried to sound resolute and inflexible, which was very difficult for a Cinrusskin empath even when he was carrying mind-partners of a more heavyweight and psychologically positive species.

"When we approached it in orbit," he said, "*Terragar* used its last reserves of power to move away from us. Its crew were willing to die rather than allow our ship, or perhaps our crew members, to make physical contact with them. The rescue team will shortly be making physical contact with them, with extreme caution, naturally. But until we discover the medical, psychological, or other reasons behind their apparently suicidal or self-sacrificing action, I am expressly forbidding *Rhabwar* to do so.''

CHAPTER 6

Sunlight shone through the ragged-edged hole where the control-room canopy had been. The heat-discolored instrumentation that the water had not already swept into tangled heaps on the deck showed dead, blank readouts. The remains of the four control couches were empty, with faintly steaming water flowing slowly between their support struts as it ran away through cracks in the ruptured deck. But life was present, and even though it was difficult to detect through the welter of emotional radiation coming from the rest of the team, he knew that it was close by.

"Naydrad, Danalta," he said urgently, "please subdue your feelings. You're muddying the emotional waters."

A moment later he pointed towards a group of four tall cabinets set into the aft bulkhead. Heat deformation had twisted one of the doors slightly open while the others looked as if they had been fused shut. They were the standard ship furniture that contained the crew's spacesuits Now they contained the crew as well, because their structures had given an extra layer of protection against the heat.

For some reason these people had been willing to die, Prilicla reminded himself again, but they had also wanted badly to live.

Quickly, Naydrad sliced off the four doors with its cutting torch. Only three of the cabinets were occupied, because earlier one of the officers had gone aft to start the main thrusters manually when the ship had made its desperate attempt to pull away from *Rhabwar*. But there was too much local emotional radiation for him to be able to detect accurately the fourth man's distance or position. He could feel, although the source was so faint that it might have been a hope rather than a feeling, that the fourth officer was still alive. But there was no time to go looking for it now because the other three needed immediate attention. Naydrad and Danalta were already removing them from the cabinets. He tried to look at their faces, but the inside of the visors were steamed up and the suits were hot to the touch.

"Finish transferring them to the litters," he said, moving closer to lay his hand gently on each of them in turn, "then remove the spacesuits and all body coverings. Friend Murchison, the vision pickups are running. Are you seeing this, and are you ready to receive casualties?"

"Yes, sir," it replied. "*Rhabwar* has lifted over the prefabricated med station, myself, and the Earth-human burn medication onto the beach above the high-water mark. Until now I was too busy even to notice if this world had a moon and tides. It does. I'll be ready to take the casualties in fifteen minutes. Have you a preliminary assessment for me, sir?"

Prilicla flew slowly over the three Earth-humans. Rapidly but very gently, their suits and underlying garments, apart from the small areas of scorched clothing still adhering to the bodies, were being cut away by Naydrad and Danalta. The Earth-humans were too deeply unconscious for their emotional radiation to trouble him, but the mere thought of what they must have suffered before they had reached that state was enough to make his hovering flight less than stable. In the hospital he had seen Chief Dietitian Gurronsevas produce synthetic meat dishes that were less well-cooked.

"All three casualties are suffering from advanced heat prostration and massive dehydration," Prilicla replied in a clinical voice that belied his underlying feelings. "Undoubtedly this followed the overload and apparent recent failure—very recent, otherwise the casualties would have terminated by now—of their suits' cooling systems. There is localized surface and subdermal burning, with escharring in several areas to a depth of two centimeters, where the internal metal stiffening of the suits made contact through the clothing, or the wearer lost consciousness and allowed the front or side of its cranium to fall against the heated interior of the helmets. There are third-degree burns to the hands, feet, and crania, plus a narrow band encircling the waist, with an estimated total body area of ten to fifteen percent.

"Interim treatment will be to place the casualties into individual litters," he went on, giving the information friend Murchison needed while at the same time issuing polite instructions to the two team members working beside him, "with the canopies sealed and the refrigeration units reducing the ambient temperature. Rehydration is a matter of urgency but must wait until your facilities are available. Friend Naydrad will convey the three litters to you and assist while I . . ."

"Then the fourth officer terminated?" it broke in softly.

"Perhaps not," he replied. "I have a feeling, very tenuous and more likely only a wish, that it is still alive somewhere aft. Friend Danalta will remain here to help me find it."

Even at one hundred meters distance he could feel Murchison's sudden burst of negativity and deep concern.

"Sir," it said, "the captain has just informed me that the continuous strain on the fabric of that ship caused by the braking action of the tractor beam, together with the atmospheric buffeting during reentry, will have converted the interior into a heap of wreckage that could collapse at any time. As well, the hull temperature at the stern is still unacceptably high for would-be rescuers. You will be at serious risk and may wish to reconsider your recent decision. I suggest you send Naydrad with Danalta to recover the missing casualty . . ."

Well," said the Kelgian, its fur rippling under the protective garment, "isn't it nice to be considered expendable?"

". . . while you bring in the other litters," it went on. "From the condition of the first three, it looks as though your surgical experience will be urgently required here."

"I agree, friend Murchison," said Prilicla. "But if Danalta or Naydrad found the fourth crew member, neither of them would be able to know whether they were recovering an unconscious or dead casualty without removing its suit, which would be contraindicated in the high temperature levels aft. You know very well that only I can feel and specify at a distance whether it is a casualty requiring urgent attention, or a cadaver that can await recovery at more convenient time."

He moved to the fourth litter and climbed inside, sealing the pressure canopy behind him for maximum protection before signaling with a forward manipulator for Danalta to proceed aft.

"Please refrain from going into maternal mode, friend Murchison," he added. "I promise to be very careful."

The situation aft was much worse than he had expected with an almost solid plug of wreckage barring their way. Atmospheric heating and the tractor-beam stresses had caused the interior hull plating to buckle and open up so that ragged, metal edges projected into their path and opened wide cracks that allowed long, uneven triangles of daylight to show through. He could feel the buildup of heat even through the litter canopy and his own suit's laboring cooling system. But Danalta, as it had done on many previous rescue operations, was proving once again that its polymorphic species was the closest thing to a general-purpose organic tool in the known universe.

His limbs were showing a faint tremor which his polymorphic friend had noticed, but was forbearing to mention, because the emotional radiation causing it was due to Prilicla's own cowardice.

It was a terrible psychological burden to be afraid all the time, of everything and everybody, and of the harm that might be done him by accident or intention. But there were compensations. A life-form with hostile intent could not hide its feelings towards him, so he could either take evasive action or, if it was intelligent, try to change the other's hostility to feelings of disinterest or even friendship towards him. As a matter of pure survival as well as to secure a pleasant emotional environment for himself, he had made many good and protective friends. But there was nothing he could do about stupid pieces of sharp-edged, inanimate matter except try to avoid them.

There was another ship's officer to find, if it was still alive and emoting. Prilicla tried to allay his own fear and widen his empathic range while he followed and coordinated his litter's movements with those of the shape-changer.

Danalta was always a minimal source of emotional interference because it rarely encountered situations that caused it to have unpleasant feelings, and it was never afraid because nothing—short of a major explosion, or being crushed between two closing faces of massive colliding objects—could harm it. Now it was opening a path through the hot, steaming devastation by extruding appendages of the length, shape, and strength necessary to move obstacles aside or, with the whole of its body, taking shapes that it was better not to think about as it used itself as an organic pit prop that lifted masses of tumbled wreckage in order to enable the litter to go through.

Fotawn, the planet where Danalta's species had evolved, had been one of the least hospitable worlds to be discovered by the Galactic Federation. It had a highly eccentric orbit and consequent climatic variations so severe that an incredible degree of physical adaptability had been necessary for its flora and fauna to survive on a world of animal and vegetable shape-changers.

Danalta's people, its dominant life-form, were of physiological classification TOBS. They had developed intelligence and an advanced civilization based on the philosophical rather than the physical sciences, not by competing in the matter of natural weapons but by refining and perfecting their adaptive capabilities. In prehistoric times, when members of the species were faced with stronger natural enemies, their defensive options in order of preference had been protective mimicry, flight, or the adoption of a shape frightening to the attacker. The speed and accuracy of the mimicry suggested the possession of a high degree of receptive empathy of which the species was not consciously aware.

With such effective means of physical adaptability and self-protection available, the species was impervious to disease and normal levels of physical injury, so that the concepts of curative medicine and surgery had been completely incomprehensible to its people. In spite of this, Danalta had applied for and been accepted at Sector General for medical training.

Danalta's purpose in coming to the hospital, it had insisted, had been selfish rather than idealistic. The sixty-odd different life-forms who worked there were a unique and continuing challenge to its powers of mimicry. Admittedly, it was being forced into using all of its polymorphic abilities—to reassure beings who might be suffering from serious physical or psychological malfunctions, by mimicking their shape and vocal output if there were no members of their own species present to give reassurance; or, in an accident situation with associated toxic pollution, it could adapt its shape and tegument quickly so that urgently required treatment would not be delayed because of time wasted in donning protective garments; or during surgery it could extrude limbs and digits of the indicated shape and function which were capable of quickly repairing damage to otherwise inaccessible areas where organic damage or dysfunction had occurred. But it was simply reacting to a challenge that no shape-changer of its race had ever faced before and, while it was deriving much pleasure from the experience, it was not and should not be called a doctor.

In turn, the hospital authorities had insisted, gently but very firmly, that if it planned to continue doing that kind of work at Sector General, there was nothing else they could call it.

"Sir," said Danalta suddenly, bringing his mind back to

present time and space, "we've reached the power room. The ambient temperature is unacceptably high for an unprotected Earth-human DBDG, but the structure here is robust and less likely to collapse on us. You may safely leave the litter. I'm trying to reduce my emotional radiation. Can you feel the casualty?"

"No," said Prilicla; then immediately contradicted himself. "Yes."

It was a feeling almost without feeling, a mere expression of individuality and existence that was characteristic of an entity very close to termination. It was tenuous with extreme weakness or distance or both. Before signaling to move farther aft, he looked quickly around the room. It, too, had been cracked open, but compared with the wreckage-strewn compartments they had already passed through, this one was almost neat except for an untidy heap of tools that looked as if they had been thrown haphazardly onto the deck in front of a low, closed metal cabinet. Perhaps someone had been urgently in need of shelter.

"In there," he said, pointing and moving quickly towards it.

As they forced open the cabinet there was a sudden explosion of black, oily vapor from the sponge plastic lining that had been melted by the heat, but the casualty's suit was still intact so it had not breathed any of the highly toxic gas. Inside they found the fourth officer on its knees and bent almost double. Without trying to straighten the body they quickly lifted the spacesuited figure onto the litter and laid it on its side. Apart from the deep red coloration, the details of the face were blurred by internal condensation. The emotional radiation suggested a life expectancy that could be measured in minutes rather than hours.

"Friend Danalta," he said, glancing back at the way they had come, "this casualty is close to termination and the temperature in here means that we can't afford the time or the risk of opening its suit. Please look for a faster way out of here. Try to find an opening in the hull large enough to allow the litter through so we can . . ."

"Doctor," the voice of the captain broke in, "we can make that opening for you, as large as you need. I've been monitoring your progress, I'm familiar with the ship's layout, and I know exactly where you are. Please move clear of the hull on the landward side and hold on to something solid.

"Haslam," he continued quickly, "tractor beam, narrow-focus rapid push-pull to the aft hull plating, just there."

The whole power room began to vibrate in sympathy around them as a sudden, metallic screeching sound came from a small area of the hull interior. The existing cracks in the structure opened up as a large section of plating and internal trim was pulled outwards and pressed inwards at a rate of once a second. For a moment the plating fluttered like a metal flag in a high wind before it was whipped out of sight. Sunlight poured into the compartment and with it, a clear, close view of the beach and medical station.

"Thank you, Captain," he said. "Friend Murchison, to save time I'm sending friend Danalta with the fourth litter. The canopy will be sealed and the cooling system set to maximum in the hope that the reduction in external temperature will be conducted to the occupant. The casualty is still inside its suit which should be removed as quickly as possible in a less hostile environment. I will follow at once to assist you."

"Maybe not at once, Doctor," said Danalta. Its voice was coming from what seemed to be a small storage compartment farther aft.

He had been aware of a sudden burst of emotion an instant before the shape-changer had spoken. Its feelings were complex, a mixture composed predominantly of intense surprise and curiosity. Before Prilicla could ask the natural question, Danalta gave the answer.

"Doctor," it said, "there is another casualty here. The physiological classification is strange to me but, but I think I've found a stowaway."

CHAPTER 7

The creature appeared to be wearing a spacesuit so close-fitting that it seemed highly probable that its general body configuration was identical in size and shape to its protective garment. Physically the creature was a flattened ovoid with six appendages growing at equal intervals from the perimeter, each terminating in long, flexible digits encased in gauntlets that fitted like a coat of metallic paint. There was a variety of what looked like specialized tools on the fingertips of each of the thin, metal gauntlets. The rounded projection on what was presumably the forebody, was almost certainly the cranium, but it was covered by sensors rather than a transparent visor so that he was unable to obtain a direct view of the facial tegument and features. There was a large area of scorching covering the upper surface, or possibly the underside, of the body. He couldn't be sure without removing the suit.

"What is it, Doctor?" said Danalta. "Is it alive?"

"I'm not sure," he replied, and indicated the fourth litter. "Move the Earth-human casualty ashore, quickly, and assist Murchison and Naydrad with it until I join you or send for another litter. I'll need this area to be clear of all other sources of emotional radiation if I'm to be absolutely sure whether or not life is present."

The emoting of Danalta and the Earth-human casualty diminished with distance to merge with the faint, background feelings of the medical team and the rest of the casualties. Without false modesty Prilicla knew that out of the entire Cinrusskin race he possessed one of the most sensitive and analytical empathic faculties his planetary history had ever recorded. For several long minutes he concentrated on using it.

And found nothing.

His disappointment was severe enough to make his limbs tremble. He knew that he was capable of detecting the emotional radiation of every species known to the Federation, right down to the tiny, savage feelings of non-sapient insects, but this was a thinking member of a new star-traveling species. Perhaps he had finally encountered one that thought and felt on a sensory level that was beyond his detection range. He was having feelings of personal doubt and inadequacy as well as disappointment.

Sometime and somewhere, he told himself as he lifted the scanner and keyed for the metal penetration setting, *everything has to happen for the first time.*

Prilicla moved closer until his head was only a few inches from the bulbous swelling in the protective garment which, in the majority of life-forms, was the location of the cranium and the nerve center of the sensory equipment. Slowly and carefully he passed the scanner over the area, continuing for several minutes to scan with his feelings at ultra-short range while at the same time searching with the instrument for clinical signs of life in any underlying organic material. He could not believe it when he found neither. He even had trouble finding his voice.

"Friend Murchison," he said finally, "I have a casualty here which requires further examination. Do you need me there?"

"We do, but not urgently," the pathologist replied. It emitted a sudden burst of concern before it brought the feeling under control. "You have been with that one for over half an hour. The situation here is that all four casualties have been cut free of their suits but there are a few small areas where pieces of burned clothing and charred body tissue are adhering, which will require surgical separation. The escharred areas and deeper burn locations where obvious necrosis has taken place will need to be trimmed away and the sites covered with surrogate skin until proper replacement surgery is available at the hospital. Meanwhile, IV nutrients, rehydration, and replacement of lost protein is currently under way while the casualties are being supported on cushions of cool, sterile air. Their present condition is critical but stable, and one of them, the last one you sent to us, is barely on the plus side of terminal. We may lose that one. Earth-human vital organs don't take kindly to being casseroled in their own juices. But you sound as if you might have another casualty for us. Is it a new boy on the block?''

Prilicla hesitated, then said, "I'm not yet certain whether it is a casualty for treatment or a new specimen for postmortem investigation. Certainly I've never encountered a life-form like this one before, or seen references to anything like it in the literature.''

"Sounds interesting,'' said Murchison, its matter-of-fact tone belying the mounting curiosity it was feeling. "When can we see it? Shall I send Naydrad with a litter to—''

"No,'' Prilicla broke in. He could feel the other's surprise because normally he would never have spoken so sharply to a subordinate. In a gentler voice he went on. "I have the feeling that you have the clinical situation under control over there. Continue as you are doing, but do nothing else until or unless I tell you otherwise.''

"Sir,'' it said, emoting intense puzzlement. The feeling was being shared and reinforced by Naydrad, Danalta, and the officers on *Rhabwar* who were monitoring the images and conversations coming from *Terragar*. But Prilicla needed answers himself before he could try to give them to others, and he had to pause for a moment to steady his shaking limbs before he could return to the scanner examination.

Since he was the only empath present, there was of course

nobody to know of or feel his fear. The minds of the medical team were engaged exclusively with their own clinical concerns, but the people on the ambulance ship had little more to do than to monitor and observe his actions, and those observations would have included the minor and continuing tremor in his limbs. Very soon friend Fletcher would deduce the reason for his terror, if it and the others hadn't done so already.

They knew as well as he did that the crew of *Terragar* had sought desperately to avoid all contact with their fellow officers and would-be rescuers, and that it was a virtual certainty that the entity he was trying to examine was the reason. It came as no surprise when the long period of silence was broken hesitantly by the captain.

"Doctor," it said. "Possibly this is none of my clinical business, and I'll understand if you tell me to shut up in your usual polite fashion, but your examination of the alien casualty puzzles me. I've been watching you for the past half an hour and have observed that while you began by closely approaching but not touching the creature, for reasons that I think we both understand, you are now making continuous contact with it. In what way has the situation changed? Is the creature no longer a threat to you, and, if so, why is your body language suggesting otherwise? And why are you examining every square inch of the body surface, including its hands and individual digits which, in my layperson's opinion, are not usually the site of life-threatening injuries?"

Prilicla was silent for a moment while he tried to organize the results of his examination in a form that would not embarrass him when the recording was played back, as it would be many times, by the cultural-contact people.

"I began by assuming that the air inside its suit was one of the oxygen-and-inert combinations used by warm-blooded oxygen-breathers, and identified the species tentatively as physiological classification CHLI. Sub-surface scanner investigation of the suit, and a deeper, detailed examination of its content, revealed the presence of unique technology of a level of complexity that I am not qualified to assess. The subsequent forensic investigation suggests that the position and sharply defined area of heat damage to the suit—the head section, forward pair of limbs, and particularly the attached digits which are literally fused together—was sustained before, rather than after, the subject was taken on board *Terragar*. The later atmospheric heating effects suffered by the ship had no effect on the occupant. No doubt, friend Fletcher, you will wish me to help you to make a more thorough investigation at a more convenient time.

"To summarize," he ended, "life—as we understand the term—is no longer present. I very much doubt that it ever was."

He felt the sudden burst of surprise and curiosity from the medical team, but it was on a low level because their attention was being concentrated on their Earth-human casualties. The captain's emotional radiation was accompanied by words.

"Wait, Doctor," it said. "Do I understand you correctly? Are you saying that the subject is a robot of unique and advanced design, and, and that it may be a casualty of war?"

"I'm unwilling to speculate on the available evidence, friend Fletcher," Prilicla replied, "but judging by the sophistication of design and construction in this mechanism, it may even be possible that we have discovered a non-organic form of intelligent life. But I advise extreme caution during any subsequent examination, because the actions of this creature or others like it may be the reason why *Terragar* was trying so hard to avoid contact with us. We won't know more until or unless the ship's officers are able to talk to us.

"Friend Murchison," he added, "I'll be with you in five minutes."

"The sooner the better," he heard Naydrad say. In spite of Murchison's earlier, reassuring situation report, he could feel that it was speaking for all of them.

The field medical station was a prefabricated, modular structure designed for use at the scene of space construction accidents or planetary disaster-relief operations. It comprised a self-contained, multiple-species operating room to which recovery wards, medical-staff accommodation, and ancillary equipment could be added as required. The OR was already in use and *Rhabwar*'s pressor beams had lifted in the less urgently required sections together with a couple of general-purpose robots that were busily attaching them as he approached.

As if it were an unconscious emotional preparation for the serious clinical problems ahead, a childhood memory of his home world, like a waking dream, came flooding back to calm his mind. In those days it had been himself who had been assembling brightly-colored structures out of building-blocks on the sand, and peopling them with legendary creatures out of his imagination who had strange and varied capabilities for performing great deeds of good or evil on those in their power—short of ending their lives, that was, because violent death was something that even an adult Cinrusskin did not willingly think about. This stretch of golden beach could have been the same, as was the green fringe of vegetation inland that was too indistinct to appear alien and therefore different. But there all similarity ended.

The steep, low-gravity waves of Cinruss had been replaced by the low, smooth rollers that peaked and foamed only as they broke in the shallows; and here the people inhabiting the bright building blocks were more varied and wonderful than anything he could ever have imagined as a child, and death was something that they thought about, faced, and, in the majority of their cases, conquered every day of their lives.

But not today.

From Murchison and the other team members he felt the sudden burst of sorrow, self-criticism, and near anger characteristic of healers who had just lost a patient.

CHAPTER 8

When he joined them a few minutes later, Naydrad was moving the deceased casualty to an adjoining compartment on a litter with a closed, opaque cover. The features of Captain Fletcher looked silently down from the wall communicator screen, the fleshy edges of its mouth pressed tightly together and its strong feelings tenuous with distance. Two other casualties had been given preliminary treatment and were floating above an enclosed, air-cushioned bed while Murchison and Danalta were working on the remaining one. They were concentrating all of their attention on excising the areas of charred tissue while covering the less severely affected sections of the body surface with the thick, creamlike, clinging medication that had been developed for the treatment of DBDG burn cases. It would aid tissue regeneration, deaden pain on the patient's return to consciousness, and protect against same-species airborne infection. The latter was the reason why it was the pathologist alone who was dressed for a full aseptic operational procedure.

Microorganisms that had originated on one planet could not cross the species barrier to affect or infect life-forms who had evolved on another. Naydrad felt the downdraft from Prilicla's wings on its uncovered fur and looked up.

"I'm beginning to feel like a redundant limb here," it said, looking at the newly arrived casualty with feelings of concern and impatience ruffling its mind and its fur. "Will I help you to cut off its suit?"

As a specialist in heavy rescue, Naydrad was the hospital's acknowledged expert at cutting all shapes and sizes of injured space casualties out of their environmental protection and underlying body coverings, if the species concerned wore them, without inflicting further damage to the living contents. It made no effort to salvage any part of the suit, but instead used its high-speed cutter to section the entire surface, leaving it with so many connected incisions that the pieces could be peeled away and discarded like the shell of a multiply cracked egg. Except in the places where the material and underlying skin had fused together into a single, charred mass, the uniform went the same way. While it was dealing with those areas, Naydrad positioned the patient for him on its frictionless bed of cooling air and began the rehydration process. Murchison and Danalta joined them without comment and smoothly took over the procedure while he withdrew to hover above the patient.

"How is it, sir?" said Murchison. They both knew that it wasn't asking about the patient's physical condition, which was clear to see, but the unseen emotional radiation that only he could detect. "Can it withstand major surgery?"

"It is better than I would have expected, and yes," Prilicla replied. "It has suffered major trauma and as a result is deeply unconscious, but the emotional radiation is characteristic of a being who, unconsciously, is still fighting to survive. That situation could change for the worse if we don't operate quickly.

"This patient," he went on for the benefit of the recorders, "took shelter in a heavy metal equipment cabinet. It was found in the kneeling position with its body folded forward at the waist and steadied by one hand. That hand and its lower limbs were in lengthy contact with metal whose heat was conducted through the suit fabric to the feet and knees so that these areas have sustained deep charring that involves the underlying circulatory system, muscles, and associated nerve networks. The other two casualties have already lost their feet and lower limbs. We may be able to save the hand on this one, which seems to have been holding a non-conducting tool to keep it from direct contact with the hot metal. Your feelings, friend Murchison, and those of the rest of you, indicate that you have come to a decision, but I must ask the question verbally.

"Is there general agreement," he ended, "that the lower legs should be removed without delay?"

He was aware of their feelings, so there was no real need for them to speak, but Murchison, who had its own, peculiarly Earth-human form of empathy, was feeling Prilicla's need for support and reassurance.

"Yes," it said firmly.

Before anyone else could reply, there was an interruption in the form of the captain clearing its breathing passages. It said, "Much as I dislike watching major operative procedures, especially on fellow officers of my own species who are personally known to me, I've been forcing myself to do so. The reason is that, to my medically untutored mind, and considering the literal hell they went through on that ship, it seems to me that there is a strong possibility that none of these casualties will survive."

It hesitated for a moment, and he was able to detect distant feelings of embarrassment mixed with determination as it went on. "To me the most urgent priority here is the gathering of information, knowledge that could be of vital importance to a great many beings throughout the Federation. After all, your patients were intent on killing themselves, so restoring one of them to a condition in which he can tell us why is . . ."

"Friend Fletcher," Prilicla broke in gently, "your words are giving rise to intense feelings of disagreement and anger which the medical team is trying hard not to verbalize, and in the present circumstances those words are an unwanted distraction. The clinical condition of the three casualties is critical but stable, and it is possible that they may not survive, much less regain consciousness.''

''In that case,'' the captain said, ''why not bring one of them round in case they die before they can give us the information we need? It will be tough on the person concerned, but they are Monitor Corps, after all, and would be the first to understand the priorities in this situation.''

For a long moment Prilicla tried hard to reduce the tremor that the other's suggestion had caused in his limbs, but succeeded only in keeping his operating hands steady. Finally he spoke.

''We will discuss this matter at a more convenient time,'' he said, without his customary politeness. ''You may continue to observe, but you will refrain from making any further suggestions until the procedure has been completed.''

The captain remained silent but watchful during the remainder of the operation, and the additional surgery needed on the other two casualties. Prilicla assumed that the other was breathing through its nasal openings because never before had he seen Earth-human lips pressed so tightly and continuously together. But when it was obvious to the layest of laypersons, which the captain was not, that the procedures on all three patients was completed, it spoke again.

Dr. Prilicla,'' said the captain, ''we must have a serious talk as soon as possible after—''

''Captain Fletcher!'' Murchison broke in, its words calm and cold and quiet, although the feelings that accompanied them shared none of those qualities. ''Dr. Prilicla has been operating here for nearly two hours, to which must be added its rescue time on *Terragar*. By now a space officer in your position must be aware of the physical limitations of the GLNO life-form, including its lack of stamina which requires that it rest frequently and often. We're all tired right now, and not just the boss . . .''

It broke off as the captain raised a hand for silence and said sharply, ''I'm well aware of my senior medical officer's requirements, and I had been about to say that we must talk very seriously as soon as possible after it has rested. It may well be that the situation we have here transcends any considerations of medical ethics. Sleep well, Doctor."

After a final check of the patients' monitors, Murchison, Naydrad, and himself retired, leaving Danalta on watch. In the shape-changer's utterly savage home-planet environment, all lifeforms who required regular periods of unconsciousness to recharge their organic batteries had not survived their unsleeping natural enemies to develop intelligence, so remaining awake was no hardship for it. In the present situation it extruded an eye and a large, sensitive ear which it kept trained on the patient monitors. There were times when Prilicla almost envied the unsleeping Danalta, but not often, because normally he needed and welcomed those periods of non-thinking and non-feeling when he did not have to empathize with anything or anybody.

When Cinrusskins slept, there was an external sensory shutdown. Neither loud noises nor bright lights nor the most acrid of smells would awaken them. Only a sharp, physical stimulus or the close presence of a source of danger, a legacy of his own prehistoric past, could do that. Even Cinrusskin dreams were brief, being nothing more than a few subjective seconds of bright, confused imagery from the recently experienced past or, as some of the more unorthodox Healers of the Mind argued, from possible futures. They were nothing more than the steeply shelving shallows at each end of a journey across the ocean of sleep.

In the fleeting dream before awakening he had been examining the non-organic casualty on *Terragar* again, but this time he was working in a thick, unseen cloud of anxiety and there was a pair of Earth-human hands assisting him. He dismissed the dream as another meaningless and random discharge of unconscious brain activity, chose a favorite breakfast from his food dispenser, then spent a few moments on the improvement of his appearance. He used an aromatic sponge to oil and polish his head, thorax, exoskeleton, and limbs, even though he knew that nobody on the ship would notice any difference, before he contacted the casualty deck.

Danalta reported that all three patients were in a stable and clinically satisfactory condition, and that they remained deeply unconscious with the monitors registering a slight but continuing improvement in life signs. Prilicla's empathic readings gave confirmation. Murchison and Naydrad were still in their quarters and emitting the emotional radiation characteristic of deep and undisturbed sleep. He decided to leave them in that condition, and face the coming confrontation with the captain without their moral support—always bearing in mind, he reminded himself dryly as he pressed the communicator stud, that for a Cinrusskin a very gentle and flattering attack was the best form of defense.

"Friend Fletcher," he began as the other's face appeared on his screen, "you displayed great sensitivity, understanding and kindness in allowing me to rest my fragile body and mind before discussing your own urgent concerns. But before we do so, you will be pleased to know that the clinical condition of the three injured officers is stable and their prognoses give grounds for guarded optimism. At present they are deeply unconscious and are likely to remain in that condition for many hours, perhaps up to few days. Following massive trauma that stops short of termination, you Earth-human DBDGs have a great capacity for physical and psychological recuperation, and in the present situation it is the mental aspect which must be given consideration if useful information is to be obtained from them.

"However," he continued quickly, "should an attempt be made to revive one of them prematurely, the consequent withdrawal of their anesthetic medication would have two effects. The sudden return to high levels of pain, combined with the medication-induced mental confusion, would render the necessarily short conversation with them, especially any specific, technical information they might try to give you during questioning, of doubtful value. As well, the general shock to their systems might cause them to terminate before they were able to produce sense-bearing sounds.

"Other than the clinical condition of my patients, friend Fletcher," he ended, "was there anything else you wanted to discuss with me?"

The captain remained silent for a long moment, then he heard it give a long sigh. Even though the emotional range was extreme, he could almost feel the disappointment that accompanied it.

"Dr. Prilicla," it said finally, "my primary need is for information regarding the reasons for the earlier abnormal behavior of your patients. You've effectively closed the first and most obvious source by pulling medical rank on me, for which we are all relieved. But I still need that information, urgently. Can you suggest another source?"

This time it was Prilicla's turn to be silent.

"Perhaps you are not yet mentally awake, Doctor," it went on. "Let me remind you that we're here in answer to three distress calls. Two of them may or may not have been due to the discharge of weapons by or at the alien ship, and the third was a standard subspace distress beacon released by *Terragar* which was later augmented by what seemed to be hand-signaled warnings to stay clear of the alien vessel. As the ambulance ship in attendance, *Rhabwar* is expected to report on the disaster and the action being taken to deal with it, or to request and specify the help needed if we are incapable of handling the problem ourselves. For technical reasons, that report will be necessarily brief, even terse, but it must contain the essential information . . ."

"Friend Fletcher," Prilicla broke in gently, "I am fully aware of the problems and shortcomings inherent in subspace radio communication and, considering my long service as *Rhabwar*'s senior medical officer, it is impolite of you to suggest otherwise. But if you are truly feeling concerned, I can assure you that I am physically rested and mentally alert."

"Sorry, Doctor," said the captain, "I was being sarcastic. The point I'm making is that twenty-one standard hours have passed since we arrived and no situation report signal has gone off because, frankly, I have nothing to say about it that makes sense even to me. But I have to say something or they will send another ship, or, more likely, warships, to find out what happened to us, and that ship or ships might also suffer the same fate as *Terragar*. That damage by beings unknown could be construed as a hostile act and we might have the beginnings of a war—pardon me, police operation—against the same persons unknown."

It took a deep breath and in a calmer voice went on. "I still need solid information, no matter how sparse, if for no other reason than to support my intended action of placing all three of the ships involved in indefinite quarantine. The reasons must be credible; otherwise our authorities might think that we have been so affected by the situation that we must be considered psychologically suspect, in which case they will send another ship anyway. But other than telling them to stay away from us, what can I say? Have you a suggestion, Doctor? I hope."

"I have, friend Fletcher," Prilicla replied, thinking how good it felt to be in possession of a clear mind in a rested body. "But it may involve a small personal risk for you."

"If the risk is warranted," said the captain impatiently, "the size is unimportant. Go on."

Prilicla went on. "Until I know the exact nature of the threat, infection, or whatever that seems to have been picked up by *Terragar*, I have asked that *Rhabwar* remain separated from the medical team. That stricture still holds, but I may have been a little overcautious because none of the team suffered any detectable ill effects as a result of our brief visit to the ship, nor myself from my examination of the damaged life-form found on board. I feel sure that, provided the normal safety precautions are taken and we subject ourselves to external sterilization procedures before and after the visit, we could conduct a forensic examination of the wreck in safety. Whatever the damage inflicted by the alien ship, or by that life-form found on board, it must have left some evidence of the kind of weapon used—enough, perhaps, to complete your report. And the quality of the information could well be better than that supplied by a semiconscious casualty in intense pain. Do you have any comments, friend Fletcher?"

The captain nodded and showed its teeth. "Three of them," it said. "The first is that you should rest and clear your body and mind more often. The second and third are, how soon can we meet, and where?"

Less than an hour later Prilicla was watching the captain's Earth-human hands beside his as they began the reexamination of the strange life-form, and suddenly he remembered his odd waking dream. He was about to mention it, then had second thoughts. The captain was not the sort of person with whom one discussed one's dreams.

CHAPTER 9

Murchison reported that the condition of the three casualties remained stable, and asked permission to go along to assist with the forensic examination. It had insisted that as an other-species pathologist its field covered all forms of intelligent life, and not just the organic variety. Prilicla had heard few lamer excuses for satisfying professional curiosity, which in Murchison's case was every bit as intense as that of the captain and himself, but he had agreed. Murchison was his principal assistant and the person most likely to inherit the senior medical officer's position on *Rhabwar*—and besides, he was curious to see how it dealt with a totally new situation.

That was why most of the talking was being done into the recorder by Captain Fletcher, with Murchison making an occasional interjection, while Prilicla spent long periods saying nothing at all. Following a meticulous examination with the special scanner provided by Lieutenant Chen—a scanner normally used to detect obscure symptoms deep inside ailing machinery—the captain straightened up, placed the instrument gently on the deck, and spoke with feelings of excitement and enthusiasm.

"This creature, entity, artifact, or whatever," it said, "displays a degree of design and structural sophistication well beyond the Federation's present capabilities—if it was, in fact, built by anyone or anything but itself. The internal circuitry and actuator mechanisms are so incredibly fine and intricate that at first I couldn't recognize them for what they are. This thing wasn't just put together by watchmakers but by the mechanical equivalent of a microsurgery team. I've traced several of the peripheral nerve networks to a processing area in the central body which seems to house the brain and heart equivalents. I can't be sure of this because that location has been damaged and the contents fused by the heat and radiation discharge that destroyed the creature. The sensory circuits underlying the surface in the same area have also been burned out, probably by the same agency, which may or may not have been a wide-focus heat weapon of some kind.

"But there is clear evidence throughout the whole body," it went on, "of a highly developed self-repair capability of apparently indefinite duration. Until it sustained that blast injury, this thing would have been capable of regeneration and growth. Any organism that can do that is technically alive."

Prilicla had a question but Murchison asked it for him. Quickly it said, "Are you sure that your subject isn't alive now?"

"Don't worry, ma'am," the captain replied. "How sure would you be if your subject's brain and heart had been burned to a crisp? Besides, its muscles—I mean its actuator linkages—are designed for light, precise work and are not all that robust. Physically it would not represent a serious threat"—it smiled—"except possibly to Dr. Prilicla."

Murchison returned the other's smile, because practically everything larger than an Earth kitten was a serious threat to Prilicla.

"Something else is worrying me," Murchison said, "I watched your internal scanner examination, Captain, and saw that the subject's body is solidly packed with circuitry, metal musculature, and sensory receptors. But why is it that particular shape?"

Fletcher remained silent, radiating the confusion and impatience characteristic of a mind that had been expecting a different question.

"Robotics isn't my specialty," Murchison went on, "but isn't it usual for one to be mechanically more functional? I mean, shouldn't it basically be a box with locomotor appendages simpler and more versatile than the six limbs we are seeing here; with a variety of specialized manipulators sprouting out of the body without regard to aesthetic balance; and with all-around visual sensors instead of just two in the head section? If this thing had been normally organic we would classify it as a CHLI. Rather than adopting a functional robotic shape, it seems clear that this body configuration is decidedly organimorphic. My question is, why would a non-organic intelligence copy itself on a CHLI?"

"Sorry, ma'am," the captain replied, looking and feeling apologetic. "I have no answers, just a wild guess."

Murchison nodded and said, "Which is?"

The captain hesitated, then said, "This isn't my field, either. But think about the evolution of an organic life-form as opposed to that of an intelligent machine. Ignoring the religious perspective, the first begins as an accidental grouping of simple, cellular forms which takes several millions of years of environmental adaptation with other competing species to become the dominant intelligence. The second doesn't do anything like that because, no matter how long it is given, a simple tool like a monkey wrench can never evolve through the intermediate stage of a lawn mower to become a superintelligent computer, at least, not without outside help. That simple tool has to be created by someone in the first place, and at some later stage the creator has to provide the machine with self-awareness and intelligence. Only then would there be the possibility of further self-evolution.

"I'm speculating, of course," the captain went on, "but a further possibility is that the beings who first bestowed on their machines the gift of self-aware, intelligent life are a permanent part of their racial memory—or inherited design—and that they were made, or in gratitude made the choice to remain, in their CHLI creators' image."

"In your opinion, friend Fletcher," Prilicla asked, "would this entity have been capable of disabling a starship?"

"No, Doctor," the captain replied firmly. "At least, not directly. Although composed of metal with plastic-insulated circuitry, the appendages were designed for precise and delicate work rather than hard labor or fighting, although there would have been nothing to stop it using those digits, as we DBDGs have been known to do, to operate a variety of destructive weapons. I'll be looking for anything like that when I'm searching the ship. All the evidence points to our robot friend being dead on arrival, and the type of heat and blast injuries it sustained were too unfocused to be caused by a Corps hand-weapon.

"And now," it went on, looking at the opened seams in the hull plating of the ship all around them, "I have to examine the body of a larger, metal cadaver, one that is more familiar to me."

Prilicla used his antigravity belt to move outside and fly forward to the control deck while Murchison stayed with the captain, both to satisfy its curiosity and to help move aside troublesome debris. There was minimal risk because both of them were experienced in negotiating ship wreckage, and he was pleased that neither their voices in his headset nor their feelings indicated that they were taking risks.

When they rejoined him, the two crescents of facial fur above the captain's eyes, and its emotional radiation, were indicating extreme puzzlement.

"I don't understand this," it said, gesturing aft. "Discounting the effects of atmospheric heating and buffeting on the hull on the way down, the ship's systems and linkages—power, guidance, life support—are all in pretty good mechanical order. Why should one of the officers have had to go aft to operate the main thrusters on manual? But that is what he did, and the answer has to be here somewhere in control."

"Including, friend Fletcher," said Prilicla, "the reason why the casualties wanted us to stay away from their ship?"

"That, too, Doctor," it replied. "And thank you for the reminder and gentle warning, which I'm pretty sure is unnecessary. Pathologist Murchison reported earlier that, apart from their severe burn trauma, there is nothing clinically abnormal about the patients' condition. On the way here she also told me that the only microbes present were the usual harmless, Earth-human bugs that came on board with them and were trapped in the air-circulation system, plus a few airborne varieties native to this world which cannot cross the planetary species barrier and so need not concern us.

"I agree with everyone exercising a high degree of caution," it went on, its feelings if not its voice registering impatience, "but surely it is no longer necessary to wear sealed suits, or for your team to continue working in an isolated, prefabricated unit with limited facilities rather than on *Rhabwar*'s casualty deck. There is nothing to threaten us here."

"It must be nice," said Murchison, radiating sarcasm, "to feel so sure of yourself."

"Friend Fletcher," Prilicla said quickly, in an attempt to reduce its growing irritation and head off a possible exchange of verbal violence, "no doubt you are quite right in everything you've said, but I, for physiological reasons that have made my people a species of arrant cowards, am extremely cautious. Please humor me."

The captain nodded and its feelings once again became calmly analytical as it began its examination of the damaged control consoles around them. It trained the vision pickup on each and every item and discussed its observations for the recorders. Apart from a few minutes checking with Naydrad on the condition of the casualties, they watched in silence the progress of a technically-oriented postmortem as painstakingly thorough as any the pathologist had performed on organic cadavers. Prilicla had always derived pleasure from watching an expert at work, and he knew that his feelings of appreciation and admiration were being shared by Murchison. But finally the work was done and the captain was staring at them with an expression and emotions that could only be described as a large and perplexed question mark.

"This doesn't make sense," it said. "The main and secondary computer systems are down. That shouldn't happen. They are strongly encased, protected physically and electronically in case of damage during a major malfunction or collision. They perform the function of the black boxes in atmosphere craft so that, in the event of an accident, the investigators have some idea of what went wrong. But there was nothing structurally wrong with *Terragar* except that all its computers are dead, or as good as. This is ridiculous. With all our fail-safe systems and protective devices, that should not have happened. . . ."

It broke off for a moment, then with a sudden burst of emotion intense enough to make Prilicla tremble it said, "Are you thinking what I'm thinking?"

"We're not telepaths, friend Fletcher," said Prilicla gently. "You'll have to tell us what you're thinking."

"I'd rather not tell you anything just yet," said the captain, "in case I'd be making a complete fool of myself." It reached into its equipment satchel and indicated one of the consoles whose plastic trim was only slightly heat-discolored. "There may still be some life left in that one. Instead of talking to you, maybe I'll be able to demonstrate my idea with this tester. The instrument has a small screen so you'll have to move closer. But don't touch it, or allow any of your equipment to make contact with it. That is very important. Do you understood?"

"We understand, friend Fletcher," said Prilicla.

"We think," Murchison added.

With the pathologist's feeling of bewilderment matching his own, they watched in silence as the captain expertly removed the console cover to lay bare the underlying circuitry. Then with a magnetic clamp it attached the tester to a convenient bulkhead, activated the display screen, unreeled one of the device's many probes, and went slowly and carefully to work. If it had been a sick patient rather than a malfunctioning machine, Prilicla thought, the other's movements could not have been more delicate or precise.

Many minutes passed while the display screen remained lit but blank, then suddenly it flickered and a schematic diagram appeared. The captain bent closer, excitement diluting its intense concentration.

"I'm into the ship's main computer now," it said, "and there's something there. But I don't recognize the . . . What the hell!"

The image was breaking up and generating random, geometrical lines and shapes that were drifting off the four edges of the screen until all that remained was an expanse of sparkling white noise. The captain swore and jabbed at several of its control studs without result. Even the green POWER ON light was dead.

The type and intensity of the captain's emotional radiation was beginning to worry Prilicla. He said, "Something has happened, friend Fletcher. What is troubling you?"

"My tester just died," said the captain. Suddenly it grabbed the instrument in both hands, raised it high above its head and slammed it downwards with all of its strength against the deck before adding, "And I was expecting it to happen, dammit!"

"Temper, Captain," said Murchison, radiating irritation and surprise as it bent down to pick up the remains of the device.

"No!" said Fletcher urgently. "Stay away from it. Probably there's no physical danger to yourselves because it's dead, defunct. But don't touch it until we know the technical reason for what happened here."

"Which was what?" said Prilicla.

He spoke very gently because the other's feelings were confused, fearful, excited, and radiating all over the emotional spectrum. It was an unprecedented mental condition for the usually calm and imperturbable captain to display. Murchison's feeling of irritation at the other's brusque manner was being replaced by the clinical calm of a physician towards someone who might shortly become a patient. But before the captain could reply, there was an interruption from Naydrad speaking on their headsets.

"Dr. Prilicla," it said. "One of the casualties, the last one you brought in, has returned to partial consciousness. Judging by its manner, it was the ship's commanding officer. It is greatly agitated, its speech is slurred and unintelligible, and, in spite of being immobilized, it is fighting all attempts at administering further sedative shots. The self-inflicted additional trauma is causing a marked deterioration in its clinical condition. If we patch you through, will you speak to it? Or better still, come back here and try your projective empathy on its mind?"

While the charge nurse was speaking, Prilicla had been trying not to tremble at the thought of what the severely burned and prematurely conscious patient was doing to itself. He said, "Of course, friend Naydrad. I'll talk to it now and while I'm flying back to join you. If it is *Terragar*'s captain, then *Rhabwar* will have its family and personal names on file. Quickly, please, find out what they are. Using them in conversation will help reassure it, but I'll speak to it now."

"No," said Fletcher. "I know his name. Let me talk to him."

He felt Murchison's earlier calm disappear in an uncharacteristic flare of anger as it said, "What the hell's got into you, Captain? This is a clinical matter. It is definitely *not* in your area of expertise."

Both of their faces were showing the reddening of temporarily elevated blood pressure, but the anger of the captain was being overlaid by feelings of increasing certainty as it said, "Sorry, ma'am. In this case it is, because right now I'm the only one here who knows what happened."

CHAPTER 10

The captain was not allowing the intense sympathy and concern it was feeling to affect the calm, unemotional tone of its voice as it spoke via the communicator screen to the patient, but considering the urgency of the situation, Prilicla thought that friend Fletcher's long-range bedside manner was very good.

"Captain Davidson, George," it began. "This is Don Fletcher, *Rhabwar*. We were able to land your ship, cool it in the sea, and recover your crew. Apart from the burn injuries, which are severe, you are in no immediate danger, and—please believe me—neither are we. . . ."

No sentient creature, Prilicla thought as an uncontrollable tremor shook his body, should ever have to suffer such an intensity of pain, much less have to fight through it in an attempt to produce coherent words. The captain's voice remained steady but its normally pink, Earth-human face had paled to a bloodless yellow-grey.

"George," it went on, "please stop threshing about in that litter and trying to fight your medication, and most of all, stop trying to talk. Believe me, we know what is troubling you and what you're trying to warn us about, and we appreciate the effort. But right now you must relax and just listen to me. . . ."

Captain Davidson was still trying desperately to talk rather than listen, but its words lacked coherency even to the listeners of its own species who did not need translators. The high levels of pain and fear and urgency it was feeling had not diminished.

". . . We received and understood the hand signals and emotional radiation from your control canopy," the captain went on, with a nod towards Prilicla, "and at no time was direct physical contact made by *Rhabwar* either with *Terragar* or the alien ship, and that situation will continue until the threat is fully understood. In the meantime *Rhabwar* has been positioned at a safe distance along the beach from this medical station that we have deployed to treat your survivors, and the remains of your ship are also at a safe distance from both. Following the recovery of your casualties, *Terragar* was boarded again and your ship interior and the remains of the alien robot we found on board were thoroughly investigated. As a result we know the reason for your desperate and apparently suicidal attempts to avoid contact with our own ship. We deeply appreciate what you were trying to do and tell us, but now we have received the message and probably know more about the threat from that alien ship than you do."

Prilicla detected the change in emotional radiation several seconds before Danalta spoke.

"The patient's struggles have diminished slightly," the shape-changer reported quietly without looking up from the patient. "It is no longer trying to speak, but the monitor indicates continued muscular tension and elevated blood pressure. You are getting through to it, Captain. I don't understand one word of your explanation, but for the patient's sake, keep on talking."

"From the evidence so far uncovered," Fletcher went on, ignoring the compliment and at the same time trying to reduce Danalta's level of ignorance, "I would say that the robot was floating free outside the other ship's hull and you recovered it hoping that it might be a survivor or, if not, that it would at least give you some idea of the form of life you were trying to rescue. When they didn't respond to your radio signals, you sent across a contact-sensor plate and connecting cable which you attached magnetically to the hull, hoping that it would be able to detect life signs or movements that your computer would be able to process to give the exact locations. But it was the direct cable connection between the sensor plate and your computer that wrecked *Terragar*. In short, George, that alien vessel doesn't affect or infect living people, it kills ships. It also infects, disables, or kills any lesser form of computer-controlled device that comes into contact with it.

"You turned up an alien hot potato this time, George," the captain ended softly, "but now it's our problem. So just relax, go back to sleep, and let us worry about it."

Several minutes passed without anyone speaking. From the medical team Prilicla detected feelings of surprise, curiosity, and excitement caused by Fletcher's explanation, while Captain Davidson's emotional radiation was that of a mind that was slipping back into unconsciousness.

"The patient is again responding to the sedative medication," he said, "and its life signs are stabilizing. Thank you, friend Fletcher."

"Yes, indeed," said Murchison, radiating relief and gratitude. "That was very well done, Captain." It looked at the broken test device lying on the deck and added, "Now we know why you lost your temper and trashed that thing. I'd probably have done the same."

Prilicla was feeling friend Fletcher's gratitude and pleasure at the compliments, as well as its increasing embarrassment. He said, "Have you enough information now to send your subspace signal?"

"On the *Terragar* situation, yes," the captain replied. "But I'd like to make the report as informative as possible. We have to go into space to send it, so I want to take a closer look at that alien ship before I do. Don't worry, I won't make direct contact or do anything stupid like deploying another sensor connection cable. *Rhabwar* will be back in three to four hours. And Doctor, we'll be visiting a hunk of sick machinery so there will be no need for a medical presence."

"There is, friend Fletcher," said Prilicla gently. "You are visiting a ship disaster situation and, regardless of the type or condition of the casualties, as the senior medical officer I should be there. About this I must insist."

Before any of his team could voice their objections, which were based principally on concern for his safety, he went on. "Don't worry, I shall take no unnecessary risks nor allow friend Fletcher to do so. Are there any decontamination procedures you can suggest before I transfer to *Rhabwar*?"

Murchison and Fletcher looked at each other for a moment while their feelings changed from concern to a grudging acceptance of the inevitable.

"The usual organic decontamination drill at the airlock," said the captain, "which is almost certainly unnecessary, but I don't believe in taking chances, either. . . ." It gestured towards the tester lying on the deck. ". . . And, of course, don't bring any computer viruses on board."

Even though the alien vessel was clean, bright, shining, and highly streamlined—a clear indication that it had taken off from a planetary surface rather than being assembled in space—among themselves, *Rhabwar*'s officers were calling it the Plague Ship. As a vessel crewed by robots it was probably as clean inside as it was out, Prilicla thought as he watched the image enlarge beyond the edges of his viewscreen, but then they were not talking about that sort of plague.

They moved in to a distance of two hundred meters and began a series of slow circles around its longitudinal axis. At close range, the only blemishes visible on the sleek hull were the two small craters with the heat discoloration around them and an open access hatch cover with heat-damaged equipment of some kind projecting from it.

"There's something odd about that hull damage," said the captain. "I would like a closer look at it, or better still, a hands-on examination. I'm thinking aloud, you understand, but what if I was to go over there in a lightweight suit, and didn't touch it with any computerized test equipment, and even retracted the suit antenna to reduce the risk of making metal-to-metal contact with the hull? It would also mean not carrying a weapon, but that is normal practice in a first-contact situation. At this short range I wouldn't need the antenna, and as an added precaution I could wear non-conducting gauntlets, and insulated covers for the boots, during the . . ."

"Pardon the interruption, friend Fletcher," said Prilicla quietly, "but I feel you radiating intense curiosity. I have similar feelings and would like a closer look, too. Admittedly the contamination we would be investigating is non-organic, but the presence of a medical advisor could be an advantage."

The other radiated indecision for a moment, then it made the soft, barking sound that Earth-humans called laughter and said, "Right. But I have the feeling that if Pathologist Murchison had been here she would give you an argument about that, as well as subjecting me to a great deal of verbal abuse for allowing you to take the risk. Chen?"

"Sir," replied the engineering officer.

"We intend closing to a distance of twenty meters, very slowly," Fletcher went on. "Be ready to pull us out again faster than that."

By the time Fletcher and himself had suited-up and flown clear of *Rhabwar*'s personnel lock, Prilicla had had time for many second thoughts and had foolishly discarded all of them. It was not always an advantage to carry Educator tapes whose donors were less cowardly than himself, especially when he allowed them to influence his own thinking. The alien vessel was now rolling ponderously at a distance of about thirty meters, but no attempt had been made to kill its spin because the tractor beam might have furnished an avenue for electronic infection. As they compensated for its movement with their suit thrusters, it felt as if they were tiny insects sandwiched between the vast white wall that was the ambulance ship's hull and the silvery surface of the alien vessel, with a broad, circular band that was divided into star-sprinkled space above and the mottled carpet of the planetary cloud blanket below them.

They used their suit thrusters to bring themselves to a halt within three meters of the open hatch cover. After a moment's hesitation, Fletcher edged closer and one of its hands made fleeting contact with the metal projection, then gripped it firmly in both.

"No harmful effects noted," it said for the benefit of the recorders.

"The mechanism projecting from the small compartment behind the hatch cover," it went on, "appears to be a simple, extendible metal arm with a hinged outer section that is capable of rotation horizontally and vertically through one hundred and eighty degrees, and there is a gripping mechanism at its extremity. It has the appearance of being an unsophisticated device used for placing in position on, or removing objects from, the external hull. There is evidence of scorch damage. . . ."

While the captain continued to describe in meticulous detail everything it was seeing and thinking, Prilicla waited until the slow, rolling motion of the vessel caused them to move close to the cratered area. With small, precisely timed bursts of thruster power he maintained position about two meters above them. He was not a forensics expert, but his visual acuity was exceptionally good and the type of damage he was seeing, although probably caused by the same agency, displayed a major inconsistency in its effect.

The first crater showed a normal, circular depression whose depth was approximately half of its diameter and with the interior and lip edges compressed and fused by the explosive pressure of a high-temperature blast of some kind, but the second one was entirely different. It had a shallower, ringlike formation with an area at its center that showed pressure but minimal heat damage. Deep scratches covering the area with what looked like small traces of silvery metal were adhering to some of them. Even though he was trusting to visual observation alone, Prilicla was sure that the metals of the hull and of that adhering to the scratches were markedly dissimilar. He edged closer to make absolutely sure before he spoke.

"Friend Fletcher," he said, "there is something very odd here that I would like you to see."

"The compartment behind this access hatch looks very odd, too," said the captain. It moved to join him and looked in the direction of his pointing digit for a moment before it added, "But you first, Doctor. What am I supposed to be seeing?"

"The difference in the extent and depth of the damage at this and the other crater," he said. "You can see that this crater is shallower than the first one and, while the perimeter of this one has been fused by intense heat, the central area has been depressed but is not as badly burned. There is deep scratching that contains small traces of a brighter metal that is foreign to the surrounding hull. It looks as if a large, fairly smooth metal object made heavy contact at this spot. Friend Fletcher, the size and outline of the unburned area are suggestive."

"You've got organic microscopes there instead of eyes, Doctor," it said. "But suggestive of what? I'm seeing what you're seeing, with great difficulty, but what should I be thinking about it?"

"Your pardon, friend Fletcher," said Prilicla. "I cannot be absolutely certain without analyzing a specimen for purposes of comparison, but the traces of foreign metal you see suggests that this is where the alien robot we found on *Terragar* sustained its injuries or—since it was not an organic life-form—damage. The weapon or other agency which blew a crater in the front of its body, also blasted it backwards against the hull with the results you can see. Perhaps it was trying to protect its ship from something, or someone. If the crew were defenders rather than attackers, their lethal assault on *Terragar*'s computer systems may have been due to a panic reaction following an earlier attack as well as a simple, first-contact misunderstanding."

"You could be right," said the captain, "but I think you're giving them the benefit of a very large doubt...." It reached towards the equipment satchel at its waist. "Grab my backpack and use your thrusters to hold me steady while I scrape off a specimen."

"Friend Fletcher...!"

"Don't worry, Doctor," said the other, radiating reassurance as it produced a short, broad-bladed screwdriver. "This thing is too simple and stupid to be infected by a computer virus.... Oops. That's strange."

While it had been scraping hard to remove the largest of the specimens, the tool's sharp blade had penetrated the hull and torn out a narrow triangle of metal. It was surprisingly thin, structurally weak, and its underside was covered by the fine, geometrical shapes of integral circuitry. When it had bagged the original specimen, Fletcher removed the hull sample and placed it in an insulated box as a precaution against possible electronic infection. The captain's accompanying feelings of impatience and barely controlled excitement suggested that it would rather be doing something else.

"I feel that you, too, have found something interesting, friend Fletcher," said Prilicla. "What is it?"

"I don't know," the other replied. It secured the two specimens in its sample box before going on. "I had time for a quick look into what seems to be a long, thin and apparently empty compartment or corridor behind the access hatch. It would be easier to show you, Doctor. There's enough room for both of us, and your extra helmet light will help us see whatever is in there, and, if necessary, make a fast retreat."

CHAPTER 11

Their lights showed a length of corridor leading inboard whose walls, except for a large cylindrical structure on one side that was enclosed by seamless metal plating that was warped and heat-discolored, were composed of a lightly-built, boxlike framework that appeared to be non-metallic. Continuous lengths of open-mesh netting were secured to and stretched tightly along all four inner surfaces of the framework and, about thirty meters inboard, a similar netted passageway intersected theirs at right angles. When the captain's foot caught accidentally in the netting, the whole corridor vibrated for a moment before returning to stillness.

"That wall netting tells us one important fact about their level of technology," said Fletcher, for the benefit of the recorder as well as Prilicla. "They don't have artificial gravity. And look at the internal supporting structure of the hull. It reminds me of the interior of one of Earth's old-time zeppelins—it's just a light framework on which to hang a streamlined skin that will aid passage through a planetary atmosphere."

"A skin," Prilicla reminded it gently, "that your second specimen suggests could be one single, overall, multipurpose sensor."

"Yes, indeed," Fletcher said. It pointed at the warped metal cylinder near them and went on. "I want to take a closer look at that later. From its size and shape I'd say that it houses one of a pair of matched hyperdrive generators which malfunctioned, either by accident or through malicious intent, and caused them to detonate a distress beacon."

Fletcher moved its vision pickup carefully so as to sight it inboard between the open mesh of the net. Prilicla pointed his helmet light in the same direction.

"Several more enclosed structures are visible," it resumed. "All are solidly-built, some with complicated shapes and many projections which badly needed that streamlined outer hull. They appear to be joined to each other by a latticework of structural-support members. All of the ones we can see are linked together externally by short stretches of open-weave corridors like this one. But our point of entry, which may not be the only one, was by a simple, close-fitting, hinged cover that appears to allow access deep into the entire ship. It was not a pressurized seal, and nowhere can we see anything like an airlock.

"But then," the captain added, allowing itself a small bark, "a crew of intelligent robots wouldn't need air.

"There is no obvious threat here at present," it went on, "so I shall continue the investigation deeper inside the ship. In case of unforeseen developments, Doctor, would you like to remain here so that you can make a fast getaway?"

Prilicla was silent for a moment while common sense and his evolutionary imperative of survival through cowardice warred with the intensity of his curiosity, and lost.

"I would like to remain here," he said, "but I won't. Lead the way."

The captain didn't reply but its feelings regarding such stupid behavior were very plain.

Slowly and carefully and with many pauses while Fletcher directed its vision pickup at objects that might or might not be of importance, they continued to move inboard while Fletcher described everything it saw and deduced in its flat, unemotional, observer's voice.

Their helmet lights showed many cable looms running along the members that joined the large and small structures and mechanisms that were coming into view. Some of the cable runs were attached to the outer framework of the passages they were traversing, and clearly visible. The individual lengths were color-coded, their graduation in coloration and shading suggesting that the visual sensitivity of the ship's crew was slightly higher than that of Prilicla's Earth-human companion, but lower than his own. When they drew level with a large, blocky mechanism of indeterminate purpose with what was obviously a control panel and two access hatches on it, the captain's curiosity became so intense that Prilicla felt obliged to issue a warning.

"No, friend Fletcher," he said. "Look but don't touch."

"I know, I know," it replied with a flash of irritation. "But how else can I find out what it is and does? I can't believe that these people—robots or whatever—would plant a virus to booby-trap every internal control panel and hatch. That wouldn't make sense. It would lead to a lot of unnecessary accidents among the crew."

"The robot crew," said Prilicla, "should be resistant to their ship's computer viruses."

"Good point," said the captain. "But so far there has been no sign of them. Are they in their quarters? If so, what would the accommodations for a crew of robots look like?"

It didn't speak again until they came to the next intersection, a T-junction leading into a passageway that led fore and aft to the limit of visibility provided by their helmet lights. The support frames carried what seemed like hundreds of differently-coded cable runs and the new passageway was obviously a main trunk route for crew members, but it was no wider or deeper then any of the others they had encountered.

That suggested infrequent traffic, Prilicla thought, or a small crew.

"We have to find out what this ship can do," said the captain suddenly, "apart from simply killing other ships. For our own defense we must learn and understand its weapons capability and, if possible, that of its attacker. Next time I'll bring something more intelligent than a screwdriver. A radiation sensor, perhaps, that will work without being in direct contact with the target object. . . ."

"Friend Fletcher," Prilicla broke in, "would you please be silent and absolutely still?"

The captain opened its mouth and shut it again without speaking. As it waited motionless, the curiosity, puzzlement, and increasing anxiety it was radiating hung about it like a thick fog.

"You may relax, friend Fletcher, at least for a few minutes," said Prilicla finally, directing his helmet light forward. "I thought I detected vibration in the corridor netting that was not being made by us, and I was right. Something is moving aft towards us. It is not yet visible. Shall we withdraw, I hope?"

"I want a look at it first," said the captain. "But stay behind me in case hostilities break out. Better still, you head back to *Rhabwar*, now."

The calm, controlled expectancy with a minimum of fear that was being radiated by the other compared very favorably with Prilicla's own cowardly feelings. He moved a few meters behind the captain but no farther.

In the netting around them the vibration increased, and suddenly it was within range of their helmet lights, a flattened, ovoid shape that moved like an enormous blob of animated quicksilver. The digits of the six short appendages spaced equally around its body were grasping the netting expertly and using it to pull the creature rapidly towards them, but at a distance of ten meters or so it slowed to a stop. Obviously it was watching them.

"Friend Fletcher," Prilicla said anxiously, "don't open your satchel—a tool could be mistaken for a weapon—or make any movements that might seem threatening."

"I know the first-contact procedures, Doctor," said the captain irritably. Slowly it released its hold on the netting and extended its two empty hands palms-outward.

A subjective eternity passed that must have lasted all of ten seconds without a response from the alien. Then its body rotated slowly through ninety degrees until the back or underside was directly facing them. Its six tiny hands were tightly gripping the netting all around it.

"It doesn't seem to be armed and its action isn't overtly hostile," said the captain, glancing backwards over its shoulder, "and plainly it doesn't want us to go any farther. But what can the rest of the crew be doing? Moving to cut off our retreat?"

"No, friend Fletcher," said Prilicla in gentle disagreement. "I have a feeling that . . ."

"Doctor," the other broke in incredulously, "are you saying that you're detecting feelings from this, this robot?"

"Again, no," he replied, less gently. "It is what you would call a hunch, or a guess, based on observation. I have the feeling that we are meeting half of the ship's crew and that we met the damaged other half on *Terragar*. There are small differences in size and body configuration which lead me to think that the damaged specimen was the male and this one is the female equivalent. . . ."

"Wait, wait," the captain broke in again, its emotional radiation a confusion of surprise and disbelief with a flash of the unsubtle humor associated with the cruder aspects of reproduction. It went on: "Are you saying that the design of these robots is so sophisticated that they have the means to reproduce sexually? That would imply the implantation of a metallic sperm equivalent and an exchange of non-organic DNA and . . . It's ridiculous! I just can't believe that robots, even highly intelligent robots, would need a sexual act to reproduce their kind, and I didn't see anything resembling sex organs on either of them."

"Nor did I," said Prilicla. "As I've already told you, it was a simple matter of differences in body mass and configuration. This one appears to be slimmer and more graceful. But now I would like you to do something for me, friend Fletcher. Several things, in fact."

The other's emotional radiation was settling down but it didn't speak.

"First," Prilicla went on, "I want you to move forward, slowly, until you've closed to half the present distance from the robot, and observe its reaction."

The captain did so, then said, "It hasn't moved and I think its hands are gripping the net even more tightly. Obviously it doesn't want us to pass. What's the next thing?"

"Move around behind me," said Prilicla. "It may consider you to be a threat even though you've taken no hostile action. Your body mass is over twice that of the robot, your limbs are long and thick and strange to it. My body is also strange but I don't believe anyone or anything would consider me a threat or, hopefully, wish to harm me physically.

"Then I want you to return to *Rhabwar*," he went on before the other could respond. "Move the ship away, a distance of half a mile should be enough, and come back for me when I signal. You will not have a long wait because fairly soon I will be close to the limit of my physical endurance."

The other was radiating such a combination of surprise, bewilderment, and intense concern for his safety, that it was making his limbs tremble.

"Friend Fletcher," he said firmly, "I need the area of this ship to be totally clear of all extraneous emotional interference, especially yours."

The captain exhaled so deeply that the sound in his headset was like a rushing wind, then it said, "You mean you want to be left alone and unprotected in an alien ship while you try to pick up emotional radiation from a machine? With respect, Doctor, I think you're mad. If I allowed you to do that, Pathologist Murchison would have my guts for garters.''

It was a colorful and physiologically-inaccurate Earth-human expression Prilicla had encountered before, and knew its meaning. He said firmly, "But you will allow it and do exactly as I say, friend Fletcher, because this is a disaster site and I have the rank.''

Gradually the principal source of emotional interference that was Fletcher diminished with distance as the captain retraced its path to their entry point and jetted towards *Rhabwar*, and a few minutes later the faint background of emotional noise from the ambulance ship's crew was gone as well. Very slowly and cautiously Prilicla extended one long, fragile arm and moved close to the robot.

"I think I'm mad, too," he said softly to himself.

Lightly he touched the robot in the center of what he assumed was the cranial swelling on its forebody. His gloves were insulated but very thin and he was expecting anything from a faint, tingling sensation to a lethal bolt of lightning, but nothing happened at all.

He concentrated his entire mind on his empathic faculty to force it into maximum sensitivity. As well as receiving the emotional radiation of patients, injured casualties, and accident survivors, he possessed a projective empathic ability which, if the receiving entity was not too distressed by fear or pain, could be used to pacify and reassure. It was the reason why most people felt good around him and why he had so many friends. As an aid to focusing the effect rather than in an effort to communicate, he began to speak.

"I mean you no harm," he said. "If you are in trouble, sick, injured, or malfunctioning, I want to help you. Disregard my outer shape and that of the other person who was with me, and the others you may meet. We must look strange and frightening to you, but we all mean you well. . . ."

He repeated the message while continuing to project reassurance, sympathy, and friendship at maximum intensity and, while doing so, he moved his hand to the middle of the robot's body and changed his touch into a soft, gentle push.

Abruptly it released its grip on the netting with four of its hands and used the other two to pull itself rapidly away from him. It was about to disappear forward beyond the range of his light when it paused and began to move back towards him again. When it was about five meters distant it stopped, then began to move away more slowly.

Plainly it wanted him to follow it, which, after a moment of fearful hesitation, he did.

The passageway was leading directly towards a complex structure that seemed to fill the interior of the vessel's bow section. The bracing members radiating from it and the framework of the passageway he was following were festooned with cable looms, many showing the distinctive color-coding of the outer hull's sensor network.

He was beginning to feel something.

"Are you doing this," he called ahead to the to the robot he was following, "or is it your superintelligent captain robot?"

It continued moving forward without replying. There was nothing on its silvery body surface that resembled a mouth, so probably it couldn't.

The feeling that came to him was so tenuous that it verged on the insubstantial, but it was increasing slowly in strength. At first he was unsure whether it was originating from one mind or a group of them; then he decided that it was coming from two separate thinking and feeling beings. Both of them felt distressed and frightened, and, as well, one was puzzled and intensely curious while the other was radiating the claustrophobic panic characteristic of close confinement and sensory deprivation.

So far as he could feel, neither of them were in any pain nor were they exhibiting the fear characteristic of imminent termination, but then, he thought, thinking robots might not have such feelings. For a more accurate emotional reading he needed to get much closer to them, but that was triply impossible.

He was at the end of the passage and facing the solid wall of the structure that probably housed them. Although there was a convenient panel filled with colored buttons and switches, he had no idea of the operating principles of the actuator mechanism that would allow entry or the damage he might do—not least to himself—if he tried and failed. And most important of all, he was fast running out of conscious time.

Prilicla was still frightened but for some odd reason he no longer felt threatened by his situation. Still, it would be considered an act of utter stupidity and carelessness if he were to fall asleep in the middle of an alien starship.

CHAPTER 12

When Prilicla wakened he felt rested and clearheaded but he was also feeling, in spite of the source being half the ship's length away, the angry impatience of the captain. He had been semicomatose from fatigue when he had returned from the alien vessel, and had not been able to make a coherent report, and now friend Fletcher was waiting to talk to him. The trouble was that he was still feeling so confused by his discoveries inside the ship that the report would sound incoherent. He needed more time to think.

Cowardice—both physical and moral—and procrastination were second nature to him. He flew down the central well to the casualty deck and used its communicator to contact Pathologist Murchison for a detailed report on the condition of *Terragar*'s casualties.

It told him that Captain Davidson and the two surviving officers were stable, responding to the limited treatment available in a temporary medical facility, and being maintained on a regimen of IV feeding and heavy sedation. Personally, it felt that the quarantine arrangements between the patients and the ambulance ship were totally unnecessary, and a rapid casualty transfer to *Rhabwar* and a fast return to Sector General for more aggressive treatment were indicated. It ended by saying that the investigation and first-contact situation with a bunch of intelligent robots was a technical matter and none of their medical business.

Prilicla was unable to detect the pathologist's emotional radiation from orbit, naturally, but he could imagine the intense irritation and concern it and the rest of the team were feeling for their patients. He also knew that friend Fletcher would be routinely monitoring all radio traffic between the ship and the surface so that what he was about to say would mean that he could not delay speaking to the captain any longer.

"Friend Murchison," he said gently, "I don't foresee an immediate return to Sector General because the situation here is becoming more complicated. There are two other-species casualties on the alien vessel who may also require attention. . . ."

"Other-species casualties!" it broke in. "Sir, with respect, we're not running a bloody robot-repair shop down here."

"You are assuming that the alien casualties are non-organic life forms," he replied. "That may not be so. But I have no wish to answer the same questions twice, so keep your communications channel open and listen in while I talk to the captain. I can feel friend Fletcher very badly wanting to talk to me."

"You're right, Doctor," said the captain as he flew onto the control deck a few minutes later. It gestured towards the communicator whose monitor light was showing and went on, "What was that all about? Other-species casualties? What did you find after I left you alone back there?"

Prilicla hesitated, but not for long because the other's impatience was so intense that it was making him tremble. He said, "I'm not sure what it was that I found, and even less sure of what it means. . . ."

Briefly he described the events following the captain's departure for *Rhabwar*, the silent but obvious efforts of the robot crew member to entice him to follow it forward to the end of the central passageway where he could go no farther, and all that he had seen, thought, and felt there.

". . . On the way back," he continued, "I decided that I had enough time to spare before I fell asleep to explore the ship's stern, and followed the passageway all the way aft. The inside of of that ship is like a three-dimensional spider's web, with thin supporting and bracing members, open-netting passageways, and, most of all, cable runs linking the major internal structures. Considering the color-coding on the majority of the cable looms I saw—especially those linking the microcircuitry underlying the ship's outer hull to what is presumably the control center forward—there are close similarities in the overall structure to the layout of major organs, musculature, and central nervous system of an organic life-form. The skin is highly sensitive and we know how it can react to an attack, or what it thinks is an attack, by an outside agency.

"We were safe," he went on quickly, "because we entered through the damaged hatch, which is analogous to a traumatized and desensitized surface wound. The forward structure obviously houses the brain and . . ."

"Wait, wait," said the captain, holding up one hand. "Are you telling me that the whole ship is alive? That it's an intelligent, self-willed star-traveling machine like its robot crew members, only bigger? And that all that stopped you getting into its computer superbrain—or, from what we overheard you tell Pathologist Murchison, its *two* superbrains—was a simple, structural impediment and your lack of physical endurance?"

"Not exactly," Prilicla replied. "There has to be a nonorganic interface, but I'm beginning to suspect that the two controlling brains belong to organic life-forms, with feelings. I won't be able to prove that until you find a way of getting me into the brain housing.

"I need to go back inside that ship," he ended, "for an extended stay."

The captain and everyone else on the control deck were staring at him, their emotional radiation too complex for individual feelings to be isolated. It was Murchison on the communicator who broke the silence.

"Sir," it said, "I strongly advise against this. We're not dealing with ordinary casualties here . . ."

"Define an 'ordinary casualty,' " said Prilicla quietly.

". . . being recovered from the usual run of space wreckage," it went on, ignoring the interruption. "This could be—in fact it was, so far as *Terragar* was concerned—an actively hostile vessel. Its hyperdrive is out, but otherwise there appears to be only superficial hull damage. In spite of your theory that its sensors are only skin-deep, there may be internal booby-traps that could injure or kill you because you don't understand the technology behind them. Captain Fletcher is the specialist in other-species technology. At least let him open up this metal cranium before you go in."

While Murchison had been speaking, the captain had been nodding its head and radiating agreement.

"I agree with both of you," Prilicla said. "The trouble is that while the captain is a topflight solver of alien puzzles, it is not an empath. The moment-to-moment feelings of the beings we are trying to recover could be a very important guide to whether or not we are doing the rescue work properly. The captain and myself will do it together.

"Friend Fletcher," he said, gently changing the subject, "is the information you have now enough to send that hyperspace message?"

"Enough for a preliminary report," the captain replied, radiating anxiety. "My problem will be making it short enough not to drain our power reserves."

Prilicla was well aware of the problem. Unlike the detonation of a hyperspace distress beacon, which was simply a location signal and an incoherent cry for help, this message had to carry intelligence. It had to carry it in spite of all the intervening sunspot activity, charged gas clouds, and other forms of stellar interference that would be tearing it into incoherent shreds. The only solution that had been found was to make the message brief and concise and to repeat it as many times as the transmitting station's available power would allow so that a receiver could process it, filter out the interstellar mush, and piece the remaining fragments together to obtain something like the original signal. A surface station with virtually unlimited power reserves, a major space installation like Sector General, or even one of the Monitor Corps' enormous capital ships could send messages lengthy enough for later processing with clarity. Smaller vessels like *Rhabwar* had to reduce the possibility of additional local interference from a planet's gravity field by transmitting their signals from space, and even then they had to trust to the experience and intuition of the person manning the receiver.

But the captain was radiating a level of anxiety greater than that warranted by simple concern over the wording of a condensed situation report.

"Is the necessarily compressed wording of the signal your only problem," Prilicla asked, "or are the two new aliens a complication?"

"Yes, and no," the captain replied. "There will be too few words available for me to include either complicated arguments or reasons for what I want done. Are you quite sure that the two new ones you found are organic rather than robotic life-forms? And would you object if the signal expressed doubt on that point?"

"No, and no," said Prilicla. "The emotional contact was tenuous. Perhaps it is possible for a really advanced computer to have feelings, but there is doubt in my mind. Something else is worrying you, friend Fletcher. What is it?"

The captain sighed, and embarrassment diluted its feelings of anxiety as it said, "This whole situation is potentially very dangerous and, if it isn't handled correctly, it could develop into a greater threat to the Pax Galactica than the Etlan War . . . I mean, police action. I want to order this solar system to be placed in quarantine, interdicted to all service and commercial traffic and contact forbidden to all personnel other than those presently on-site. That includes medical assistance, first-contact specialists, or technical investigators, and there must be no exceptions.

"My worry," it ended quietly, "is whether or not my superiors will obey that order."

In spite of its efforts at emotional control, the captain was radiating a level of concern that verged on outright fear. Fletcher, as Prilicla knew from long experience of working with it, rarely felt fear even in situations where it would have been warranted. Perhaps, considering their initial contact with the outwardly undamaged but utterly devastated *Terragar*, the other was frightening itself needlessly. Or, more likely, it understood the nature of this technological threat better than could a medic like himself. Either way, it was a time to offer reassurance.

"Friend Fletcher," he said, "please remember who and what you are. You are the Corps' most experienced and respected specialist in the investigation of unique other-species technology, otherwise you would not have been given operational command of this, the greatest and most non-specialized recovery vessel ever built. When your superiors consider this fact, I have no doubt that your orders will be obeyed.

"I'm assuming," Prilicla went on, "that the medical team will remain here with *Rhabwar* since we are best-suited to solving a unique problem that is both technological and medical. However, allowances must be made for the natural curiosity of your higher-ranking colleagues. They will probably send at least one fast courier vessel for information-gathering purposes, in addition to the ship we need to transfer the *Terragar* casualties to Sector General. . . ."

"My point exactly!" Fletcher broke in, a burst of anger briefly overshadowing its anxiety. "A quarantine is either in force or it isn't, but for what may or may not prove to be good, medical reasons, even you are willing to break it. Everyone must be made to realize that we are faced with the technological equivalent of a plague. You and your team know this, you've seen what it can

do for yourselves, and still you are willing to compromise by ..."
It raised its hands briefly and radiated helplessness. "If I can't
convince you, what chance is there of a mere captain and glorified
ambulance driver telling fleet commanders and and higher what
to do and making it stick? I don't have enough bloody rank."

"Together, friend Fletcher," said Prilicla, "we might have
enough. I suggest you draft the signal you wish to send, and if
you wouldn't mind, let me see it and perhaps suggest amend-
ments before transmission with a view to increasing its effectiveness. ..."

"I'd do that anyway," the captain broke in angrily, "as a
matter of professional courtesy. But I won't promise to insert
your changes. Considering the power requirements, that signal
must be clear, concise, and contain absolutely no excess verbi-
age."

"... While you're doing that," Prilicla went on gently, as if
the interruption was a figment of everyone's imagination, "I'll
check on the condition of the Earth-human casualties before trying to get close enough to identify the two on the alien ship."

The captain was radiating feelings of disbelief. "You mean
you want to go back in there?"

"As soon as possible," he replied.

Within the first few minutes it became clear that he was not
urgently required in the medical station. *Terragar's* casualties
were stable, responding well to treatment, and showing signs of
significant improvement although the grafting, reconstructive
surgery and lower-limb replacements should be done as soon as
practicable at the hospital. But if he was reading correctly between the lines of dialogue, there was a problem. Unlike his em-
phatic faculty, intuition was not affected by distance.

"I think there is something other than the patients' clinical
condition worrying you, friend Murchison," he said. "What is
the problem, and does it require my presence?"

"No, sir," the other replied quickly. "I'm ashamed to say,
the problem is sheer boredom. We're all cooped up in this bunch

of high-tech medical shoeboxes with virtually nothing to fill our time except watch the patients getting better while outside the sun is shining, the sea is blue, and the sand is warm. It's as environmentally perfect as the hospital's recreation deck except that it's bigger and it's real. Sir, it feels as if we're on vacation but confined to our hotel bedrooms.

"Subject to the usual safety checks," it went on, "we'd like permission to take turns exercising and relaxing outside. This really is a lovely place. The casualties would benefit from the fresh air and sunshine as well, especially if our stay here is likely to be extended. Is it?"

"It is," said Prilicla. "*Rhabwar* will have to remain in orbit to investigate the alien vessel and its crew, who may themselves be with you soon as casualties. Permission granted, friend Murchison. But remember that this is a completely strange as well as a pleasant world, so be very careful."

"You, too, sir," she replied.

He ended the transmission as the captain pointed at its own screen and spoke.

"You wanted to see this before I send it off," it said. "Well, what do you think?"

Prilicla hovered above the screen for a moment, studying it, then he said, "With respect, friend Fletcher, I think it is too polite, too subservient, and too long. You should tell your superiors what you want done, as I will also do, without regard to the high rank of those concerned. Because of our knowledge of the situation here, limited as it is, we have the rank. May I?"

He felt Fletcher's agreement before it could reply, and dropped his feather-light digits onto the keyboard. The original draft, scaled down, moved to the corner of the screen and the new one appeared. It read:

TO: GALACTIC FEDERATION EXECUTIVE; COPIES FEDERATION MEDICAL COUNCIL; SECTOR TWELVE GENERAL HOSPITAL; MONITOR CORPS HIGH COMMAND; SECTOR MARSHAL DERMOD,

FLEET COMMANDERS, ALL SHIP CAPTAINS, AND OFFICERS OF SUBORDINATE RANK.

WITH IMMEDIATE EFFECT THIS SOLAR SYSTEM IS TO BE PLACED IN QUARANTINE.

REASONS: UNIQUE TECHNOLOGICAL AND/OR MEDICAL THREAT BY DISTRESSED ALIEN SHIP MOUNTING UNIQUE WEAPONRY CAPABLE OF DESTROYING ALL SPACE VESSELS REGARDLESS OF SIZE OR POWER RESOURCES. DISTANCE IS ONLY KNOWN SAFEGUARD.

THREE *TERRAGAR* SURVIVORS RECOVERED. *RHABWAR* INVESTIGATING ALIEN SHIP AND TRYING TO CONTACT CREW.

REQUEST TWO COMMUNICATIONS VESSELS TO BE STATIONED MINIMUM OF FIVE MILLION MILES DISTANCE TO RELAY LATER INFORMATION AS IT BECOMES AVAILABLE. ALL OTHER VESSELS AND PERSONNEL REGARDLESS OF SPECIALITY OR RANK ARE EXPRESSLY ORDERED TO STAY CLEAR.

NO REPEAT NO EXCEPTIONS.

FLETCHER, COMMANDING *RHABWAR*

PRILICLA SENIOR PHYSICIAN, SECTOR GENERAL

For a long moment the captain stared at the screen while it regained control of its feelings, then it said reluctantly, "It's shorter and . . . well, better. But Sector Marshal Dermod doesn't usually receive messages like this from subordinates. He and his staff will probably have a collective fit. I didn't realize, Doctor, that you could be so, so . . ."

"Nasty?" said Prilicla. "You're forgetting, friend Fletcher, that your sector marshal is halfway across the Galaxy, and I am unable to detect its emotional radiation over interstellar distances."

CHAPTER 13

It was a rule of interspecies medicine to which no exception had ever been found that pathogens which had evolved on one world could not affect or infect any creature belonging to another. There was nothing in this world's microbiology, therefore, that could threaten her. But that did not stop Danalta, in the respectful manner befitting a subordinate, from insisting that Murchison take no chances with the life-forms that were large enough to see.

The shape-changer had already scouted the beach, shallows, and the trees and undergrowth inland to a distance of five hundred meters, for evidence of large and possibly harmful life-forms. A few varieties of water-breathing and amphibious creatures inhabited the shallows, tiny animals and insects crawled or flew among the tree roots and branches, but none of them were large enough to constitute a physical threat. This did not mean that they could be completely ignored. Pathogens could not jump the off-world species barrier, Danalta reminded her unnecessarily, but insects secreting organic toxins in poison sacs were capable of delivering painful if not lethal stings, the crablike sea-dwellers could nip, and all of them, should they feel threatened or hungry enough, could bite.

That was why she was walking along a golden beach without

feeling the gentle abrasion of hot sand between her toes while, apart from her uncovered face and the backs of her bare hands, much of the sun's heat was being reflected away by her white coveralls. In this situation she would have preferred to wear much less, and the other members of the team would neither have cared nor noticed if she had worn nothing at all because Earth-humans were one of the few intelligent species with a nudity taboo. The others covered themselves only when their working environment required the wearing of body protection. In spite of her advancing years, Peter kept telling her with maximum ardor and minimum poetry—and when his brain was not so busy with other-species mind partners that he was unsure of who and what he was and why they were lying together—that she was in very good shape.

She wished he were with her now, under this real sky rather than the artificial one on the hospital's crowded recreation deck, with his mind his own, its professional concerns forgotten, and his attention concentrated entirely on her. But, she supposed, being the life-mate of the renowned Conway, Sector General's Diagnostician-in-Charge of Other-Species Surgery, had to have a few disadvantages. He couldn't take a vacation of opportunity like this just because she wanted to and he probably needed it. She sighed and continued walking.

Beside her Danalta rolled silently over the sand. In keeping with the occasion, and because it liked to give gratuitous exhibitions of its shape-changing prowess, it had adopted the form of a recreational plaything much-favored by Earth-humans, a large beach ball. It was covered overall by triangles of garish red, yellow, and blue; the eye, ear, and mouth were inconspicuous and the visual effect was quite realistic, but the track that it made in the sand was too deep to have been made by an air-filled ball. Danalta, regardless of the shape it took, was unable to reduce its considerable body-weight. The pretty ball would never bounce.

"Would you like to move inland?" said Danalta, stopping suddenly and extruding a bright green, Earth-human hand and index finger to point. "That hill is only a mile away and seems to be the highest point on the island. From there we might be able to see features of special interest to explore later, and possibly the nearer islands."

As well as being a show-off, the polymorph was intensely curious about everything regardless of shape or size, and the harder it was to mimic, the better it liked it.

"Fine," said Murchison. "But in case we're needed urgently I want to stay as close as possible to our patients. There's a stream that runs past the med station into the sea. We'll go back and follow it inland to its source, which should be on high ground. Do you agree?"

It was a rhetorical question, and even though she wasn't in the habit of pushing her rank, they both knew it.

For the first hundred meters or so, the nearby environment could have been that found on any sun-drenched, tropical island on her home world. The stream was less than two meters wide but fast-flowing so that the stones on its bed were washed clean and showed many different colors and patterns of veining. It was only when her walk, and Danalta's roll, took them inland and under the trees that the differences began to show. The chlorophyll-green of the leaves looked the same but the shapes were subtly different as was the soft carpet which was not of grass that grew along the banks of the stream from damp earth that was not of Earth. A little shiver of pure wonder made her twitch her shoulders, as it always did when she encountered a completely alien planet that looked and felt so entirely familiar. Then as they moved deeper under the trees, the amount of vegetation bearing large, sunflower-like blooms increased. The petals on many of them had dropped away to reveal clusters of pale green fruit buds. There would be no problem with cross-pollination here, she thought as the insects began to swarm.

Very definitely they were like nothing on Earth.

They ranged in size from the virtually invisible to several stick-insect varieties whose bodies were nearly six inches long. A few of them were rounded, black and shiny, with wings that beat so rapidly that they seemed to be surrounded by a grey fog, but the majority were brightly colored in concentric circles of yellow and red with multiple sets of wide, slower-beating gossamer wings that threw back constantly changing, iridescent highlights. They were gorgeous, she thought, and some of them made even Prilicla look dowdy.

Most of them were heading towards Danalta, obviously attracted by the garishly colored beach-ball body it had adopted.

"They seem to be curious rather than hungry," said the shape-changer. "None of them has tried to bite me."

"That's sensible of them," said Murchison nervously as they lost interest in Danalta and began moving towards her. "Maybe they've realized that you're indigestible."

"Or I have the wrong smell," it replied. "I've just now extruded an olfactory sensor pad. There are a lot of strange smells in this area."

Smells, Murchison thought, was not the word she would have used to describe them. The subtle combination of scents being given off by the aromatic vegetation around them was something that the fashion perfume houses on Earth would have sold their souls for. But the insects were now homing in on her.

Instinctively she wanted to swat them aside, but knew that might make them excited and hostile. Instead she raised one hand very slowly to her opened helmet visor so that she could snap it closed at the first sign of an attack. Her hand remained there, tense and motionless, for several minutes while the insects large and small swarmed around her head without actually touching her face, until they lost interest and returned to their own concerns.

Relieved, she lowered her hand and said, "Apparently they're non-hostile, They don't want to bite Earth-human DBDGs, either."

Which meant that, should their stay on this island paradise

be delayed for any reason, the *Terragar* casualties could be moved outside for a few hours every day. She had always been a believer in the efficacy of natural fresh air and sunshine in the post-op treatment of casualties, a form of treatment not available in Sector General.

Puzzled, she said, "No animal or insect species, regardless of its size, can be universally friendly and hope to survive. These seem to be the exception that proves the rule. Let's move on."

The ground began to rise gently, the trees opened out into a large clearing and the stream became a wide, shallow pool whose bottom was covered by broad-leafed plants, each of which floated a single, radiant bloom on the surface, and they saw their first non-insect life-form.

Three fat, piglike animals with mottled yellow-and-brown skin, narrow, conical heads, and sticklike legs were wading in the shallows, nibbling at the flowers or pulling up the subsurface greenery. When Murchison's shadow fell across them they made bleating noises and ran splashing up the bank to disappear into the long vegetation that was not grass. From all over the clearing and under the surrounding trees came the sound of more bleating, and a much larger version of the same animal pushed through the greenery to stand and look at them for a moment before apparently losing interest and moving away.

"That must have been Mama or Papa," said Murchison. "But have you noticed, even the adult life-form is placid and unafraid and without aggressive tendencies or obvious natural weapons, and so far we've seen no sign of any predators or prey. Prilicla would just love this place. Have you seen any signs of bird life?"

Murchison went down on one knee and shaded her eyes with both hands in an attempt to reduce sky reflection while she studied the subsurface features more closely. A few minutes later she stood up again.

"None," said Danalta, "but one must expect strangeness on a strange planet. Are you ready to move on?"

The ground ahead began to slope more sharply, and a few minutes later they found the natural spring that was the source of the stream bubbling out of a crevice in the ground that was now showing several flat outcroppings of rock. The trunks and branches of the trees competing for the green areas between them were stunted and carried fewer blossoms and buds so that the insect population was proportionately diminished. But it was still a beautiful and relaxing place, especially with the breeze off the ocean finding its way through the thinning vegetation and cooling her face. Murchison took a deep breath of fresh, scented air and let it out again in a sound that was a combination of a laugh and a sigh of sheer pleasure.

Danalta, who found no pleasure in fresh air, smells, or environmental beauty, extruded a pointing hand and said impatiently. "We're within fifty meters of the highest point of the island."

The rounded summit was covered sparsely by trees, but not enough of them to obstruct their all-around view over the island. Through the gaps in the intervening foliage, Murchison could make out tiny areas of ocean, beach, and a section of the white medical-station buildings. A scuffling sound on the ground made her swing around to look at Danalta.

Its beach-ball configuration was collapsing, flattening out and spreading across the ground like a mottled red, yellow, and green pancake. Suddenly it rolled itself up into a long, cylindrical, caterpillar shape with a great many legs, before heading for the highest tree. She watched as it wound itself around the lower trunk corkscrew-fashion and began to climb rapidly.

"The view from up there will be much better," it said.

Murchison laughed and moved to follow it. Silently she was calling herself all kinds of a fool because if she were to become a casualty through falling out of a tree she would never live it down. But she was feeling like a child again, when tree-climbing had figured high among her accomplishments, and the sun was shining and all was right with this world and she just didn't care.

"Earth-human DBDGs can climb trees, too," she said. "Our prehistoric ancestors did it all the time."

A few minutes later she was as close to the top as it was safe to go, with one arm wrapped around the trunk and a branch that looked strong enough to bear her weight gripped tightly between her knees. Danalta, whose latest body-shape enabled it to distribute its weight more evenly than her own, was clinging to the thinner branches a few meters above her. The view over the island and beyond was perfect.

In all directions they could see across the dark green, uneven carpet of treetops and clearings to the ragged edges where it met the beach. The medical station looked like a collection of white building-blocks standing in the dark, lengthening shadows of approaching evening, and the ocean was empty except for a tight group of pale blue swellings that were probably the mountaintops of a large island that was below the horizon. Danalta extruded an appendage to point slightly to one side of the distant mountains.

"Look," it said. "I can see a bird. Do you?"

Murchison stared hard in the indicated direction. She thought she saw a tiny, fuzzy speck almost touching the horizon, but it could just as easily have been her imagination.

"I can't be sure. . . ." she began, and broke off to stare at the thick cylindrical member that was growing out of the top of Danalta's head. "Now what are you doing?"

"I'm maximizing my visual acuity," it replied, "by positioning a lens of long focal length the required distance from my retina and making small focusing adjustments. Since the material is organic and the viewing base is moving perceptibly in the wind, some distortion is to be expected, but I'm sure that I can resolve the image to show . . ."

"You mean you're growing a telescope?" she broke in. "Dr. Danalta, you never cease to surprise me."

"Definitely some kind of bird," it said—obviously pleased at the compliment—and went on, "with a small body, wide, narrow wings and a triangular tail whose outer edges are uneven. At this distance the size is uncertain. It appears to be dark brown or grey in color and non-reflective. It has a short, thick neck but I cannot resolve any details of the head and there are no other body projections, so presumably its legs are folded for aerodynamic reasons. The wings do not appear to be beating and it seems to be soaring on the air currents. It is close to the horizon and shows no sign of dropping below it.

"Birds did not evolve on my home planet," it went on, "but I have studied the various species with a view to possible mimicry. So far, the general appearance and behavior of this one resembles that of a carrion-eater found on your own planet. At this range anything else I could tell you would be mostly guesswork."

"Let's go back to the station," said Murchison quietly. "I want to be there before sunset."

Danalta had spotted the planet's first bird, she thought, as she climbed to the ground, and it seemed to be the equivalent of an outsized vulture, with all that that implied. It was silly to feel so disappointed just because this perfect-seeming world had shown its first imperfection.

CHAPTER 14

Captain Fletcher and Lieutenant Dodds were being extremely careful, Prilicla noted with approval, and displaying a level of vigilance that elevated caution to the status of a major art form. This time they were using *Rhabwar*'s pinnace, a vehicle normally used for evacuating space-wreck casualties whose condition was not serious enough to require litters, to move a variety of specially insulated test equipment to a more convenient distance from the investigation site. All of the analyzers had one or more backups, in case they probed a sensitive area and the alien ship killed the instrument stone-dead as it had done to *Terragar*'s sensors.

Not for the first time the captain was reminding them that the test instruments and even the pinnace were expendable, but not the people using them, which was the reason why they were wearing insulated, self-powered spacesuits.

Rhabwar maintained its distance with a communications channel open while they edged to a stop a few meters above the damaged area of the alien's hull, then tethered their vehicle loosely to it with a simple magnetic pad attached to a non-conducting cable.

"Sir," the lieutenant said as they were exiting the vehicle, "Dr. Prilicla says that this damaged area of hull—what it calls the surface wound—has apparently become desensitized to outside stimuli and we can safely make contact there. But shouldn't we check to make sure that other areas haven't been affected by now, due to a power leakage or other deterioration in its sensor circuitry? I suggest making a few random tests. It might be that this metal carcass is dead by now and our precautions are wasting time."

"If it can be done without you killing yourself, Lieutenant," said the captain, "then do it. You agree, Doctor?"

"Yes," said Prilicla. "That information would be helpful, friend Dodds. Especially if you can find another access hatch that is closer to the ship's brain section. From here we'll have to travel the internal walkways for more than half the length of the ship. But be very careful."

"Of course," said Dodds. "This might be the only life I've got."

They watched as it positioned its powered suit a few meters from the hull and began the first slow, lateral circuit of the ship that became a spiral leading forward. Several times the lieutenant disappeared from view and Prilicla felt the captain's controlled worrying, but Dodds was in sight when it made its find.

"Sir," it said excitedly, "I've found what could be a cargo loading hatch. It's about ten meters in diameter, flush-fitting, and the joins are so fine I almost missed them. Inset is a two-foot rectangle, that looks as if it might give access to the actuator controls. Along one side there is a group of three recessed buttons, but I won't touch them until I have some idea of what they do and, in case they're booby-trapped in some way, the order in which they should be pressed. I'm moving closer with the sensor now. The magnetic pads are holding it to the hull. I've switched on. So far, no response from the ship."

The captain's level of worrying peaked then began to subside. It didn't speak.

"I'm using minimum power on the sensor," the lieutenant went on, "so the image I'm getting is by induction rather than direct contact with the underlying circuitry, and pretty vague.

The wiring is complex, and active. To trace the leads to the three actuator buttons, I'll need to clarify the picture by using a little more power. . . . Bloody hell, the ship just did a *Terragar* on it! I'm sorry, sir, we need another K-Three-thirty sensor. This one just died."

"Don't worry about it," said Fletcher. "It's expendable. You're not. Continue your search aft, report anything you find, and then get back here and follow us inside. We'll have to go in the long way."

To Prilicla it went on. "This vessel's weapons system baffles me. So far there has been no sign of missile launchers, focused radiation projectors, or anything that might be an other-species equivalent. They could still be there and I just didn't recognize them, but . . . I'm reminded of a porcupine."

Prilicla didn't ask the obvious question because he knew it would be answered when the other's thoughts stopped moving too fast for any possible verbal communication. They were inside the ship at the first junction of the netting walkways and turning in the direction of the control section before the other spoke.

"It is a small, non-sapient Earth life-form," the captain went on, "with a soft body that has no natural weapons of attack, but it possesses an overall covering of body-spines that are long and sharp enough to discourage predators. If that was the situation here, then killing *Terragar*'s operating systems could have been a mistaken act of self-defense because the aliens didn't know our ship was simply trying to give assistance."

"A not entirely comforting theory, friend Fletcher," said Prilicla. "It infers that there are other species, or perhaps other members of their own species, who wanted to attack it. Why? Do they consider it a threat of some kind, or their prey? Either way, they were able to inflict heat and blast damage. Remember, offensive weapons were used against this vessel."

"I know," said the captain. It continued pulling itself along the netting for a moment before it added, "But I'm beginning to wonder about that, too."

It did not elaborate although its emotional radiation was characteristic of a mind engaged in intense cerebration. Dodds reported finding another large hatch, presumably used for loading fuel or cargo, close to the stern thrusters, then it rejoined them while they were still halfway along the central walkway and heading forward. There it was that a robot crew member—perhaps the same one, Prilicla suggested quietly, or maybe it was the only one—emerged from a side walkway and began pulling itself rapidly along the netting to meet them. It stopped about five meters from the captain, who was in the lead, and spread itself out starfish-fashion with its six hands gripping strands of the netting and barring their path towards the control section.

"The last time this happened, Doctor," Fletcher said, "you were alone, you gave it a gentle push, and it moved back. Presumably the action was not meant as an obstruction so much as a warning to move carefully. Do you agree? I'll try a very gentle push, with my feet. In case it tries to shock me, my boots have thicker insulation."

The captain moved close, spread out its hands to grasp the netting on both sides to stabilize itself, then very slowly and carefully brought its feet forward to stop a few inches from the center of the robot's body. Its push was gentle to the point of imperceptibility.

There was no response. It pushed a little harder, then with steadily increasing pressure, but the robot only clung more tightly to the netting without moving back an inch.

"Friend Fletcher," said Prilicla, "move back a little and let me past."

Without speaking but radiating puzzlement and impatience, the other did so and flattened itself against the netting while Prilicla's pressure globe squeezed past. A few seconds later he touched the robot's body gently. Immediately it released its grip on the netting and moved back slowly towards Control. Prilicla did likewise, but as soon as Fletcher and Dodds began to follow him, it barred the way again. The meaning of its action was plain.

"Why will it allow you past and not us?" said the captain. "Does it think Earth-humans are stronger and more of a physical threat to it than a Cinrusskin? It's right, of course. But I've made no threatening moves towards it or . . . I don't understand this."

"Maybe it doesn't like you, sir," said Dodds, laughing nervously, "because your feet's too big."

Fletcher ignored its lieutenant's insubordination as well as the anxiety that had caused it, and said, "With respect, I don't intend to wait here doing nothing while you and your robot friend socialize. Dodds and I will follow you to the next intersection, then we'll try to find other walkways that will take us around to the control section. Earlier you suggested that our metal friend might be the only surviving crew member. If you're right, then it can't bar our movements and stay with you at the same time. Keep your communicator channel open at all times, Doctor, and have fun."

The robot hesitated in obvious indecision when the two officers turned into a side walkway, although Prilicla could not detect the emotional radiation that should have accompanied it at such short range. But its movements were communicating feelings—someone or something else's feelings—in a subtle form of body language that he could read. There was a tenuous wisp of emotional radiation in the area, much too faint to be readable, and he was now quite sure that this robot was a highly sophisticated construct of limited intelligence which was little more than the hands and eyes of an entity who, for reasons still to be discovered, could not move.

But if he was being seen or his presence sensed in some other fashion through this robot, it or they might have their own reasons other than sheer physical size why they preferred the close approach of a Cinrusskin to that of Earth-humans. In which case it might even be possible, considering the robot crew member's lack of hostility, that they wanted to make contact with him.

That was why, when he reached the point of his previous closest approach to the control section when fatigue had forced his return to *Rhabwar*, he stopped to hang motionless with one hand holding lightly onto the netting. The robot did the same.

For a moment he looked at the small, recessed panel with the three colored buttons, which was plainly the actuator for the nearby door, then with his free hand he reached forward very slowly to bring a digit to a stop one inch above each button in turn, then he withdrew the hand and used the same finger to point at the robot. He repeated the process several times before the crew member reacted. It moved back quickly the way they had come, to stop at and block the nearest walkway intersection.

Bitterly disappointed, he thought, *Now it doesn't want me here for some reason.* Or did it? The background emotional radiation was still too tenuous for clear definition, but he could not feel anything that resembled strong rejection.

"Friend Fletcher," he said into the communicator, "I have a feeling that I may be about to make progress. But the robot, or the agency presently directing it, is uneasy and has placed it on guard at the entrance to the walkway you and friend Dodds are using. Our radio traffic must be detectable so they know that I'm talking to you although they won't know what I'm saying. That will have to wait until we're able to program our translation computer for their language, which will be a separate problem. But right now I want to reassure these people by appearing to give you orders which you will plainly be obeying without delay or question. Will you comply, friend Fletcher?"

"What orders?" said the captain in a guarded voice.

"To vacate the forward section of the ship," said Prilicla, "and move back to the place where we came on board. We must make it plain that you are no longer investigating the control area. Please do that immediately."

"But temporarily," said the captain firmly. "This ship is crammed with unique technology which includes a weapon that could threaten the peace and stability of the Federation. It has to be investigated."

"Of course, friend Fletcher," said Prilicla, "but not right now."

"Very well," the other replied, radiating equal levels of irritation, disappointment, and impatience. "I won't promise not to look around back there, especially at the circuitry of the hull sensors. But don't worry, we won't do anything to worry your robot friend. And if you should get into trouble, Doctor, there's something you should know.

"From where we are now," it went on before he could respond, "we have a clear view through the netting of a strongly supported, square-sectioned metal-walled passageway leading from the big forward hatch that Dodds found to Control. I'd say it was used to load bulk consumables or heavy equipment. Internally, the structure shows no sign of the circuitry that underlies the hull. So if you should need help quickly, we can cut a way into the passageway and get into Control by the back door. I don't think a computer virus could travel up the flame of my cutting torch.

"Keep this channel open, your recorders on at all times, and be careful," the captain ended, its feeling of concern for him making it give unnecessary warnings. "We're moving back now."

Prilicla watched as they withdrew towards the stern. When it was clear that they were not intending to double-back to Control, the robot moved back quickly to Prilicla and the actuator panel. This time he could sense no hesitancy in its body language, or that of its controller, as it began tapping keys. He was noting the colors and sequence for future reference when the forward wall became a large door that began sliding into a recess.

When it was fully open, bright orange lighting units placed at two-meter intervals and recessed into what was presumably the ceiling came to life along the length of another passageway that stretched ahead for close on thirty meters to another intersection. All four surfaces were opaque, made either from metal or hardened plastic, and covered with netting where it was not interrupted by transparent access hatches. Deliberately he moved past them slowly so as to give his vision pickup and himself a chance to see what lay on the other side. Through one he had a foreshortened view of the passageway leading from control to the hull that Fletcher had mentioned earlier, but mostly there were only regimented tangles of color-coded wiring. He was sensing faint but definite feelings of uncertainty and impatience from somewhere.

As he reached the intersection the robot remained clinging to the netting of the surface facing him. It made no move to guide him or block his way, so it seemed that the choice of direction was being left to him. Prilicla was aware of two distinct sources of emotional radiation, both of them organic. The robot followed him as he moved into the side passage on his right and towards the stronger of the two. The passage ended at another door and actuator panel.

The source of emotional radiation strengthened almost to the level of readability.

CHAPTER 15

Again he positioned his hand a few inches from the panel and, without actually touching the buttons, moved his index finger from one to the other in the same sequence the robot had used while opening the first door, then waited. Hopefully he was displaying intelligence and memory as well as asking permission to proceed.

If the combination on this door was different, and it was booby-trapped and he was being allowed to make a mistake, then he might not survive the experience. The robot moved closer to him but it did not interfere. He pressed the buttons, the door slid open, and he moved slowly into the middle of another shorter, brightly lit passageway, then stopped.

His emotional radiation was so confused that for a long moment he could scarcely analyze it himself.

"Are you getting this?" he said finally.

"Yes, Doctor," Haslam's voice replied from *Rhabwar*. It sounded excited. "But remember to—"

"Getting what?" the captain's voice broke in impatiently.

"I don't know, sir," Haslam replied. "You'd have to see it for yourself. And Dr. Prilicla, please remember to move your head and your helmet vision pickup very slowly, and hold it steady on each area you are describing. In case of, well, accidents, that is very important if we're to have sharp images for later study."

Prilicla was well aware of that fact, but perhaps the other was trying to reassure both itself and himself that he wouldn't be speaking for posterity.

He ignored the remark and went on. "As you can see, the surfaces of the walls, floor, and ceiling of this stretch contain more transparent hatches than there are opaque surfaces, and there is a major change in the configuration of the netting. It is no longer attached to the wall surfaces and has instead been replaced by what appears to be a light, open-lattice metal cylinder. It runs along the center of the passageway, is strongly supported at each end and, I would say, forms a convenient working position for crew members needing access to the systems behind the transparent hatches. Between the cylindrical net and the transparent hatches there isn't much room for maneuvering . . ."

But then, I don't need much, he added silently.

He moved forward along the cylindrical net in a slow spiral so as to cover all the inner surfaces of the passageway, speaking as he went. At one particularly large transparent panel he moved a hand close to its actuator buttons without touching them. Immediately the robot moved closer to nudge the hand away. He braced himself against the net and pressed his helmet and vision sensor firmly against the transparency. The robot did not react.

"Plainly this is a case of 'Look but don't touch,'" he went on. "The wiring behind this panel is similar to that in the damaged robot crew member we found on *Terragar*. I'm holding the vision pickup motionless against the panel so that you'll be able to use high magnification on the image . . ."

"I am," said Haslam with enthusiasm. "That looks good, Doctor, whatever it is."

There was an impatient sound of an Earth-human throat being cleared and the captain said irritably, "Dammit, will I have to go back to *Rhabwar* to find out what you're doing here?"

Prilicla didn't reply at once because he had moved to another panel. Even though the view revealed mechanisms and connections much cruder in design and fabrication than the previous one, once again his hand was pushed away from the actuator mechanism.

He continued to describe clearly everything he was seeing and thinking, but not what he was feeling. The emotional radiation in the area was strengthening as he moved towards the other end of the passageway, but it was not yet clear enough to describe even to himself.

". . . This area appears to be dedicated to complex plumbing," he continued. "There are single and grouped pipes, from half an inch to two inches in diameter and distinctively color-coded. The fact that I was gently discouraged from opening the access hatch is a measure of their importance. I can't remember seeing piping with these codings on the way here. This makes me suspect that they are a local phenomenon, and probably the conduits and metering devices for the crew's air supply, water, or whatever other working fluid they use, and their food. Now I'm moving closer to another large door and actuator panel at the other end of the passageway and will try to open it. . . . No, I won't."

While he had been speaking the robot had swarmed along to the opposite side of the cylindrical net and interposed its body between Prilicla and the actuator panel. Gently he slowly extended a hand and tried to move it aside.

It resisted strongly but took no other action.

"Interesting," he said. "Apparently it trusts me, but not enough to let me go all the way in." To the captain he went on, "Friend Fletcher, earlier you mentioned returning to *Rhabwar* to see what I am doing. Are you and the lieutenant engaged on anything of vital importance at the moment?"

"We're investigating the interior hull circuitry and the leads to the power source aft. But the short answer is no, so stop wasting time being polite. What do you want me to do?"

"I want both of you to go back to *Rhabwar*," said Prilicla, "and await further instructions. . . ."

"That means leaving you alone here," the captain broke in. "I don't feel happy about that."

". . . Depending on how well things go here," Prilicla continued, ignoring the interruption, "I want you to send friend Dodds back with the portable holo projector and the standard first-contact tapes. I detect no strong feelings of personal animosity here, but if it will make you feel better, then the lieutenant may remain here. But it must stay well away from the control section. For some reason the Earth-humans, or maybe just the DBDG body configuration, make these people very much afraid."

"Not all humanoids are good guys," said Lieutenant Dodds. "Maybe they ran into some hostile elements during the Etlan War. . . ."

"The Etlan police action," Fletcher corrected automatically, and went on. "They could have had a bad experience with Earth-human look-alikes during the hostilities, or have entirely different reasons that we don't yet understand. But Doctor, are you saying that you're ready to open communications with them?"

"I'm ready to try," said Prilicla.

He moved his helmet as close to the door as the robot would allow, then closed his eyes and tried to empty his mind of all distractive thoughts and feelings except for the tenuous fog of emotional radiation that he was trying to isolate and identify.

As he had expected from a survivor of a wrecked ship, the strongest emotions were negative. There was fear that was being controlled with difficulty, and a deep, corroding despair and concern that might or might not be personal, and pain. The pain was not the acute form characteristic of trauma, although there was a little of that present, too. It seemed to be more emotional than physical, and associated with a feeling of imminent loss. But within that dark fog there was a pale glimmer of curiosity, and wonder, trying to shine through.

It was time Prilicla shone a little light of his own. Literally. Describing aloud what he was doing and thinking, he began switching on and off his helmet spotlight, low enough to be barely perceptible by his own eyes at first, then gradually increasing the intensity. He didn't want the alien survivor to mistake the light for a weapon, but he also wanted to know if he was being seen through the robot's eyes or if there were other visual sensors in operation. When he began to detect feelings of physical discomfort that were characteristic of sensory overload, presumably a reaction to a light that was now dazzling it, he reduced the brightness until its feeling of discomfort went away. Next he began flashing his light in an attempt to transmit intelligence in a form that he hoped the other should understand—simple arithmetic.

One flash of light followed two seconds later by another, then two flashes in rapid succession. He repeated the process with three, four, and five flashes as he tried to demonstrate simple addition as well as his own possession of intelligence. A change in the other's emotional radiation, a sudden feeling of interest, an understanding combining with the background curiosity, told him that he had succeeded.

It was an immediate and present response to his first attempt at communication, but now he needed to know if he could continue the process at long range.

"Friend Fletcher," he said, "you've seen and know what I've been doing. I'm going to stop using my helmet light. Instead I want you to duplicate the sequence and timing, but using your ship's external hull lighting. I won't be able to see *Rhabwar* from here, so please tell me as soon as you begin."

"Right, Doctor," said the captain. "I'll need a moment to . . . You've got it."

He didn't need the other's words because the survivor was reacting exactly as it had done to his helmet light, although the curiosity it was radiating was becoming tinged with impatience.

Plainly it was wondering what he was going to do next. That made two of them.

"Thank you, friend Fletcher," he said. "You can stop signaling now."

He had expected but was still relieved at the confirmation that the visual communication could be continued from the ambulance ship, either by himself or—if he was undergoing one of his frequent periods of regenerative unconsciousness—by one of the others. But abruptly his relief was obliterated by a sudden explosion of fear from the survivor. Even the movements of its robot had become agitated.

"I'm not doing anything," he said sharply into his communicator. "What's happening out there?"

"Nothing much," the captain replied promptly. "In order to save time loading and off-loading it from the pinnace, Dodds is using his suit thrusters to bring the holo projector to you. It's an awkward piece of equipment but he can manage; in fact he's about to land on the hull as we speak. . . ."

"Dodds," said Prilicla urgently, "don't move! The alien survivor is terrified. Turn back until I can find out why."

But he already knew why. The holo projector was a large, intricate, and completely harmless piece of equipment, but the survivor didn't know that. While its attention was being directed at *Rhabwar*'s lights, it had seen Dodds, one of the DBDG life-forms which for some reason frightened it, about to land on its ship with what it must have thought was a weapon. Except in the areas where the hull was damaged the ship had external defenses. *Terragar* had learned that, to its cost. But now it seemed there were no comparable internal defenses.

A porcupine didn't need spines on the inside.

As well as being sensitive to others' emotions, Prilicla knew that he was a good projective empath. But he also knew that there was no way to make a being who was in the grip of intense fear feel good, or at least a little better, without first removing the source. That was why he concentrated all of his considerable empathic ability into the projection of reassurance, sympathy, and trust at a level of intensity that he could not maintain for more than a few minutes. He also gesticulated on the off-chance that the survivor could understand the gestures he was making while he spoke into his communicator.

"I'm pointing back the way I came," he said, "then making pushing motions with my hands to give the impression that I'm barring entry to anyone else. By now the survivor should have seen friend Dodds turning back. I think it's working. The fear is diminishing. . . ."

Prilicla continued to emote feelings of reassurance and sympathy until he was forced to stop and rest his brain for a moment, but by then the survivor's feelings had returned to normal, or at least to the level they had been before the approach of Dodds. But there was still concern in the other's mind which was not for itself.

The robot followed close behind him as he turned and moved out of the passageway, past the T-junction to the door opposite. It made no attempt to interfere when he pressed the actuator buttons on the opposite door. As well as being its sole protector, he was beginning to think that it was the only source of vision that the first survivor had.

The door opened into another passageway that was identical in size and layout to the one he had just left, but there the resemblance ended. Only two of the lighting units came on as the door opened so that he had to use his helmet light to see through the transparent access hatches.

"Are you seeing this?" he said again, unnecessarily. "The plumbing and circuitry in this area has sustained damage."

"We see it, Doctor," replied the captain, who must have joined Haslam in control. "And there are signs that someone has been trying to effect repairs."

Two of the pipe junctions had been wrapped in some form of metalized, adhesive tape, but not tightly enough to prevent a haze of air or vaporized fluid from fogging the joints. Behind the other hatches he could see that many of the visible cable looms were showing patches of heat discoloration, and several had been ruptured. One group, which bore the color-coding indicating that it led from the hull sensors, had been pulled apart, opened up, and the fine, hair-thin individual strands of wiring fanned outwards in preparation for splicing.

The repair work was nowhere near completion.

Prilicla indicated the areas of damage in turn, pointing at the robot each time, then he pointed several times towards the damage and to himself. He was trying to ask two questions—whether the robot was responsible for the attempted repairs, and if Prilicla would be allowed to help complete the work. If the robot or its director understood him, there was no way as yet that they could answer. He moved to the inner door.

It was no surprise that the robot was there first, its body covering the actuator buttons to bar his entrance. But for now he would be content to touch the mind rather than the body on the other side of the door.

The general emotional texture was the same as he had detected from the other survivor, but the content was shockingly different. This time there was physical as well as emotional trauma. He couldn't even guess at what was causing the physical discomfort, but there was a feeling of constriction, possibly of suffocation, that was overlaid by fear, despair, and the dreadful, negative emotion characteristic of utter isolation. He edged a little closer to the door and, as he had done earlier, concentrated on projecting reassurance, friendship, and sympathy.

It took longer this time, possibly because he was tiring again, but finally there was a reaction. Faintly, through the cloud of negativity he detected surprise, curiosity, and a feeling of hope. He began using his helmet light, but there was no change in the other's emotional radiation. He asked the captain to duplicate the sequence with the ship's lighting. Still there was no response.

"Friend Fletcher," he said, hiding his feelings with unemotional words, "I have detected the presence of a second alien survivor. Its emotional radiation suggests that they are not in contact or presently aware of each other. The first one is distressed but not seriously injured. The second one, whose sensory and life-support systems are compromised as a result, I feel sure, of it being closer to the damaged side of their ship, is injured and short of food, air, and water. It is also deaf, dumb, and blind.

"Full communications with and between the two aliens must be established as soon as possible," he ended, "and both survivors must be extricated and treated without delay."

"Doctor," said the captain, "just how will we manage that?"

"Thankfully I am not the specialist in other-species technology, friend Fletcher," he replied. "I'm returning to my quarters now to rest. Perhaps the solution will come to me in my sleep.

CHAPTER 16

The *Terragar* casualties were progressing well enough to have their litters moved outside for a few hours each day so that the psychological therapy of fresh air and sunshine could reinforce the effects of her medication. The sun would warm and relax and tan the pallor of long service in space from their bodies and, because this world's ionization layer was intact, there would be no harmful aftereffects. But she could not spend all of her free time in ministering-angel mode and saying reassuring things to her patients even though, because of them being officers and presumably gentlemen, they did not object to her company or comment on her abbreviated dress. Now that their burns were healing to the point where there was no longer the risk of her Earth-human pathogens getting to them, she was not wearing her breathing mask and white coveralls.

Murchison's intention was to walk completely around the island over the firm sand by the water's edge. From their first hilltop observations three days earlier, she had estimated that the trip would take just under two hours and, while nobody had ever accused her of being antisocial, she would have preferred to walk alone and avoid having to tell therapeutic half-truths to a colleague.

The casualties had progressed to the stage where they were

becoming restive and worrying less about whether or not they would survive than how soon the transfer to Sector General for their reconstructive surgery would take place. Danalta and Naydrad were asking the same questions, which were valid and deserving of straight answers, but she had no hard information to give them because she hadn't been given any herself.

When asked, during her daily report to *Rhabwar*, the captain had stated that it was a medical matter and referred her to her boss. Prilicla, in its gentle, inoffensive, but totally immovable fashion, said that the timing was uncertain because they were trying to communicate with and extricate two other-species casualties from the alien vessel, that there were complications and the answer was "not soon."

She had passed this information on to Naydrad and Danalta but not to the patients. They might be disturbed by the thought that very soon the two beings who had been responsible for destroying their ship might be lying in the beds beside theirs.

Obviously Danalta had grown tired of being a multicolored beach-ball shape and had changed itself into a more challenging shape, that of a Drambon Roller.

Outwardly it was a perfect replica of the CLHG physiological classification native to the planet Drambo, although she doubted that even Danalta could mimic the complex movements of the original creature's internal organs which enabled it to roll continuously from the moment of partuition until the end of its life. Physically, a water-breathing Roller resembled an animated donut that rotated vertically on its outer edge, with a fringe of short, manipulatory tentacles sprouting from the inner circumference and curving outwards on both sides to give balance at slow speeds. Between the roots of the tentacles she could see that the shape-changer had perfectly reproduced the series of gills as well as the visual equipment which operated coeleostat fashion to compensate for its constantly rotating field of vision. The original life-form had used a gravity feed system for circulation rather than a muscular pump, which was why they died quickly when age, weakness, accident, or an attacking predator caused them to fall on their sides and stop rotating. Her first experience of giving CPR to a stopped Drambon had been like rolling a floppy, half-inflated ground car's inner tube around underwater. She laughed suddenly.

"That's very good, Doctor," she said. "If there were another Drambon on the island, it would find you irresistible."

Ahead of her, the donut shape made a right-angle turn, stopped, and bent almost double in a bow of appreciation at the compliment. Then it melted and slumped into a shapeless mound of green jelly which sprouted vertically into a tall, erect, yellowish-pink shape which oozed and melted into a near-perfect, two-thirds–scale replica of Murchison herself.

It was smaller than she was because Danalta was constrained by the limits of its own body mass and, although the detail in the eyes, ears, and fingernails was very good, the edges of her white swimsuit, hair, and eyebrows merged into the adjacent skin coloration like the uniform and features painted on a toy soldier. She gave an involuntary shudder.

Murchison had seen Danalta take some weird and often repulsive shapes with a minimum of inner distress, but for some reason this one was making her feel really uncomfortable.

"Why don't you go for a walk up to the hill?" Murchison said, more sharply that she had intended. "I'm safe enough here on the beach. No insects, no crabs, no fish or amphibians in the water to crawl out and attack me. You might find something more interesting to mimic inland."

"No danger large enough to see," said the smaller Murchison, "but we're on an alien planet, remember?"

Being reminded of the obvious had always irritated her, especially when, as now, she needed the reminder. Even so, it was very difficult to believe that this wonderful place was not on Earth. She didn't reply.

"So far we've seen only one species of animal," said Danalta, "unless the others are hiding from us, and that one is boring to mimic. But I sense your annoyance. I'm sorry. Pathologist, is this body configuration not to your liking?"

The half-sized Murchison, with the exception of its communications-and-translator pack, began to subside like melting wax into a pink, sluglike shape with a tiny mouth and a large, single eye. The real Murchison concentrated on looking out to sea.

Apologetically, it went on. "If you would rather walk alone without distractions, I can take on an aquatic form and keep pace with you without holding conversation. Or if you would like to immerse yourself for a while, I can serve as a protective escort, should one be necessary, although there is no evidence of any threat here, from the land, sea, or air."

"Thank you," she said.

That was what she had most wanted to do since the beginning of today's walk, although, perversely, she didn't want to appear too eager. As she continued walking, her peripheral vision showed her Danalta entering the water and spreading out into a flat, carpet shape resembling an Earthly stingray with the addition of a high, dorsal fin which had an eye at its tip to give both lateral stability and all-around visibility.

She laughed suddenly and thought, *The people I have to work with!*

Gradually her path curved until the waves were breaking over and cooling her feet, then her calves and around her knees. Her back was to the beach as she suddenly broke into a long, high-stepping, splashing run, dived in, and began to swim.

The water was cold, pleasantly so, and so clear that if there had been anything on the sandy bottom larger than her thumbnail she would have seen it. After a few minutes of fast swimming, most of it underwater, she rolled onto her back and floated with only her face above the surface, comfortable in the embrace of an alien ocean which, on this world as well as on Earth, had been the mother of all life. She was looking up at the deep-blue sky and thinking that the casualties were well enough to profit from a therapeutic, closely supervised immersion, when she saw the birds.

There were two of them, not quite overhead and circling, dipping and banking slowly to take advantage of rising air currents. They were so high, a few thousand feet at least, that they were almost hidden by the glare from the sun, and at that altitude they could scarcely be considered a threat. Nevertheless, feeling guilty rather than anxious over the way she had been enjoying herself, Murchison raised an arm to wave at Danalta, pointed up at them and then towards the beach.

It was time they returned to their patients

And even higher above the birds, in the orbiting *Rhabwar*, a similar thought was going through the mind of Prilicla regarding a different set of patients. There was very little that he could do for them until they had learned to trust not just their physician, himself, but the DBDGs and their portable equipment of which, for some reason, they were so afraid, because the specialized knowledge and experience of the Earth-humans were vital if the treatment that one of them so urgently needed was to have any hope of success.

"In my cubicle I've been thinking as well as sleeping, friend Fletcher," he said. "Our first problem here is one of communication and, more importantly, of reeducation, but without the use of the portable audio-visual devices that are usual in first-contact situations. Any such equipment—especially, it seems, when it is carried by Earth-human DBDGs—is considered a threat. It also appears that suit ancillary equipment such as helmet lights, thrusters, and even our vision pickups which they may consider too low-powered to be dangerous, is allowable. That is why I want you to—"

"We are agreed," the captain broke in, "that they feel comfortable with you and are afraid of us. It must be that physically your smaller size, physical weakness, and obvious lack of natural weapons make you much less of a threat to them. Doctor, against my advice you insist on going back alone into that ship. Why not take the first-contact equipment with you?"

"Because," said Prilicla gently, "I'm not sure whether it is certain types of equipment, you DBDGs, or both that they are afraid of. So far, my close presence has been acceptable to them. Carrying the equipment with me might not be acceptable and I might destroy their feeling of trust in me. I don't want to risk losing that."

The captain nodded. "We know you can detect their emotional radiation and to a lesser extent project your own feelings of friendship towards them. That is communication of a sort, but it isn't the same as exchanging the words and concepts necessary for them to trust the rest of us as well. You have a problem, Doctor. Do you also have a solution?"

"I may have," said Prilicla. "We already know from our simple light signals that they have visual sensors on the undamaged area of their hull. The solution will involve my presence inside the control section, where I will be able to monitor their emotional responses, while you execute the first-contact visuals, highly magnified and edited to fit our situation, outside the ship. Is this technically feasible?"

The captain was silent for a moment, radiating concern for his safety as well as the anticipation of overcoming a technical challenge; then it said, "So you want me to project tri-di images into the space between our ships. How big do they have to be?"

"At least twice as large as the other ship, friend Fletcher," he replied. "As yet we don't know the degrees of resolution of their external visual equipment, so I want every detail of your display to be clearly visible to all the sensors on that side of their ship. Can do?"

The captain nodded again and said, "Modifying the portable equipment to project externally will take time, Doctor. More than enough time for you to sleep and think again on the problem, and maybe find a solution that involves a lesser element of personal risk for yourself."

"Thank you, friend Fletcher"—ignoring the implied criticism. "I enjoy resting, even, and especially, when it isn't strictly necessary and other people are doing the real work. But first I must discuss with you the exact content and presentation of the projection we will use, and, second, I need to pick your brains."

The captain radiated a silent mixture of curiosity and caution, as if it were expecting another surprise. It wasn't disappointed.

"In simple, non-technical terms," he went on, "I would like guidance on how and what to do in the damaged control section, as if you yourself were doing it. Naturally this will mean us studying the visual records together."

"It took many years of training in other-species technology to fill the brain you wish to pick, Doctor," said the captain, sarcasm thick in its voice and its emotional radiation. "Is that all?"

"Not quite," said Prilicla. "I'll have to remember to check on the condition of my less urgent, Earth-human patients. But that will not involve extra work for you."

By the time the captain and himself had completed their discussion, to the satisfaction of neither of them, Prilicla got very little additional rest. Before releasing his consciousness for sleep he called Murchison. The pathologist reported seeing two high-flying birds and, following its brief swim with Danalta, that the sea was safe for short-term Earth-human occupancy. It said that as Naydrad hated getting its fur wet and Danalta would be posted to seaward as a probably unnecessary guard, it suggested that their patients, although not yet ambulatory, would benefit both physically and psychologically from a brief daily immersion in the sea followed by a lengthier exposure to what was for Earth-human DBDGs fresh air and sunshine. Understanding as he did from long experience of working among them the emotional attraction that existed between Earth-human males and females, he knew that the casualties would derive much pleasure from being bathed by an entity of the opposite sex, and so would his assistant. He acquiesced.

He was dreaming of sunshine and sand and the soft crashing of the high, low-gravity waves of his native Cinruss when the idyllic scene was dissolved by the insistent sound of his communicator and the voice of the captain.

"Doctor Prilicla," said the captain. "Wake up, it's show-time."

CHAPTER 17

This time Prilicla made the trip alone, with the pinnace being guided by Haslam to the entry point on remote control. If the robot crew member or, through its sensors, its superior noticed the miniature, eye-level repeater screen that had been added to the interior of Prilicla's helmet, it was not considered a threat because nothing was done to impede his trip back to the control section. It wasn't absolutely necessary that he have a picture of what would shortly be going on outside since Fletcher could have told him about it via his communicator, but words took time and good pictures were always faster, clearer, and less susceptible to misinterpretation.

When he was deep inside the control section he drifted as close as possible to the inner door that would give access to the least injured of the ship's two organic survivors, a position where he could monitor the other's emotional responses with optimum accuracy. The robot drifted passively less than a meter away. He knew that the tiny metal digits encircling its body were capable of ripping open his spacesuit in a matter of seconds, but he also knew—or rather he felt fairly sure—that it would remain passive unless he tried to open the inner door.

"Ready when you are, friend Fletcher," he said.

A few seconds later an immediate change in the alien's emotional radiation as well as the image on his helmet screen told him that, in the space between *Rhabwar* and the distressed alien ship, the show had begun.

"It sees the external image," Prilicla reported excitedly. "There are feelings of awareness, curiosity, and puzzlement."

The captain didn't reply but one of the other officers laughed softly and said in a voice not meant to be overheard, "I would feel puzzled, too, if somebody projected the image of a star field onto another star field."

The projected star field remained unaltered for a few seconds, then slowly it began to shrink and condense so that more and more stars moved in from the edges of the three-dimensional projection until it took on the glittering, unmistakable, spiral shape of the Galaxy itself.

The survivor's concentration was now total.

Gradually the fine detail of the image coarsened, the wisps and streamers of interstellar gas were erased, and the number of stars was reduced to a few hundred which became large enough to have been counted individually. One of them was highlighted inside a circle of bright green and the circle increased rapidly in size until a stylized representation of the star and its system of planets filled the projection volume for a few seconds before the image changed again.

The viewpoint zoomed in on that solar system's inhabited planet, showing the swirling, tattered cloud formations that could not quite hide the continental outlines. As it swooped closer and lower it slowed until the viewpoint was giving panoramic views of the planetary surface, seascapes, ice fields, mountains, tropical greenery, and great, sprawling cities with their interconnecting road systems. Then the image was reduced suddenly in size and moved to one side so that it filled only half of the projection.

The other half displayed an equally detailed representation of the world's dominant intelligent life-form.

It was the picture of an enormous, incredibly fragile flying insect with a tubular, exoskeletal body that supported six sucker-tipped, pencil-thin legs, four even more delicately fashioned and precise manipulators, and two sets of wide, iridescent, and almost transparent wings. The head was a convoluted eggshell so finely structured that the sensory organs, particularly the two large, glowing eyes projecting from it, seemed ready to fall off at the first sudden movement. The head, manipulators—some of them holding tools—and legs were bent or rotated to demonstrate their limits of movement while the wings wafted slowly up and down as they broke up and reflected iridescent highlights like mobile rainbows. It was the picture of a Cinrusskin, one of the race generally held to be the most beautiful and delicate life-forms known to the explored reaches of the galaxy.

Then the limb motions ceased, the wings folded away, and the body was suddenly encased in a spacesuit identical to the one Prilicla wore.

"As well as the background discomfort, I detect feelings of surprise and growing curiosity," Prilicla reported. "Go to the next stage."

They had shown a picture of Prilicla's race first because he had already been seen by the alien casualty and seemed to be trusted by it. But now its education and, hopefully, its ability to trust had to be widened.

Next was shown the solar system, planet, meteorology, rural and city environments of Kelgia, accompanied by a picture of a single member of its dominant species. The undulating, multi-pedal, caterpillar-like body with its silver, continually mobile fur, the narrow cone of a head, and the tiny forward manipulators, aroused no feelings of antipathy in the casualty, nor did the similar material on the crablike Melfan or the six-legged, elephantine Tralthan life-forms that followed it. But when the Hudlar planet and species were shown, there was a subtle change.

Hudla was a heavy-gravity world pulling four Earth Gs whose nearly opaque atmosphere resembled a thick, dense soup that was rich in the suspended animal and vegetable nutrients on which the Hudlars lived. It was a world of constant storms that had forced its natives to build underground. Only a Hudlar could love it, Prilicla thought, and then, not very much.

He said, "Now there are feelings suggestive of fear and familiarity. It is as if the casualty is recognizing a habitual enemy. To most people, Melfans and Tralthans are visually more horrendous than the smooth-bodied Hudlars, so it may well be that it is the planet Hudla itself rather that its native life-forms that is causing this reaction."

"Is this a guess, Doctor," said the captain, "or one of your feelings?"

"A strong feeling," he replied.

"I see," said the other. It cleared its throat and added, "If your casualty considers Hudla as something like home, I can feel a certain sympathy for it in spite of what it did to *Terragar*. Shall I proceed?"

"Please," said Prilicla, and the lesson continued.

Showing the planets and living environments of the sixty-seven intelligent species that comprised the Galactic Federation had never been their intention because the process would have been unnecessarily long and this was, after all, a primary lesson. The widely different types like the storklike, tripedal Nallajims, the multicolored, animated Gogleskan haystacks, the slimy, chlorine-breathing Illensans, and the radiation-eating Telfi, among others, were included, but so also were the DBDG classifications from Earth, Nidia, and Orligia. Those three were there deliberately because the prime purpose of the lesson was to instill in the alien casualties a feeling of trust for their Earth-human rescuers.

"It isn't working," said Prilicla, disappointed. "Every time you showed a DBDG, regardless of its size or whether it was a large, hairy Orligian, an Earth-human, or a half-sized, red-furred Nidian, the reaction was the same—one of intense fear and hatred. It will be extremely difficult to make these people trust you."

"What on Earth," said the captain, "could we ever have done to make them feel that way?"

"It was not done on Earth, friend Fletcher," said Prilicla. "But the show isn't over yet. Please continue."

The format changed again. Instead of showing individual planets and subjects, two- and three-member groups comprising different species were shown meeting and talking, sometimes with their children present, or working together on various technical projects. In some of them they were encased in spacesuits while they rescued other-species casualties from damaged ships. The pictures' application to the present situation, he hoped, was plain. Then the scene changed again to show all of the subjects, forming the rim of wheel and shown in scale, from the diminutive Nallajims and Cinrusskins, up to the massive Tralthans and Hudlars of more than ten times that body-weight. At the hub of the circle was shown a tiny, glittering representation of the galaxy, from which radiated misty spokes joining it to the individual species on the rim. Then the individual species were pictured again, this time with all of them displayed as being the same size, in order, it was again hoped, to illustrate equality of importance.

Several seconds passed. At this extreme range Prilicla could not feel, but he could imagine the captain's anxiety as it spoke.

"Well, Doctor," it said urgently, "was there a response?"

"There was, friend Fletcher," he replied, "but I'm still trying for an exact analysis of the emotional radiation. In conjunction with the background feelings of anxiety, which may be caused by worry over its companion who it can no longer contact, there are strong feelings of excitement, wonder, and, I feel sure, comprehension. I'd say that it understood our lesson."

When he didn't go on, the captain broke the silence. It said, "I've the feeling that you're going to say 'but.'"

"But," Prilicla went on obligingly, "every time you showed a DBDG, the casualty also radiated deep suspicion and distrust. These feelings are better than the earlier ones of intense fear and blind hatred, but only fractionally. I feel certain that the casualty still doesn't want you DBDGs anywhere near it."

For the first time in Prilicla's long experience on ambulance-ship operations, the captain used words that his translator had not been programmed to accept, and went on. "Then what the hell am I expected to do to change that?"

Before replying, Prilicla looked slowly around the compartment, pointed at one of the transparent inspection covers, then moved close and began opening it. The robot drifted nearby but made no attempt to interfere, even when he reached inside and, after hesitating and looking back as if to ask permission for what he was about to do, he gently touched one of the cable looms. When he replied, he knew that his vision pickup was showing the captain everything he had been doing.

"In very simple pictorial terms, we've been talking big," he said, "by telling it about a few of the Federation's species and the cooperation that exists between their worlds and in space, like assisting distressed ships and—"

"If you remember my advice," the other broke in, stressing the last word, "it was to follow through on the ship-rescue sequence and show the casualties receiving medical treatment. That, Doctor, would have clearly demonstrated our good intentions."

"And I did not take your advice," Prilicla replied gently, "because of the possibility of a misunderstanding. In the present climate of fear and distrust, the emotional reaction of an alien— who would have been witnessing a multispecies medical team, which would certainly have included at least one DBDG, carrying out a surgical procedure on a casualty—could not have been taken for granted. We know nothing about the alien's physiology, environment, or medical practices, if it has any. It may have decided that we were simply torturing captured casualties.

"You, friend Fletcher," he said, when the other remained silent, "can do nothing right now, apart from furnishing me with technical advice when needed. I've already mentioned this idea to you, and your lack of enthusiasm for it was understandable. But the time for showing pictures is over. As my Earth-human gambling friends keep telling me, I must put my money where my mouth is.

"So now," he ended, "we– or rather, I—must try to reinforce those pictorial lessons with deeds."

He withdrew his hand slowly, closed the transparent cover and pointed along the linking passageway in the direction of the identical compartment on the damaged side of the ship. Had the robot crew member been an organic life-form, he thought, it would have been breathing down his neck. But it made no move to hinder him.

In the darkened compartment he used his helmet light to open inspection panels and look and, if it didn't look dangerous, to touch the scorched or ruptured cable looms and plumbing inside all of them in turn. Still there was no interference from the robot. He was beginning to feel less sure of himself and his ability to do this job when the captain, demonstrating the strange mixture of empathy and understanding possessed by Earthhumans, answered his question before it could be asked.

"You should start with an easy one," said the captain. "High on the upper side of the first inspection compartment you opened there are two fairly thick wires—one has what seems to be pale blue insulation, and the other red. If you look carefully you can see where they make a right-angle turn and disappear through a grommet into what is presumably the ceiling of your corridor. The force of the explosion caused a wiring break in one of them at the angle bend. Do you see the ends of the bare wire projecting from the torn insulation? Try to splice it, but be careful not to touch any metal in the area while you're working. Your gauntlets are thin and we don't know how much current that wire will be carrying. You'll need insulating tape to hold the splice together."

"My med satchel has surgical tape," said Prilicla. "Will that do?"

"Yes, Doctor, but be careful."

A few minutes later the splicing operation was complete, the join was insulated, and all the lighting fixtures in the corridor were on. The robot crew member was moving from one to the other and, Prilicla hoped, reporting on the completion of one small repair to the conscious survivor who was its chief. It wasn't much, but he had done something.

"What next?" said Prilicla.

"Now comes the difficult part," said the captain, "so don't get cocky. The other wiring affected is finer and with more subtle color-codings. Some of the ruptured strands show heat discoloration, and you must trace these back to an unaffected area so as to positively identify each end before joining them. The complexity of the wiring makes me pretty sure that most of these breaks are in the hull-sensor and internal-communications networks, and if a join were to be mismatched, we could cause all kinds of trouble. It would be like short-circuiting your hearing sensors to your eyes. We're in the strange position of making repairs to systems whose purposes are totally unknown to us. I wish I was there with the proper equipment to help you. This is going to be delicate, precise, painstaking, and exhausting work. Are you up to it, Doctor?"

Don't worry," said Prilicla, "it's a little like brain surgery."

CHAPTER 18

Even though the captain was giving him the benefit of its wide-ranging technical expertise and guiding his hands at every stage, the work went very slowly. An early splicing problem was that some of the damaged fine-gauge wiring had burned away along several inches of its length and the missing pieces had to be replaced. There was suitable replacement material on *Rhabwar* and the captain offered to bring it himself, in the hope that he would be allowed to assist Prilicla directly and so speed up the process.

"Bring some food as well, friend Fletcher," said Prilicla. "I've decided that it will also save time if I don't have to return to the ship for meals. Or sleep."

Prilicla waited politely until the expected objections were becoming repetitive, then said, "There are risks, of course, but I'm being neither foolish nor foolhardy. My spacesuit makes provision for the short-term elimination of body wastes, it has a small airlock attachment for the introduction of food, and in the weightless condition, padded rest furnishings are unnecessary for comfort. My thinking is that if we want the survivor to trust us, we must show that we trust it."

"I agree, reluctantly," the other replied after a long pause.

"But if I can make it plain that I'm helping you help it, maybe it will begin to trust me, too."

"That is the general idea, friend Fletcher," he replied. "But at this delicate stage in the contact procedure we shouldn't rush things."

"Right," said the captain. "I'll bring the food, replacement wiring, and some simple, non-powered tools that I think will help in your work. They will be inside a transparent container so that the survivor and/or its robot will be able to see exactly what it is getting. I'm coming now."

But when it was approaching the alien ship, the emotional radiation of the survivor became apprehensive and its robot left the compartment quickly on what was obviously an interception course. Prilicla followed it and, when it was plain that the captain was not to be allowed to enter the ship, he relieved the other of its package.

"Sorry, friend Fletcher," he said as he did so, "I'm afraid that you're still unwelcome here. But I've been thinking about a possible explanation for that, and for the high sensitivity these people have towards external physical contact, allied to the strange fact that, in both the ship and its crew robots, their defenses are ultra–short range. Surely that is a strange type of weapon to use in space."

"The weapon used against them was not short-range," said the captain. "It blew a large hole in their hull and, to a lesser degree, in the defunct crew robot we examined. But go on."

"During your show," Prilicla resumed, "I received the feeling that the survivor was being given information for the first time. There was excitement, wonder, but a strangely reduced level of surprise. It was almost as if the survivor was expecting, or maybe just hoping, to meet other life-forms in space. If I'm right, that would mean that interstellar travel was new to it, or that this was its first time out and it was exploring, perhaps even searching for the planet it has found. But when you showed the Hudla sequence, there I detected subtle changes in its emotions. There was an odd combination of fear, dread, hatred, and, strangely, familiarity. Hudla is not a pleasant world to people who are not Hudlars and, I would guess, neither is the survivor's. I realize this is speculation but I have the feeling that it went out looking for another and better world. The presence of its ship in close orbit could mean that it found it."

The other made a gesture of impatience. "An interesting theory, but it doesn't take into account the fact that an as-yet unknown agency used an offensive weapon against it."

Prilicla hated telling the captain that he thought it was wrong, especially at this short range because he would feel the other's annoyance at full intensity. He said gently, "Are we quite sure about that? Consider the type of blast damage to the ship and the robot taken aboard *Terragar*, and that this species may be new to interstellar and hyperspatial flight and the distress beacons associated with it. Let's suppose that they found an uninhabited planet, green and pleasant and without the violent meteorology of home and that they signaled its position by detonating—not a distress beacon because if they were new to space they would not expect rescue—but a similar device that would give an accurate position fix. The signaling device was untried and it blew up in their faces. That's the one we suspected might be a weapons discharge. *Terragar* responded before we could and needed to detonate its own distress beacon. But the point I'm making is that the damage to the alien ship might have been accidental and self-inflicted."

"I think you're wishing rather than theorizing, Doctor," said the captain; then, after a moment's thought, "But it's a nice theory. However, it doesn't explain why their robots as well as their ship have such prickly hides. Plainly they were expecting someone or something to attack them. And if you still think I'm wrong, don't waste time being polite about it."

"Their defenses may be automatic," said Prilicla.

The captain did not reply. It was beginning to have doubts, which meant that the reflected annoyance caused by Prilicla's words would be reduced. He went on. "Consider the surface design of the ship's outer hull as well as that of the robot's skin. Those surfaces can be touched without harm by organic digits or simple, unsophisticated, non-powered tools. If we postulate a dense or highly disturbed atmosphere on their home world, a thick, protective, and streamlined covering would be necessary for survival, as it is on the Hudlars' planet. But suppose they have an implacable natural enemy, perhaps an intelligent and technically advanced one, and the ship's defensive weapons are needed only on their environmentally-hostile home planet during the periods of construction, takeoff, and landing.

"And if their implacable enemy bears a physical resemblance to you DBDGs," he ended, "that would explain much."

The captain made an untranslatable sound. "I suppose we're lucky that they don't have a phobia about outsized crabs or caterpillars, or six-legged elephants or even large flying insects," it said, then went on briskly. "About this repair job, Doctor. There will be considerable physical and mental stress involved. The quality of any work suffers with the onset of fatigue, whatever the profession. While your mind is clear, can you estimate how long you will be able to function effectively before I should remind you to stop for rest?"

Prilicla gave an estimate that was on the generous side, knowing that the other would be sure to reduce it. Nothing more was said until he had returned to the alien's control center, after which the captain rarely stopped talking, but the words and tone were continually reassuring.

". . . Before its insulated cover was pulled apart by the accident," Fletcher was saying, "the cable loom you are working on enclosed ten individual lines. The magnifier here tells me that they are too fine to carry a dangerous level of current. But their color-coding is the same as the heavier cables that run to and spread across the outer hull, so we may assume that they perform a similar communications and/or sensory function. . . . Dammit,

I wish I could get in there with the proper tools. Don't take that as a criticism, Doctor, you're doing fine."

Prilicla remained silent because the other had repeated its non-criticism and apology several times in the last hour, and he was feeling excited and hopeful rather than irritated. An internal, light-duty sensor and communications circuit was what he had been looking for because it might mean that he had found the broken connection between the comparatively uninjured and strongly emoting crew member and its partner. Putting them in touch with each other again should go a long way to proving their rescuers' good intentions. Carefully and with the delicacy of touch possible only to one of his fragile race, he separated, stripped, and began to splice the severed ends of a wire that was almost hair-thin.

Suddenly he jerked his hands away as a burst of emotion exploded from the crew member at the other side of the control center. In spite of the distance it was strong, sharp, intensely uncomfortable, but brief. It faded within a few seconds and so, thankfully, did the accompanying feelings of anger.

"What happened?" said Fletcher sharply. "You jerked your hands away. Are you hurt?"

"No," Prilicla replied; then after a moment's thought he went on, "I must have joined two of the wrong wires. It made the survivor, maybe both of them, very uncomfortable for an instant. The emotional radiation was characteristic of a sharp, unpleasant sensation, as if someone was to cross our optic nerve with our aural input then make a loud noise. Sorry, I'll have to be more careful."

The captain exhaled loudly and said, "Yes. But it was a natural mistake because all the wiring in that loom has the same color-coding with subtle variations in shade. The magnifier's enhanced imaging barely picks them up but your unassisted vision can't, good as it is. Next time hold the wire ends to be joined where I can see them clearly for my okay, then, if it doesn't cause an adverse reaction, shield the other wires from it while you spray on the insulation. That way you won't risk a bared, spliced length making contact or short-circuiting against an adjoining bare wire. Tell me if you've any doubts or problems about anything you intend doing, Doctor, otherwise carry on. I think you're getting there."

Prilicla carried on while the captain furnished technical and moral assistance. There were no more accidents, but there was an increasing level of emotional radiation emanating from the survivor on the undamaged section of the control center. It was not the sharp reaction characteristic of sudden discomfort, but a mixture of fear and hope so intense that his empathic faculty received it almost as a physical pain. Then suddenly there was a double explosion of feeling that made him pull back because his whole body, as well as his hands were trembling. Slowly he moved to the the inner door that he had not been allowed to enter and placed his stethoscope against the bare metal.

"Doctor, you've got the shakes," said the captain urgently. "Is there anything wrong with you? What's happening?"

"Nothing is wrong with me," said Prilicla unsteadily as he sought for his customary clinical calm. "To the contrary, friend Fletcher. The two survivors are now communicating with each other, presumably via the repaired circuitry. I'm trying to pick up their language sounds, with a view to programming it into our translation computer, but I can't hear anything. Possibly there is not enough air to conduct sound or their speaking and hearing organs are enclosed in some kind of helmet."

"Almost certainly that is due to their control sections losing internal pressure," the other said excitedly. "How are they feeling now?"

"At present their emotional radiation is complex and confused although it is beginning to clear," Prilicla replied as he tried to describe feelings that could not be adequately conveyed in mere words. "There is a combination of relief, excitement, and concern that is due, I feel sure, to the reestablishment of inter-personal communication and the up-to-the-minute exchange of information. That information would include the first survivor's reaction to the things we have been doing for it as well as a description of the physical condition of the second survivor which, my empathy tells me, is not good. Something will have to be done for the second one as a matter of clinical urgency. Underlying the emotional radiation from both sources, but still strong enough to be unmistakable, there are feelings of grati-tude."

"Good!" said the captain. "If they're feeling grateful then they must know that you're trying to help them. But do you think they're ready to to trust us, all of us, after your good deed?"

Prilicla was silent for a moment as he concentrated on the two sources of emotional radiation, one of them attenuated with distance and the closer one faint because of physical weakness and distress, then he said, "There is still a persistent background fear in both entities that is due, I feel sure, to the fact that both of them are now aware of the presence of their feared and hated DBDG bogeyman. I may be wrong because I'm am empath, rather than a telepath, but I feel that they aren't yet ready to make friends with their worst nightmare. Something more must be done to help gain their trust, and my good deed has yet to be completed."

The captain did not ask the obvious question because it knew that the answer was forthcoming. Prilicla went on. "My close-range analysis of the second survivor's emotional radiation indicates that its body is so debilitated that it barely retains the ability to think coherently. There is increasing physical discom-fort, combined with a feeling of urgency and intense, personal fear that is characteristic of a being who is close to terminal suf-focation, or dehydration, or both. To complete our good deed, more repairs are needed, to restore their air and working fluid supply."

"So now you've delusions of being a plumber as well as an electrician," said the captain, and laughed. "Right, Doctor, what exactly will you need?"

"As before, friend Fletcher, I need directions," Prilicla replied, "because I have no idea how to proceed. But first I want to show the robot, who is the eyes for at least one of the survivors, the sections of damaged piping that I'll be trying to repair or replace. While I'm doing that, you can assess the situation and tell me what needs to be done and how to go about doing it using replacement material and basic, non-powered tools from *Rhabwar*.

"Also," he went on, "I've noticed traces of vapor around some of the fractured piping in here, indicating the escape of residual atmosphere or moisture although it could, I suppose, be the remains of a toxic fluid used in a hydraulic actuator. While you're assessing the repair requirements with me, I'll bag samples and use my medical analyzer on it. If it is air or water rather than something toxic, please reproduce it in bulk and send it over in transparent containers. If the containers are marked with the same color-codings as that of the supply pipes we're going to replace, that might further reassure the survivors. Leave everything loosely tethered to the hull where I came on board for me to pick up.

"We've fixed it so that they can talk to each other," he ended, "but the conversation will be short if one of them stops breathing."

The next two hours he passed surveying the repair job, identifying the color-codings, and isolating the fractured piping to be joined. He knew that the work would be less delicate than splicing the damaged wiring, but the captain had grave doubts about his ability to perform it.

"This isn't anything like brain surgery, Doctor," it said. "What you'll need is brute force rather than delicacy of touch. Your digits were never made to handle manually-operated metal-cutters, the only kind these people will allow near them, and heavy spanners. And your body is far too fragile to exert the leverage that may be required. A pair of Earth-human hands with muscular backup are needed for this job. I should be in there helping you."

Prilicla did not reply, and the captain went on quickly, "I'll run another external visual for them, the one showing ship repairs being carried out simultaneously by several different species including Earth-humans. After what you've already done for them, they might be more inclined to forget their DBDG phobia enough to trust me a little. I'll wear a lightweight suit, with no powered instruments other than the radio and a small cutting torch, and carry the piping and tools in transparent containers as you suggested. Working together the repairs will take a fraction of the time you'd need otherwise, and if one of them is running out of air . . ."

"I'm sorry, that will not be possible right now . . ." he began.

"At least let me try, Doctor," the other broke in. "I can be over there with all we'll need in less than an hour."

". . . Because, friend Fletcher," he ended, "in less than ten minutes' time, as soon as I finish analyzing these air and fluid samples, Ill be asleep."

CHAPTER 19

As Prilicla had expected, the robot crew member's actions showed great agitation on the part of its organic controller when the captain met him outside the hull and tried to enter the ship. He had to point several times at the lengths of piping the other was carrying and demonstrate, both by slicing one of the lengths of piping into pieces with the tiny flame of the cutter and then by turning on the cylinder taps briefly and releasing a small quantity of their contents into space to show that they contained only gas, before the captain was allowed to come on board. By the time they were in the damaged control section it was clear from the emotional radiation of both survivors that the DBDG was feared as much as it was trusted, and that the emotional balance could swing either way.

"Friend Fletcher," he said, "do not make any sudden movements that might be mistaken for a threat. In fact, until they become accustomed to your presence it would be better if you did nothing except pass tools and parts to me, and generally give the impression that I am your superior until I indicate—"

"As you are fond of reminding me, Doctor," it said dryly, "on the disaster site you have the rank."

The words were sarcastic but the emotional radiation that accompanied them was free of rancor. Prilicla went on. ". . . until

I indicate to the survivors by acting out the requirement several times that I need your physical assistance. We're lucky that their emotional radiation will tell me whether or not they understand what I'm trying to do."

It wasn't very long before he ran into trouble. One of the piping conduits had been twisted out of true so that the joints and lock-nuts were jammed. They were too tight, or at least too tight for Prilicla to move.

Several times he went through the motions of trying to loosen it, then he pointed at the captain's larger and stronger hands, withdrew, and indicated that the other should take over. The robot edged closer, its damaged metal surfaces somehow reflecting the fear and concern that its masters were feeling.

"You take over, friend Fletcher," he said. "But move slowly, they're still terrified of you."

The captain had to move slowly because it required several minutes of maximum effort, and the cooling element in its suit was just barely keeping the perspiration from fogging its visor, before the sticking lock-nut was loosened, removed, and fitted with a joint that would take the replacement piping. It chose a length that was already fitted with a T-junction and valve, and it took much less time for it to cut the pipe to size and make the join. Prilicla passed in the length of hose from the two air tanks, which was attached to the junction. Several times the captain indicated the color-coding on the old and new piping and the tanks. The robot had moved into the inspection compartment and was crowding the captain but not hampering its hands.

"I'm detecting great anxiety," said Prilicla; then, reassuringly, "but there is also a feeling of comprehension. I think they understand what we're trying to do for them. I'm turning on the air now."

The earlier analyses had shown that the survivor's atmosphere was similar to that used by the majority of the warm-blooded, oxygen-breathing species. No attempt had been made to include the trace quantities of other gases so that the mixture going in was in the usual proportion of oxygen to nitrogen. For several minutes there was no emotional reaction either from the distressed survivor or the other who was in contact with it; then, suddenly, a slow trembling shook Prilicla's whole body.

"What's wrong?" said the captain.

"Nothing," he replied. "The breathing distress of the second survivor is being treated although it is still suffering, possibly from hunger, thirst, or injuries, and both of them are now radiating intense, positive feelings of relief and gratitude which are giving me emotional pleasure. They are still afraid of you, but their hatred and distrust are diminishing. Well done, friend Fletcher."

"Well done yourself," said the captain, radiating embarrassment at the compliment. "Now that we've helped it to breathe, let's see if we can give it something to drink and eat as well. There is staining around the broken end of one of these pipes that looks like it might be dried-out liquid food. If your analyzer confirms that, we could—"

"No, friend Fletcher," he broke in, "there might not be time for that. Psychologically the second survivor's condition has improved but I feel the presence of increasingly severe debilitation associated with physical trauma. From now on we have to know exactly what we're doing, or be told exactly what to do, and do it fast. You brought spare air tanks, more than was needed for the recent first-aid operation. If we empty them, would there be enough atmospheric pressure to enable us to breathe and allow the transmission of sound?"

He felt the other's initial puzzlement dissolve into comprehension as it said, "So you're going to try talking to them and asking for directions. If we knew anything about their communications setup, especially how they convert radio into audio frequency, we could simply talk on our own radios. As it is, we aren't sure yet whether or not they have ears."

It shook its head and went on. "The answer to your question

is, I don't know. This section was close to the area of hull damage and might leak like a sieve. We could try."

Prilicla said, "Yes, but not here. We'll move back to the undamaged section with the first survivor. All of the access panels in that compartment are a tight fit, probably an airtight fit, as is the entrance door and the one into the area containing the survivor. This is probably a crew safety measure and part of the ship design philosophy. To increase the effect I'll spray on some of my plastic sealant. It won't stop the doors from being opened later, but it will ensure minimum leakage. While I'm doing that, you will want to make arrangements with *Rhabwar*."

"That I will," said the captain. It withdrew from the tiny inspection chamber, closed the access hatch tightly, and began talking rapidly into its suit radio as it followed him to the other control section. By the time it had finished talking, Prilicla had the compartment sealed and compressed air was hissing visibly and then audibly from the fully opened tank valves.

"We don't seem to be losing any air," said the captain after a few minutes, "and the pressure is high enough to carry sound, or even to open our helmets, supposing we were mad enough to do that."

"I believe we are mad enough, friend Fletcher," said Prilicla. "Folding back our helmets will be a further sign that we trust them and wish to be friends, as well as removing the small additional voice distortion caused by our external speakers. I hope our robot friend can hear and speak as well as see. Is *Rhabwar* ready?"

"Projector and translation computer standing by," the captain replied, unsealing its helmet. "You speak first, Doctor. A privilege of rank."

With the words there was a complex, background feeling of excitement, expectation, and minor relief characteristic of a personally embarrassing situation to be avoided should the attempt fail. Prilicla's own feeling was that it wouldn't.

He bent a forelimb almost double and pointed at himself. Slowly and distinctly he said, "Prilicla, Prilicla, Prilicla. I am Prilicla." Then he pointed behind towards the inner door, and waited. When there was no response he indicated the captain and nodded for it to try. The rapid, musical clicking of untranslated Cinrusskin speech was difficult for other species to follow.

"Fletcher, Fletcher, Fletcher," said the captain, indicating itself before pointing in the same direction as Prilicla.

The robot made a short, sharp sound like the squeaking of a rusty hinge.

"Was that a word, dammit," said the captain in an angry undertone, "or a malfunctioning robot?"

"A word, maybe more than one," Prilicla replied. "It heard us, and I felt a flash of understanding and urgency. Maybe its words are rapid, compressed, as in Nallajim. Let's try again, and speak very slowly. Maybe it will do the same.

"Pril-ic-la," he said slowly three times, repeating the earlier motions. The captain said and did the same.

"Keet," said the robot. A moment later it added, "Pil-ik-la, Flet-cha."

Prilicla gestured towards the sealed door in front of them and said, "Keet," then pointed back at the compartment they had just left.

"Jas-am," came the reply.

"We're talking!" For a moment the captain's relief and pleasure at the breakthrough swamped most of the survivor's emotional radiation, but not the urgency.

"Not yet," Prilicla said. "We're exchanging personal-name sounds, but it's only a start."

"*Rhabwar* here," the voice of Haslam sounding in their earpieces said. "I'm afraid the Doctor is right, Captain. The computer needs more for an accurate translation: verbs, accompanying actions, explanations, and a bigger vocabulary to link the words together."

"Friend Haslam," he said, "Show the pictures of planets and

native species again, please, but just those for Earth and Cinruss. Then patch in one of the survivor life-forms and a world with no geographical features."

Prilicla watched the tiny repeater screen in his suit as this was done. He said, "Fletcher is from Earth, Prilicla is from Cinruss, Keet is from . . ." and waited.

Without hesitation the voice from the robot said, "Flet-cha, Ert; Pil-ik-la, Cin-russ; Keet, Tro-lan."

"We're getting there, Doctor," Haslam said excitedly; then, in a tone almost of apology it went on. "Names and places of origin help, but they aren't enough for the computer to begin structuring the language. We still need verbs and related actions."

Unlike its outsize parent in Sector General, *Rhabwar*'s translation computer did not carry a record of all of the intelligence-bearing clicks, moans, hisses, and chirps that were used as speech by the members of the Galactic Federation, a vast store of data which enabled it to compare the input of the new languages that were discovered from time to time and produce a translation. But the ambulance ship had proved on several previous occasions that it could do the same job, with a little on-site help.

"Friend Fletcher," he said, pointing at the material in the other's transparent satchel, "I need a short piece of fine cable that can be pulled apart easily, and a short length of piping. Do you have one that is thin-walled and breaks without shattering into pieces?"

He felt the captain's puzzlement dissolve in a flood of comprehension. It produced the cable, wrapped it around his hand and pulled it apart, then he produced—not a pipe, but a length of thin sleeving—and snapped it in two before handing the four pieces to him. It said, "Yes and no, Doctor. This breaks without splintering, but it needs an Earth-human's muscles to do it."

Prilicla indicated a section of undamaged piping through one of the transparent access hatches, then pointed back the way they had come towards the other survivor's position. Holding a piece of the broken pipe in each hand, he brought them slowly together at the faces of the original fracture and did the same with the severed wiring. He repeated the movements several time before speaking.

"Wire, pipes," he said, pointing at the captain and himself. "We join wires and pipes. We fix wires and pipes. We repair"— he made a wide gesture that included the ship all around them— "everything."

Through its robot crew member's sensors, the first survivor already knew that they repaired things, although it had not known the word for what they had been doing. He waited, straining to detect the first feelings of comprehension that would tell him that it understood the other, more important message that he was trying to send. And when the crew robot spoke again, he knew that it did.

"Pil-ik-la, Flet-cha," it said. "Fix Jasam."

The captain gave a loud, barking laugh of sheer relief, which it cut short abruptly in case it might have been mistaken for a threatening sound by the survivor. On *Rhabwar*, Haslam sounded equally pleased.

"That's it!" said the lieutenant. "We have a translation. Just talk to it naturally and mime only if you think it might not understand a new action. The conversation will be a bit stilted until you build up a vocabulary, but the computer is happy. I'm relaying the translation through your headsets. Nice work. Any other instructions?"

Prilicla's body was shaking with a slow, even tremor of pleasure and relief that was tempered slightly by the remembered emotional radiation from the second survivor, Jasam, which indicated that clinically it was in very bad shape.

"Stand by, friend Haslam," he said. "I need you to project more pictures. Edit the previous run to show only the recovery of space-wreck casualties, then add something on their transfer to and treatment on *Rhabwar*. Be brief regarding the treatment, too much detail on surgical procedures might give the impression that we go in for physical torture. Concentrate on the before-and-after aspects, the badly injured casualties, and then showing them cured. Run them as soon as you can."

Turning towards the inner door and the robot hovering in front of it, he brought the two pieces of pipe together slowly and said, "I fix slowly," and repeated the action and words several times; then he moved them quickly into contact and said, "I fix quickly." Then he pointed back the way they had come and added, "I fix Jasam quickly," emphasizing the last word.

He felt understanding and agreement coloring the ever-present deep concern, and said, "Keet, the word for that is 'yes.'"

He pointed in the direction of Jasam and used the broken pipe to indicate, he hoped, that they were both broken. Then he raised a hand to his eyes before pointing first at an undamaged section of piping and then at the inner door of Keet's compartment.

"To fix the broken Jasam," he mimed as he said the words, "I must see the unbroken Keet."

Again there was understanding, but with it there was a sudden return of the earlier fear and hatred.

"Keep that accursed druul away from us!" it said, so loudly that it must have been its equivalent of a shout. "I don't trust it! We are both weakened and helpless and it will eat us. We thought that interstellar space, at least, would be clear of such vermin!"

Prilicla tried to ignore the captain's scandalized emotional radiation, and said reassuringly, "Don't be afraid, Fletcher won't touch you. Fletcher fixes machines. Prilicla fixes people."

The captain's low-voiced comment was lost in the sound of the inner door hissing open.

It revealed a small compartment whose interior was an almost-solid mass of support brackets, piping, and cable runs leading into a flattened oval dish at its center. The upper half of the receptacle had a sealed, transparent cover that gave a clear view of the co-captain of the ship. Physically Keet was classification CHLI and closely resembled its robot crew member in size and shape except that instead of the silvery metal skin there was the veined brownish-pink of organic tissue. A continuous control-and-sensor-input panel laterally encircled the inner surface of the body container, and the operating keys were within easy reach of the creature's short digits. Its food, water-supply, and waste-extraction systems had been surgically implanted into the relevant organs.

Prilicla's body shook briefly with a feeling composed of pity, revulsion, and the claustrophobic fear known only to free-flying beings like himself when he realized that the ship's organic crew had been confined to their control and life-support pods with no freedom to move, not even around their own ship.

They had been installed with the rest of the ship's equipment.

From his medical satchel he took his scanner, reversed it so that Keet could see the viewplate, and demonstrated its function by touching it against parts of his own body, before moving it close to the other's pod.

"This will not hurt you," he said. "It will enable me to see inside your body so that I can understand and fix anything that is wrong."   ·

"Will you be able to fix Jasam, too?"

Its speech was going and coming through his translator now, clearly and with the possibility for misunderstanding being reduced with every word. The prime rule during a first-contact situation was to find out as much a possible about the other life-form so as to further reduce that risk, and to tell the truth at all times.

But it was also sound medical practice to encourage a patient to talk about itself, or any other pleasant subject in which it was interested, so as to take its mind off a frightening or possibly embarrassing examination.

"I will try to fix Jasam," he said. "But to do that, I must first discover everything I can about you and your people. For the best results I would like to have full knowledge, even though there is no way of knowing which pieces of information will be helpful during the repairs, so just tell me about your partner, your lives, your customs, the food you eat, and the things you like to do. In the event of an unsuccessful repair, which is a faint possibility, who and where are your next of kin? You are a completely new and scientifically advanced life-form and everything you say will be interesting and useful.

"Tell me about yourself, and your world."

CHAPTER 20

A few minutes into the examination there was an interruption. The two courier ships had arrived and, although they were keeping station at the requested distance, their impatience for a full report on the situation could almost be felt. The courier captains' voices were being relayed through *Rhabwar* to the alien ship so that Prilicla and Fletcher, but not the alien casualties, could hear them.

"This is not a good time to stop and make reports, friend Fletcher," said Prilicla without looking up from the scanner. "Just tell them that . . ."

"I know what to tell them," said the other, and went on briskly. "A very delicate first-contact situation is proceeding as we speak. The alien vessel has a crew of two, both physiological classification CHLI; one is seriously injured and the other less so. The medical examination and the contact procedure are being conducted by Dr. Prilicla and are complicated by the fact that the casualties have a rabid fear of all DBDG life-forms regardless of size, apparently because of our close resemblance to a natural enemy on their home planet. All of the proceedings so far have been recorded in case of accidents, but I ask that you wait to avoid taking back an incomplete report that could be updated from hour to hour."

"Understood, sir," came the reply. "Over and listening out."

At first the casualty seemed anxious to talk about the druul, and how much its race hated and feared them, rather than about its world or itself. The proximity of Fletcher was doubtless responsible for that. Prilicla continued to speak and to radiate verbal and emotional reassurance while he plied his scanner and the captain kept its distance. Gradually the subject widened but it always veered back to the hated druul.

Keet's species called themselves the Trolanni, and their world Trolann, and over the past few centuries it had become a savage, frightful place of unending war for its diminishing resources against the druul and the other organic and inorganic pollutants that were fast making the once-populous world uninhabitable for both of its intelligent species, as well as for most other forms of life above the insect level.

Many attempts had been made to check the self-poisoning of their overcrowded world and to impose strict controls on the high degree of industrialization needed to support it if irreversible chemical changes were not to increase the level of toxicity to the point where the planetary biosphere would no longer be able to support life. But preventative and curative measures on that scale required personal sacrifices, self-control, and the cooperation of everyone concerned. A large minority of the Trolanni, and all of the druul, refused to give it.

Possibly there were individuals who thought differently, but as a population the druul decided that the problem would be solved if the Trolanni and their food supply were considered a natural resource and used exclusively for the benefit and continued survival of the druul.

As a species the druul were small, bipedal, vicious, fast-breeding, and utterly implacable where enemies, sapient or otherwise, were concerned. From the dawn of history their rate of scientific and technological achievement had been equal to the Trolanni, so that the wars they had fought had been forced to a stop rather than being won. In spite of many peace overtures by the Trolanni, the two species had lived in a state of unfriendly coexistence until a war that was no longer stoppable was being fought for the diminishing resources of the stinking, polluted, near-corpse that was their planet. For many generations the druul had practiced cannibalism, eating even the sickly young or the elderly or otherwise unproductive people of their own race. They could not be defeated because there were always more of them hungry and ready to fight. Apart from a few pockets of weakening resistance and the latest Trolanni technology which defended them, the planet belonged to the druul.

The only solution was for the Trolanni to find a new, unpolluted and peaceful home.

"You found a new home here," said Prilicla gently. "What went wrong?"

"A technical failure of some kind," said Keet, radiating feelings of minor embarrassment and apology. "I'm not the propulsion specialist. After finding an ideal world it seemed as if we couldn't return home with the news. But we had signaling devices, two of them, untried because none of the searchsuits had used them before then. The first one malfunctioned and seriously damaged the hull. The second one was modified, but it destroyed the doll who released it. Then the ship with the druuls in it arrived."

"They weren't druuls," said Prilicla. "It was a rescue ship that came to help you."

"I'm sorry," said Keet. "I know that, now."

Prilicla withdrew the scanner and moved back. He had all the physiological data he needed for a preliminary assessment of the other casualty's condition, but a lot more non-medical information was needed. He said, "I'll stay in contact with you, but we're moving over to look at Jasam now. Tell it not to be afraid; neither friend Fletcher nor myself mean it any harm. Why did you attack the first rescue ship?"

"We didn't," it replied quickly. "It attacked our protective suit . . ."

For the few minutes it took them to transfer to the other control module, Prilicla listened to Keet's reassuring words to its life-mate and felt the growing trust in Fletcher and himself that accompanied them even though they were feelings that Jasam had yet to share.

". . . That is what the druul have been doing to us for hundreds of years," it continued, "and many of our scientists think that they no longer know why they do it. As individuals they are predominantly machines designed to attack and penetrate our protective suits, as a nut is cracked to uncover its edible kernel, although all too often the kernel itself is destroyed by the ferocity of the onslaught so that there is no reward for the tiny, organic fraction that controls the machines they have become. We Trolanni, at least, are whole, sapient, and civilized, if very sickly, people inside our protective suits, although with this two-body searchsuit with its vastly greater proportion of machine–to–organic life, we were forced to become more like the druul. . . ."

So they thought of their ship as a searchsuit, a bigger, more complex and specialized version of the individual protective garment than those that the planet-based druul forced them to wear. Interesting. Prilicla could feel the captain's mounting excitement as Keet continued speaking, but he knew that friend Fletcher would not interrupt the flow of information with a question that would shortly be answered.

". . . In this instance," it went on, "our hull protection was designed to safeguard us for the short time we were in atmosphere before we entered space, where so far the druul have been unable to go. The protection operates continuously in a state of high alert, and instantly disrupts the computer-operated control and life-support systems of any attacking machine-encased druul. But we never expected to find them, or beings just like them, between the stars. That was terrifying for us and there was nothing we could do."

"It would help us to help Jasam and yourself," Prilicla said gently, "if your protective device could be switched off. Can it?"

"No," said Keet, "at least not by us. To do that, specialist knowledge and devices are needed and these are available only on our home world. It must not be switched off because its protection is needed during our second trip through atmosphere, hopefully on our way home to report success in finding a new world. But instead . . . Please, will Jasam live?"

Sometimes, Prilicla thought, as he noted the damage to its life-mate as well as the traces of dried body fluid that were staining the joins where the metal and organic interface was visible, it was not always advisable to tell the truth even in a first-contact situation.

"There is a strong possibility that we'll be able to save its life," he said.

"But not in here," said the captain on their personal frequency that did not go through the translator. Quickly and concisely it went on to explain why while Prilicla tried to provide a more optimistic translation for the two Trolanni, continuing his scanner examination of the second casualty as he spoke.

Jasam's injuries had been due to the structural damage to its side of the searchsuit, caused by the explosive failure of the first beacon they had released, which in turn had caused multiple fracturing and dislocation of the life-support plumbing that had been surgically implanted into its body. Its resultant external and internal wounds were extensive and serious, he explained, but with the right treatment they would not be life-threatening. He personally had repaired organic damage that was much more severe and had returned the entity concerned to full health.

"But in this case," he went on, "the right treatment would first involve removing Jasam and yourself from your vessel—"

"And leave us without a suit!" Keet broke in. "And, and life support? We've already lost our dolls—Jasam's destroyed, and mine damaged beyond the ability to do sensitive repair work. *No!*"

They called their robot crew members "dolls," Prilicla thought, and the accompanying emotional radiation was indicative of the feelings held for a friend and helper as well as for a pet or plaything. Curious—but satisfying that curiosity would have to wait until the more urgent problem of removing them from their ship-sized protective suit was settled.

"On Trolann," he went on, projecting reassurance with every ounce of empathic energy in his mind, "there must be doctors, healers, beings who cure or repair organic disease or damage. To perform this work effectively there must be easy access to the site of the trouble, so am I correct in thinking that they prefer the sick or injured patient to be unclothed?"

"Yes," said Keet. "But that is on Trolann. Out here . . ."

"Out here," said Prilicla gently, "you would be much safer. *Rhabwar*, the ship that you see nearby, was expressly designed for and contains all the equipment necessary to do such work, and it has done it many times. But the equipment is both bulky and highly sensitive. If it was to be moved to your vessel, a difficult job in itself, there would be a serious risk of the ship's protective devices disabling its computer-operated circuitry, as it does with the druul machines. There isn't much time left. Your life-support consumables, Jasam's especially, have leaked away and are close to exhaustion.

"If both of you are to survive," he ended, "You must agree and I must act, quickly."

There was a moment's silence while Keet radiated growing uncertainty, then it said, "Both of us? I, I thought one of us would stay in our searchsuit until the organic and mechanical repairs were done, then Jasam would be reinserted and . . . There is very little organic damage to myself."

"I know," said Prilicla. "But I will need your help and advice for the extraction process. You will be conscious and aware and will be able to tell us exactly what we have to do at every stage, and we will be able to use the experience more easily to detach your more seriously injured life-mate. We have already analyzed and reproduced your food, air, and working fluid, the last two of which are very similar to our own. My present plan is to put both of you into a covered litter that contains all your life-support requirements, and where you will be able to give close, emotional support to Jasam during the transfer to our ship and the organic-repair work afterwards.''

There was another silence, then Keet said, "Detaching Jasam is a difficult and specialized job that is done only in case of an onboard emergency by a doll. Jasam's doll was killed in the first explosion and mine was damaged in the second. The control circuitry serving the forward cluster of fine, peripheral digits, the ones needed for a complete body extraction, was burned out. My doll is incapable of the delicate work that would be required. It is certain that we will both die.''

"That is not certain," said Prilicla, "and is not even likely. Controlled by our own sensitive digits will be even finer and more delicate mechanisms that are capable of doing the work. We are widely experienced in the extraction of damaged organic casualties from the wreckage of starships, and friend Fletcher will make a very good doll.''

The captain made a noise that did not translate.

CHAPTER 21

When Lieutenant Dodds and the covered litter arrived it was met by Keet's doll and quickly escorted forward to Prilicla and Fletcher in the control section. Guided by its mistress and in spite of the impaired movement of its finer digits, the doll was able to help and occasionally hinder Prilicla and the captain during the long and physically uncomfortable process of detaching and extricating Keet from the mass of control, communications, and life-support plumbing. It was a present and obvious subject of interest to both Fletcher and himself, and in an attempt to keep the Trolanni's mind off the continuing discomfort they were inflicting as well as its deep concern for Jasam, whose communications line they had been forced to sever temporarily, Prilicla began to question it with gentle persistence about the dolls.

It was an interesting change of subject.

"I don't know why you find them of such interest," Keet protested, radiating minor embarrassment. "They are toys, playthings, used mainly by the very young, or some adults who feel the need to remind themselves of the kind of people that we used to be in the past, when we could move freely and swim and climb and play together and touch without being weighed down and smothered by heavy and uncomfortable protective suits. The dolls are lifelike, life-sized, and closely modeled after their own-

ers, and while the children's are simple both in mind and structure, those of the adults are highly sophisticated, and are capable
of a wide range of supportive functions and recreational activities
which their owners can enjoy vicariously and which in many
cases answers a psychological need.

"Jasam and I," Keet went on, "were to be enclosed per-
manently in a searchsuit where, for operational reasons, we
would be close but unable to make physical contact for the rest
of our lives. The project psychologists decided that a crew of two
specialized dolls—in design and function the most versatile and
intelligent to be built—would operate and maintain our searchsuit and, it was thought, the fact that they were exact copies of
ourselves would help reduce our feelings of loss and loneliness
and so maintain our sanity."

Prilicla reached into the restricted space the captain and the
robot had cleared for him in the dense mass of plumbing, and
put a tiny clamp on the fine tube that carried the liquefied food
from the nearly empty reservoir through Keet's abdominal wall.
It was a little like brain surgery, he thought, involving as it did
the manipulation of delicate organs in a very confined space. He
concentrated on the work for several minutes until he was satisfied with it, then withdrew before speaking.

"Did they?" he said.

"They did," it ended, "until we found this fresh, lovely, and
untouched world and our position beacons blew up, and your
rescue ship blundered onto the scene." It paused, then added, "I
don't think you, or your druul-like helper, are blundering now."

"Thank you," said Prilicla, knowing that Keet's feelings were
backing up its words. "But now we have to transfer you to the
litter and attend to some superficial wounding caused by the
extraction. The treatment will be quick and simple, a few sutures
and the application of a healing ointment suited to your metabolism. You won't have an adverse reaction to it because it is
identical to one of the medications carried in your doll's medical

kit which, you will remember, we analyzed and reproduced earlier. Ready everyone?"

It was like moving a limp, half-cooked pancake through a three-dimensional maze of barbed wire, the captain said on their private frequency. Prilicla had no idea what a pancake was, his only Earth-human food weakness being spaghetti, and had to take the other's word for it. But finally they had Keet out of its control cocoon, its wounds treated, and resting comfortably in the litter.

"What now?" it said.

"Now," Prilicla replied, "we seal the litter and move it into Jasam's section, reconnect the communications line so you'll be able to tell it what has been happening while friend Fletcher and I do the same for our own people who must make preparations to receive two new casualties. After that . . . My apologies, I need to sleep again."

While they were moving the litter to the other section of the control center, Prilicla quickly explained the situation to Pathologist Murchison while transmitting visuals of the scene that were being relayed to the surface by *Rhabwar*. The ground facility was more spacious than the ambulance ship's casualty deck, and all of his medical staff as well as the *Terragar* survivors were there. Keet and Jasam were talking together and the captain was about to begin his situation report, both of which were being recorded in case he needed to refer to them later, when he suddenly lost touch with reality.

Captain Fletcher looked at the sleeping Prilicla, lowered his voice, and, using a frequency that the two aliens could overhear, spoke briskly.

"Courier Vessel One," he said. "We can now report that the distressed alien ship is non-hostile and that the damage inflicted on *Terragar* was due to a combination of ignorance and a close-range defense system of high lethality that instantly kills any ship's computer-controlled systems, but not the living organic contents, that touches it. This defense system remains active and is an extreme danger to any investigating ship—regardless of size and armament—making a close approach. It is imperative that you remain at your present distance and that all other vessels be forbidden to enter this system until a countermeasure has been found.

"The ship's planet of origin is Trolann," it went on, "location as yet unknown, where the Trolanni are losing a war that has lasted for many centuries with another indigenous species, the druul, with whom it has been impossible to come to an accommodation. Physically the druul bear a close resemblance to the DBDG physiological classification, a fact which initially made the first-contact procedure very difficult because they looked on *Rhabwar*'s Earth-human personnel as natural enemies rather than rescuers. Now I believe that we have done enough to earn their trust . . ."

"Our limited trust," Keet broke in. "I trust Prilicla, and to a lesser extent you, because you do as it asks and seem anxious to help us, but Jasam remains fearful and untrusting. About the other ones who look like druuls, I, too, am uncertain."

"But that," said the captain, "is because you haven't seen them helping you as Prilicla and I have been doing. Their work is in the background, but it is being done. They are not, never were, nor ever will be like the druul. May I continue with my report?

"The Trolanni are of physiological classification CHLI," he went on when Keet did not reply, "warm-blooded oxygen-breathers, although there is very little breathable oxygen remaining on their heavily polluted planet. They describe themselves as an embattled minority of . . . Keet, what is the total number of Trolanni on your planet?"

"Just under one hundred thousand," it replied promptly.

"As few as that?" said the captain, its face paling as it returned to its report and went on. "In that case, and bearing in mind the fact that the Trolanni have a limited space-travel capability, I strongly recommend that the Federation mount a disaster-relief and evacuation operation to move them from their virtually uninhabitable planet to another world, the world below us, in fact, which Keet and Jasam found for their people before their ship was damaged in an attempt to signal its location. I further recommend that provision be made to interdict all druul offensive operations until the Trolanni are evacuated safely, after which, if cultural reeducation is possible, we should determine the druul's needs for continued survival and . . ."

Inside the litter canopy, Keet's body was twitching in great agitation. It said, "Aren't you going to kill them all, or at least let them die fighting among themselves? That's what they'll do if there's nobody else to fight. Or maybe you can't kill them. Maybe you're favorably disposed towards them, more so than towards the Trolanni, because the druul look like you. I'm sorry, but I think we were right about you from the start. A helpful, apparently friendly druul is still a druul. You disappoint us, Fletcher."

The captain shook his head. "Our physically similar appearance has nothing to do with it. On Earth there are creatures shaped like humans. In our prehistory, we developed intelligence and ultimately civilization, but they did not, and to this day remain non-sapient animals. They are not evil in themselves but are governed by animal instincts that sometimes make them a danger to humans, and for this reason they are confined, restricted, and cared for in their own areas where they cannot harm us. If the druul are thinking animals, implacable, vicious, unable to be taught civilized ways, or are incapable of governing their own instincts and behavior, that—if it is possible for us to do it—is what would happen to them. They would be isolated and Trolann would be interdicted by the Federation and no contact with any other species allowed.

"But we would not exterminate a species just because its long-term enemy thought it was warranted," the captain ended. "The druul and you may not be able to view each other or your problem with objectivity. Now, if you don't mind, I'd like to return to my report. . . ."

The captain resumed his description of the situation on the alien ship and their plans for resolving it while at the same time, by implication, mentally preparing the Trolanni casualties for what was to come by describing the structural problems of casualty extraction before the medical problems could be solved. But Keet was finding it difficult to remain silent.

"Prilicla and you are all right, I suppose," Keet said, "but are strangers of your kind going to be handling us? That would frighten Jasam and me very much. He might hurt himself even more trying to fight you off. We'd rather Prilicla did everything. We like it."

"Everybody likes Prilicla," said Fletcher, looking aside at the sleeping empath, "but physically it is too weak to do everything itself. That's why it will need heavy cutting equipment and the help of Dodds and Chen, two other Earth-humans like myself, to clear a path to and enclose the area in a pressure envelope before Prilicla can begin treating Jasam's injuries. But all of us, in my ship and on the surface are the same as Prilicla. We all want to help cure Jasam and yourself. While we're doing that, you'll come to know all of us, and trust us, and tell us how we can help your people."

For a long time there was silence while the captain crawled about in the wreckage surrounding Jasam's control pod, marking structural members that would have to be cut away, lengths of plumbing to be sealed off, and talking quietly. Everything he said formed part of his report including—although the Trolanni might not have realized it—the conversations with Keet and all the recorded material on the *Terragar* landing and casualties.

Everything went into a first-contact report.

"Jasam is very worried," said Keet suddenly, "in case there are healers on the surface who look like you. If there are, he doesn't want them to touch him. He says he'd rather die. Why don't we go to the hospital you showed us, where there are many healers who don't look like the druul?"

In a first-contact situation the rule was to tell the truth but to keep it as simple as possible. The captain said, "My ship has been ordered to remain in this vicinity to warn off any other vessels who might want to investigate your searchsuit and suffer damage as a result. On *Rhabwar* there are four Earth-human ship's officers including myself, and four healers. Prilicla, you already know, is in charge; then an Earth-human female called Murchison who looks, well, somewhat different than me; a Kelgian who has twenty legs and is covered with mobile fur; and a shape-changer called Danalta who can look like anything or everything, even a Trolanni if it thought that shape would be reassuring to you or your life-mate. There are also three Earth-humans who are badly damaged. The medical team, with the exception of Prilicla, are down there in a special healing facility, taking care of them. None of them, not even the *Terragar* casualties, will want to harm you while you get to know us better. Besides, the repairing of physical damage isn't everything. We think that it might make you feel better and assist your non-medical healing if you were to spend some time recuperating on the beautiful world Jasam and yourself have discovered for the Trolanni."

There was no reply, and the short silence was broken by the quiet voice of Prilicla speaking on the captain's private frequency.

"I've been awake for the past few minutes," he said, "and I could not have handled the situation better if I'd done it myself. Thank you, friend Fletcher. Keet is feeling greatly comforted and Jasam, who is still anxious and barely conscious, shares its life-mate's reassurance. This would be a good time to call in friends Dodds and Chen."

During the next three hours, while the damaged area surrounding Jasam's control pod was being isolated in a temporary pressure bubble and excised from its surrounding control actuators, plumbing, and wiring, the lines between technical and medical work were frequently blurred by the fact that *Rhabwar*'s officers were doing much more delicate work than that being performed by Prilicla. Even though he was not due to sleep for another four hours, by the time they were finished and Jasam was sharing the other half of the pressure litter with Keet, he felt so tired that it was an effort for him not to lose consciousness prematurely. The captain, who had not slept for two Earth standard days and did not seem to be affected by fatigue, was concluding its report to the courier vessels.

". . . Friendly relations have been established with the two Trolanni casualties who are ready for transfer to *Rhabwar* and immediate onward transportation to the surface medical station," he said crisply. "According to Dr. Prilicla, the being Keet has superficial injuries and is in no danger, but the other one, Jasam, is giving cause for concern. Urgent surgery is required, and the prognosis is uncertain. You have everything you need to know, but I suggest that you both remain on station, stay well clear of the alien ship's hull which is still active and a continuing danger, and wait a few hours for the latest good or bad news.

"From here on this is expected to be a routine medical matter," it ended, "and we cannot foresee anything going wrong."

CHAPTER 22

At the medical station the routines of the day had proceeded with a similar lack of drama, but the surroundings were beautiful, relaxing, and much too pleasant for boredom to be a consideration. The patients were in satisfactory medical and good psychological shape following their twice-daily immersion in the shallows and subsequent sun-drying, and had been moved indoors. The sun was within an hour of setting, with its close-to-horizontal light reflecting off the reddish-white breakers on a sea that was dark blue. It was the ideal time of day for another walk around the island.

Inevitably accompanied, Murchison thought irritably, by her shape-changing and by now totally redundant guardian angel.

There was no real reason, other than that she had never done so before and the team members and patients might worry, why she should be back inside the station before nightfall. But to reduce the unnecessary worrying all around, she decided not to break with tradition by jogging instead of walking the distance, and to stop only for a brief swim in her favorite beauty spot, a tiny, tree-fringed bay on the opposite side of the island.

She was nearing it, and the station was hidden by the curve of the shoreline behind her, when the sun began to set, although from experience she knew that there would be enough dusk left to see her way back. In the shallows Danalta was keeping pace with her, arrowing through the breaking surf and occasionally leaping into the air as it did its impression of a flying fish. She was running fast over the firm, damp sand with her eyes down so as to avoid the scattered white stones in her path when the shape-changer made a noise that did not translate, and flopped rapidly out of the water and onto the sand beside her. While it was still changing from an aquatic to a land mobile form, what had been one of its fins thickened into a hand and it pointed ahead.

This, Murchison thought as she slowed to a stop under the trees, *is certainly an interesting change in the in the usual scenery.*

It was a smooth, flattened mound covered with what looked like fibrous, greenish-brown vegetation, or possibly scales or a form of seaweed, that floated in the water with a narrow section of its forward edge projecting a few yards onto the sandy beach. It was large enough to fill a quarter of the tiny inlet and she was reminded of an outsize, beached whale.

"I'd say that this is one of the objects we saw from the high ground that first day," she said, "and now we're seeing it close-up. You have better vision than I have. Is it alive?"

Danalta, whose land shape was still indeterminate, enlarged an eye and said, "It has the general appearance of a large sea mammal, although the breathing orifices and fins are concealed from view or underwater. There is a slight overall body movement that is probably due to wave action rather than respiration. It may be alive and close to termination. But there is still a risk. Shall I investigate more closely?"

"We will investigate," she said, stressing the first word, "after we've reported this in. But I'd say the risk is minimal." She pointed to the sky above the beached creature and laughed quietly. "The vultures are gathering again and that's always a strong contraindication for casualty survivability."

The birds were circling stiff-winged as they rode the updrafts from the sandy beach that was still radiating the day's heat, and they were lower and closer than she had ever seen them before. Both bodies and their wide-spreading, leathery wings were the same color and seemed to have the same texture as that of the beached creature, and they looked mean. Instinctively she moved back under the concealment of thick, overhanging branches, hoping they hadn't seen her.

Danalta remained motionless except for lengthening his eye-stalk and bending it up to look at them.

"They aren't birds," it said quietly, "they're flying machines, unpowered gliders. Each one has a pilot."

For a moment Murchison was too surprised to react, mentally or physically. This was supposed to be an uninhabited world. According to *Rhabwar*'s sensors it was completely lacking in the signatures of cultivation, roads, electromagnetic radiation, industrial smoke pollution, or any of the signs normally produced by intelligent life, and certainly by an indigenous intelligence capable of building flying machines. It came to her suddenly that the reason why the two gliders were flying so low might be that their pilots wanted the high ground at the center of the island to conceal the operation from the view of the medical station in case someone there decided to look inland.

Fumbling in her haste, Murchison pulled her communicator out of the equipment pouch at her waist and had it almost to her lips when something large and soft and with many hairy legs landed on her back and shoulders. Simultaneously another one of them gripped her legs tightly so that she tripped and fell forwards, dropping the communicator as she instinctively put out both hands to keep her face from hitting the ground.

She was trying to reach for the communicator again when another one landed on her arm before grabbing her by the wrists and pulling them to her sides with small, hard pincers. She was lifted a few feet from the ground and her body was rotated laterally, and she felt her legs being wrapped together tightly in what felt like very fine rope. The turns continued up and past her hips, pinioning both hands and lower arms to her sides. She was able to get a close if intermittent look at her captors.

Spiders.

Two of them were holding and rolling her over while a third was producing from a body orifice the continuous, fine white strand that was wrapping her up. Three others were dropping lightly to the ground from overhanging branches on white strands that were almost too thin for her to to see, their brownish-green body coloration making them difficult to see against the vegetation until they landed. Each of them was holding a thick, stubbly crossbow with their bolts notched and bowstrings taut.

She had never had a fear of Earthly spiders, and there were many more visually abhorrent creatures among her friends and colleagues at Sector General, but that didn't mean that she liked everything that walked on eight hairy legs, especially, as now, when they were placing her life at risk.

Struggling to break free did no good because the thin strands were very tough and she succeeded only in leaving deep indentations and a few shallow cuts on her legs and forearms. She opened her mouth wide and deliberately made loud, whooshing sounds while inflating and deflating her lungs, hoping to demonstrate the need to go on breathing which she would not be able to do if the strands around her chest were too tight.

Whether they understood her body language or that had been their original intention she didn't know, but the white strands were exerting minimum compression on her rib cage. She could breathe comfortably but not too deeply unless she wanted to risk cutting herself. She could turn her head freely and even bend a little at the waist. One of them took an interest in her translator pack and tried to tug it free, but it and the medical pouch were an integral part of the equipment belt so the creature didn't succeed. When it persisted she made a noise to indicate that it was hurting her and it desisted. Then they rolled her face-upwards onto a hammock made from woven plant fiber of some kind and four of them each lifted a corner and began carrying her towards the beach while the other two followed. One of them, the one who had tried to get her translator, picked up her communicator from the ground and began poking at it curiously.

There was no sign of Danalta.

She didn't know what the shape-changer could do, but it should be able to think of something. So, Murchison thought angrily, should she. For a moment she wondered if she was generating her anger just to keep her growing fear at bay.

The sun had set but there was still enough light to see the beach clearly, and the object she had thought was a sea mammal. The smooth, outer covering was opening up to become a series of low, triangular sails resembling those of an old-time Earth felucca, and their supporting masts and rigging were still being raised, and the two flyers had landed and were half carrying, half dragging their gliders towards it. But her party, being closer, would board first. Plainly the spiders were excited because they were making low, cheeping and chittering sounds to each other or calling more loudly to the glider pilots and others on the ship.

Suddenly there was an interruption, a sound that had not come from any local throat.

"Speak, Pathologist Murchison," said the loud, irritated voice of Charge Nurse Naydrad. "If you don't want to say something, why are you using your communicator? I have work to do. Stop wasting my time."

Her bearers stopped so quickly that she almost rolled out of the litter, and the spider with her communicator dropped it onto the sand and backed away, chittering shrilly in alarm. Murchison laughed in spite of her problems. It was obvious what had happened because she could see the two indicator lights glowing. The spider who had been fiddling with it had inadvertently turned the reception volume to full as well as switching on the device. But the communicator was active and, even though it was lying in the sand several meters away and at extreme distance for a handset, Naydrad was listening.

The spiders were used to her making loud noises at them, but only when she was communicating discomfort, and now she had to talk loudly to Naydrad. But there was the danger of arousing their suspicions by making noises without a reason, when none of them was touching or therefore hurting her. If they were to get the idea that a conversation was going on, that she was calling for help, then they would immediately silence her or the communicator. They were already trying to do the latter by standing well back from it and pelting it with stones from the beach rather than shooting their crossbow bolts at it. Luckily they had missed it so far, but communicators were not robust instruments.

In an undertone Murchison used language that was unladylike—her only unfeminine trait, according to her life-mate—and thought quickly. There was very little time to send a message, and none at all if one of those rocks connected. She took the deepest breath she could without cutting herself and spoke slowly and clearly while hoping that the excited chittering of the spiders all around her would keep them from noticing the strange noises she was making.

"Naydrad, Murchison here. Listen, don't talk, and copy. We have been captured by indigenous intelligent life-forms, tentative classification GKSD . . ."

The spiders weren't paying any attention to her and were concentrating on their stone-throwing, which wasn't accurate because the communicator continued to survive and show its indicator lights.

"They appear to be sea raiders of some kind," she went on more calmly. "They use large sailing ships, unpowered aircraft, crossbows, and there is no evidence of metal weapons. I've been tightly restrained but not hurt and am unable to see Danalta . . ."

She broke off, realizing that her last few words might have been a lie. It was hard to be sure in the dimming twilight, but it seemed that the sand on one side of the communicator was showing wind ripples. Then, suddenly, they were all around it as Danalta did its impression of a patch of sandy beach. A moment later the device and its indicator lights disappeared from sight.

The spiders threw a few more stones, their voices sounding surprised and uneasy rather than angry at this apparent display of magic, but with no target to aim at they were beginning to lose interest. But a few stones would not bother Danalta, whose hide, regardless of the shape it was covering, was impermeable to most classes of low-velocity missiles. The important part was that it had rescued and was protecting the communicator and, when the spiders left the scene, it would be able to contact the medical station which would relay its report to *Rhabwar*.

Murchison was still feeling anxious about her immediate future, but more hopeful than she had been a few minutes earlier, when a loud, authoritative, chittering sound coming from the spiders' vessel drew her attention towards it.

Several of the triangular openings in the hull were open and emitting a dim yellow flickering glow which, Murchison felt sure, had to be coming from oil lamps or candles. High on the prow of the vessel and silhouetted against the darkening sky she could dimly see the spider who seemed to be making all the noise. It was holding a tapering black cone to its head that had to be a speaking trumpet. Beyond the beached vessel and perhaps half a mile out to sea there was another vessel, identical in size and shape and also showing a few patches of dim illumination. The view of it was cut off by the body of one of the four spiders who raised her litter and resumed their journey towards the beached ship.

They had not reacted adversely while she had been speaking earlier, possibly because they had been too busy stoning and talking among themselves to notice or care, so she decided to pass on the latest information before they all moved too far from the capture point.

"Danalta," she said, "the indications are that the GKSDs do

not have electric power or radio communication. Another vessel of the same size and shape is entering the bay and a third is on the horizon . . ."

Murchison broke off as the escort halted. One of them chittered loudly at her and began inserting a claw between her body and the strands binding her, possibly checking on their tightness. It was making her very uncomfortable so she shut up.

She didn't know if her words had been heard, but she hoped that the small patch of beach that was Danalta included a sandy ear.

CHAPTER 23

The captain's face on the casualty deck's viewscreen had the darkened pink color characteristic of strong emotion, strong enough to filter down the length of the ship from the control deck.

"Doctor," it said, "I have an incoming message from the medical station which is being relayed from Danalta who is somewhere else on the island. This, this is ridiculous. It says that Pathologist Murchison has been captured by pirates of some kind. But that world down there shows no evidence of sapient life. Have your medics been using their medical supplies for recreational purposes? Would you talk to them, please, before I say something grossly impolite?"

For an instant Prilicla glanced towards the forms of the unconscious Jasam and the wide-awake Keet, wondering whether or not he should switch off the translator, then decided to leave it on. Secrecy in a first-contact situation was not a good thing.

"Of course, friend Fletcher," he replied. "Patch them through."

As Danalta's report came in, with occasional interjections from Naydrad, Prilicla wondered if he had made the right decision about allowing Keet to overhear it. The Trolanni's emotional radiation was becoming increasingly disturbed, but that of the captain had changed from irritation to deep concern. When the shape-changer's report ended, Fletcher spoke before Prilicla could respond.

"Doctor," it said urgently, "you will agree that this has become a predominantly tactical and military, rather than a medical, problem. That being so, with or without your permission, I must take charge."

"It is both a medical and military problem, friend Fletcher," said Prilicla. "But the first priority, military or medical, must be to have friend Murchison returned to us safely and soon."

"My thought exactly," said the captain. "But the position is delicate. We are now faced with two first-contact situations that are running concurrently. The Trolanni one is going well, but these intelligent spiders . . . Imagine, a culture based on non-metal technology that possesses fighting ships, gliders, uses crossbows, and has no electric power generation or radio communication. They seem to have fire for lighting and perhaps cooking purposes but make no large-scale industrial use of it. No wonder the sensors found no signs of sapient life down there. An ambulance ship doesn't carry weapons, naturally, but we'd have no trouble taking them on with our tractor beams and meteorite shield . . ."

He paused and added, ". . . if we were allowed."

Prilicla knew as well as the captain how strict were the rules governing contact with any newly-discovered planet that held intelligent life. If the culture had a space-travel capability and the technology to support it, as well as the mind-set that had prepared them for the possibility of meeting other life-forms among the stars, then the contact procedure was straightforward. But if the indigenous race was primitive, then a careful and covert assessment had to be made regarding the long-term effects of making such a contact and a decision taken on whether or not it should proceed.

There was always the danger that strange beings dropping out of the sky in their thundering ships, even though the entities concerned wanted only to help, would give rise to an inferiority complex in an emerging culture, from which it might never recover. A starship, the wreck of *Terragar*, had already landed and no doubt been spotted by the reconnaissance gliders, so the damage might already have been done. But taking hostile action against them, even thought it would be in response to Murchison's abduction, would most definitely be contraregulation.

"The gliders will already have told their mother ships about the medical station," the captain added, radiating worry. "If the spiders decide to raid it from the land or sea, it has no defenses."

"Regardless of the rules, friend Fletcher," he said firmly, "we must somehow defend our people and patients there without injuring any of the spiders. Agreed? As a tactician, have you a plan for doing that?"

"I'll need to think about that for a while," the captain replied. "But what about Pathologist Murchison? We aren't trained or equipped to send in a rescue party, and getting her out any other way would mean tearing the fabric of that spider ship apart with tractor beams."

"Friend Fletcher," said Prilicla, "you have a little time to think about defending the medical facility while we are moving Jasam and Keet there or, if necessary, moving the others back on board *Rhabwar*. Regarding friend Murchison, I want to discuss the pathologist's situation with friend Danalta, who is still standing by and is close to the ships. It is a resourceful and versatile guardian and intelligence-gatherer."

"That it is," said the captain. "I'll relay my radio traffic to you so that you'll know what I'm doing. Breaking contact."

While he was speaking to the shape-changer, Prilicla could feel Keet's puzzlement and impatience, but the Trolanni didn't interrupt with questions even after he had finished talking. He knew that Danalta was concerned for friend Murchison's safety, but he was worried because the shape-changer rarely worried about anything. He gave the other advice and careful instructions and, hoping for the best, he was flying across to speak to the increasingly impatient Keet when the captain's voice sounded in the control-deck repeater.

"Courier One," it was saying. "Regarding my situation report, I have an update for you. An indigenous intelligent species has been discovered on the planet below. They are physiological classification GKSD, possibly warlike, and possessing limited, non-metal technology. Pathologist Murchison has been captured by them but the latest information is that she is unhurt. Two separate first-contact operations are now in progress. The damaged Trolanni vessel and this solar system remain in quarantine. No other vessels are to approach. Leave with this new information at once. Courier Two, you will stand by and listen out for further developments. Off."

"Prilicla," Keet said before he could speak, "I have heard and understood every word spoken by you and the druul-like person, but the meaning of the words joined together confuses me. Are Jasam and I in danger, or the Murchison person? Personally I would not find the absence of this Murchison distressing, even though you have assured me that it is a very good healer in spite of looking like a druul. But you told me that this lovely world that Jasam and I have found was empty. Where did these warlike spiders come from? We were wearing the last and best searchsuit. Our people might never be able to build another. What is to happen to us now?"

Even though a large proportion of his feelings were engaged in worrying over friend Murchison's safety, Prilicla radiated as much sympathy and reassurance as he could while explaining the situation. He spoke truthfully, but because Jasam and Keet were patients, he laced the truth heavily with optimism.

"Both of you will be moved as quickly as possible to the surface," he said, "where I and what remains of my medical team will be able to help Jasam, whose condition requires urgent surgical treatment. The spiders are hostile, for reasons we will not understand until we learn how to speak to them. We didn't know of their existence until an hour ago, but we are strangers who landed on their world without permission and that can be a strong reason for hostility. Or perhaps, as beings completely strange to their experience, they were curious and simply wanted to investigate a new life-form. But they don't pose a physical threat, except to friend Murchison, because our level of technology is far above theirs.

"However," he went on, "regardless of their species' level of intelligence or how technologically primitive they are, this is their home world. The Federation, our law-givers, would not allow the Trolanni to use your advanced technology to take it from them, or to settle on it without the expressed permission and agreement of the spiders. . . ."

"If we did not do that," the weak voice of Jasam broke in, "we would be no better than the druul."

Tactfully ignoring the remark but pleased that it was joining in the conversation, Prilicla went on, "But there are many worlds known to the Galactic Federation which are without intelligent life. When both of you are fully recovered and able to return in one of our ships to Trolann, we will show your people pictures of these worlds, and analyses of their water, atmosphere, and surface plant and animal life. Then we will make arrangements to move the Trolanni to the world of your choice. . . ."

"And will you exterminate the druul," Keet interrupted, "so that we may leave safely?"

"None of these beings," said Jasam, speaking weakly, but answering for him, "will exterminate anything or anyone, except possibly disease germs. How did they ever fight their way to the top of their evolutionary trees to became their planets' dominant species?"

"Jasam," said Prilicla, "I'm very pleased that you are awake and taking an interest in the situation, but don't overtire yourself. You ask a question that will take a long time to answer and you may be unconscious again, either from fatigue or boredom, before I finished answering it. Let me just say that in our precivilized times none of us, including my own species, were this well-behaved. The medical monitors will signal any change in your condition, so would you like me to leave you alone for a while so that Keet and yourself can talk together about your future?"

He felt a sudden burst of fear and sorrow from Keet, and one of lesser intensity from Jasam. They both knew how close Jasam was to death just as they knew that he might be giving them the chance to speak to each other for the last time. Before either of them could respond, the captain's voice sounded in the repeater.

"Doctor, I have an operational update for you," it said briskly. "We are now leaving orbit on a descending path which will bring us down close to sea level about three hundred miles from the island on the side opposite to the position of the spider vessels. We estimate arrival in just under two hours. The same high ground that they used to hide their presence from the station will also conceal our approach. Naydrad and the two servos will be standing by to receive the casualties. There has been nothing from Danalta or Murchison. Our sensors report no land, sea, or air activity in the vicinity of the three spider ships, so hopefully they are sleeping. You must be pretty close to your own limits of endurance, Doctor, so you might like to do the same."

"Thank you, friend Fletcher," said Prilicla, "that is good advice which I shall take at once."

He had folded his wings and was tethering himself loosely to an equipment support when he felt a subtle change in Keet's emotional radiation. Normally its feelings, regarding its mate, the druul, and their situation in general, were sharp and strong. It loved and hated with equal intensity. But now there was a strange blurring and softening of feeling as it spoke.

"I know that I cannot read another person's emotions as well as you can," it said slowly, "but from your words and actions here and on our searchsuit, I think—no, I believe—that you feel a deep concern for Jasam's welfare, and mine. Is this so?"

"Yes," he said, trying to keep himself awake.

"On Trolann this question would be considered an insult,"

it went on, "implying as it would a disgusting mental aberration and perversion. But I think . . . Are you feeling the same depth of concern for the safety of the druul-like healer Murchison, as you do for Jasam?"

"Yes," said Prilicla again.

CHAPTER 24

The glider pilots carrying their folded aircraft were the first to mount the boarding ramp, followed by Murchison's bearer party and with the watchful spiders who carried only weapons bringing up the rear.

The ramp, she saw, was wide, surprisingly long, and formed a gently sloping bridge over the wavelets and wet sand at the water's edge. It stretched between the large opening in the ship's bow and the dry area farther up the beach. It was an incredible idea, but she wondered if the spiders were sailors who didn't like getting their feet wet.

Inside the ship she was moved along a corridor whose roof was so low that if she hadn't been lying flat on her back in a hammock, she would have scraped her face against the rough, fibrous surface of the ceiling. Positioned at deck level about twenty meters apart were lamps that flickered and, she thought, sniffing analytically, smelled of some kind of vegetable rather than mineral oil. Each lamp floated in a large wooden pan of water and there were two larger containers, one filled with water and the other, sand, placed close by. She wondered if the spiders were afraid of fire as well as water, then remembered that in the wooden-sailing-ship days on Earth, fire had been a servant that had to be kept under tight control.

After what seemed an endless scrolling-down of dark, fibrous ceilings, her hammock was lowered to the deck in a compartment that was about six meters square and high enough to allow her to kneel upright if they untied her.

Plainly that was their intention, because three of them lifted and turned her face-downwards while the fourth opened its mouth and began to do something which softened and loosened the strands around her body. Then they rolled her over and over slowly while the fourth spider made delicate, slurping noises as the continuous strand was sucked back into its body.

When it was finished, the others left the room and it remained to wrap one of her ankles in a band of thick, soft material, which was obviously padding because around it was tied very tightly the end of another rope. It was thin, tough, and seemed to be woven from plant fiber rather than originating inside a spider. The captor's grotesque, insectile head bent over her ankle and it spat something at the rope which hardened within a few seconds and covered the knot in a solid, transparent seal. Then it tied the other end, which was long enough to enable her to move anywhere inside the room and a little way beyond it, to a structural support by the doorway and sealed it in similar fashion. It turned to look at her for a moment before pointing with the nearest limb towards a corner of the room at what looked like two low handrails with a flat wooden lid set into the floor between them.

The spider moved across to it, raised and pushed aside the lid, and indicated the square hole beneath it before waving her forward and moving back itself.

The lighting in the room was too subdued to show deep inside the opening, but even before Murchison heard the regular, gurgling wave action of water at the bottom she knew what it was—the body-wastes disposal facility. To show that she understood, but without actually giving a full demonstration, she grasped the rails, one in each hand, and hunkered down for a moment before replacing the lid. Apparently satisfied, the spider was pointing at the contents of a shelf in the opposite corner of the compartment.

It held three wooden beakers, two tall and slim and the other one short and broad, all of them with lids; one small, cuplike receptacle; a small stack of flat, wooden platters; and a large open bowl that had neatly folded squares of soft fabric lying beside it. On hands and knees she moved across to them quickly and lifted down the narrow beakers in turn. She gave them a gentle shake before removing the lids, sniffed, and decided that they contained water. The thicker one was filled with round lumps of material that looked and felt like hairy potatoes.

Murchison straightened onto her knees, turned and waved her hand vigorously at the spider, then pointed down at her equipment pouch. She wasn't simply trying to attract its attention, because it was already watching her closely, just trying to give it the impression that her next movement would be overt, innocent, and harmless.

Slowly she unfastened the flap and used one finger and thumb to lift out the narrow, white cylinder that was her analyzer, which she put in the corner of her mouth so that she had both hands free to to pour an inch of water into the drinking beaker. When she touched the sensor tip of the analyzer into it, the readout showed many trace elements but no toxicity, so she drank it down. From the solid-food container she chose a small piece and broke it. The center was pale green and spongy and gave off a faint odor that reminded her of cinnamon. She pushed the analyzer into it in several places, but none of the readings showed anything to worry her. She replaced the instrument and took a cautious nibble.

It wasn't completely nauseating, she thought, but it would require a condition of near starvation to make it palatable. Murchison was reminded of her first promotion to the Sector General permanent staff, when her mixed-species former students had thrown a party for her. On a dare she had eaten a piece of Kelgian warlgan cake. This stuff tasted a little better.

She forced herself to swallow it and say, "Thank you."

The spider chittered briefly in reply and backed to the doorway, where it continued to watch her.

For several minutes Murchison sat on the hammock, which had been left on the floor, thinking about what she should do next and, more importantly, what her captors were expecting her to do next. Their technology was primitive, but in its own way, civilized. Up until now they had shown no deliberate cruelty towards her, and they possessed a high level of intelligence and flexibility of mind, which was shown by their curiosity regarding her and their attempt to make her comfortable. It would be natural in the circumstances for her to demonstrate a similar degree of curiosity.

Using her feet with legs bent almost double and with one supporting hand keeping her from falling onto her back, Murchison began to tour the room. One wall was hung with coils of rope in various thicknesses and another had shelves of wooden implements, some of which looked like the pictures of marlin spikes she had seen in the history books. No metal tools, implements, or even support brackets were visible. Everything, even the deck, walls, and ceiling, seemed to be made of hard, dark green, tightlywoven plant fiber except for the regular lines of thin, pale grey that seemed to run through and reinforce all of them.

She was pretty sure where the grey material had come from because she had seen a few strands of it binding the crossbows together, and as a supporting latticework on the wings and fuselage of their gliders. With a tiny shiver of wonder Murchison tried to comprehend a species whose advanced technology, its homes, sailing ships, and aircraft, and who knew what else, was in part woven out of their own bodies.

The third wall was bare, except at the two top corners where there was a large wooden ratchet arrangement that enabled it to be tipped outwards from the vertical and away from the edge of the ceiling. Between them there was a six-inch gap through which fresh air, cold now that the sun had set, was blowing. Plainly this was the room's ventilation system. She moved to the fourth wall that contained the door—with her spider guard filling it—the lamp, and the fire-prevention arrangements. Intending to examine the workings of the lamp closely with a view to adjusting the setting of its floating wick to give more light, she reached forwards.

Her fingers were more than a foot away from it when she cried out in pain and surprise as a sticklike forward limb cracked down across the back of her hand.

"Why the blazes did you do that?" she cried, pressing the hand between her other arm and side to deaden the pain.

The spider unlimbered its crossbow and sent a bolt thudding into the floor in front of the lamp, then it moved into the room, and with great difficulty loosened and pulled the crossbow bolt from the floor and replaced it in its quiver before returning to the doorway.

She had the answer to her question. Clearly the message was, *Hands off the lamp.*

Up until then the spider had not deliberately tried to hurt her and might not do so again unless, as now, she tried to break their rules. She wondered how she would have felt if their positions had been reversed. In this society a moment's carelessness with a naked flame might well cause irreparable property damage in addition to personal injury.

Losing, for example, what was to them a complex, state-of-the-art aircraft would be devastating for the pilot, who had probably woven important parts of its support structure from its own body material. But the destruction of a large-scale, cooperative enterprise like this ship, which must be a continuous, floating fire hazard, would be a community disaster. Henceforth she would obey the rules and avoid having her wrist slapped, or, better still, try to communicate with and understand her captors so that such acts of minor physical chastisement would no longer be necessary.

The time to begin talking was now, but both her brain and her body were too tired to begin the long, complicated and no doubt initially frustrating process of sign language and word sounds that would be needed. She could, however, make a small start.

She moved back to the wall with the ventilator slit in it, pointed to the opening, and blew her breath out noisily for a few seconds, shivered elaborately, and returned to the floor area covered by the hammock. There she lay down lengthwise on her side along one half of it, and pulled the surplus material across her legs and body and tucking it under her chin. It was coarse-textured but warm. With the back of one hand—which was no longer hurting—supporting the side of her face, she looked along the deck at the now-horizontal picture of her guard.

"Good night," she said quietly.

The spider made a low, chittering sound.

She had no idea of how much if anything of the recent pantomiming it had understood, but Murchison hoped that she had conveyed the message that she had rendered herself voluntarily immobile and there was no danger of her breaking any more rules for a while. She lay watching it while it watched her, feeling the hard surface of the deck through the hammock material and not expecting to sleep.

She awakened to find that the lamp was out, the ventilation slit had been opened wide so that sunlight as well as air was coming through it, and that during the night another large rectangle of hammock material had been spread over her sleeping body. She felt stiff and sore, but pleased, because it seemed that the process of communication had already begun. When she raised herself onto one elbow and cleared her throat quietly, her spider guard—she was pretty sure that it was the same one—opened its eyes.

When she had stretched a few times in the limited space available, and rubbed the stiffness out of her muscles, Murchison lifted the lid of the waste-disposal opening, stared at the spider for a moment. It backed out of the doorway and moved sideways out of sight.

It was strange, Murchison thought, that all of the civilized species known to the Federation had this aversion to eliminating body wastes in public, or to witnessing the activity in others. When she had washed and eaten—she was so hungry that the food tasted horrible but on the plus side of inedible—she dissolved a small amount of the food in the remains of the washing-water and with the corner of a cloth daubed two simple sketches on the sunlit wall. Then she put her head around the side of the doorway and beckoned for the spider to come back inside.

It was time to start talking.

But her guard had other ideas. It spat accurately onto the knot holding the other end of her restraining rope, dissolving the seal, then made it into a tight coil which it grasped in one claw. With the other one it indicated its crossbow and quiver before it began tugging on the rope.

Politely she was being told to follow it, or else.

In the event, she had no need to worry because it became clear that her guard was showing her over the ship while giving the hundred or more crew members a chance to look her over. They pointed, waved limbs, and chittered excitedly at her, their body language reflecting intense curiosity. But a quiet, clicking sound from her escort made them keep their distance. She guessed that her spider was a superior officer of some kind and that it was showing off a strange and interesting specimen that it wished to keep as comfortable, if not as happy, as possible. Murchison could live with that, especially as the technology of the ship itself was so strange and interesting.

In a first-contact situation, curiosity that was strong enough to overcome xenophobia in both parties was a very good sign.

The vessel looked even larger inside than out. Its smooth outer shell contained a structure that was like a complicated

three-dimensional maze. She estimated it to be about eighty meters from prow to stern, sixty in the beam, and thirty to the
highest point of its turtlelike upper works which, so far as she
could see, enclosed five or six levels of decking that were stepped
back sharply so as to be covered by a segmented outer shell that
could be opened in whatever area and number was required, to
become sails and furnish highly directional wind propulsion. The
overall structural material must have been very light because, in
spite of its top-heavy appearance, the vessel rode very high in the
water.

She wasn't surprised to find that the two decks that were on
and just above the water line had no sail openings, ventilation,
or natural lighting. The compartments on those levels were large
and filled with coils of rope, netting, and masses of eel-like creatures, some of which were still twitching, that smelled like fish.
She was glad when her escort guided her back towards the fresh
air and sunlight of the upper decks.

But there was a steadily diminishing supply of fresh air, she
realized, and no sunlight at all. She was pushed gently against a
bulkhead and signaled to stay out of the way because it appeared
that the entire crew were moving about and working furiously
to wind in all of the sail segments and seal their outer shell. Just
before the section beside her closed to admit only a narrow band
of light, she was able to see the probable cause of all the frantic
activity.

The sun had been covered by the dark grey curtain of a rain
squall that was running in from the sea.

On the way back to her compartment Murchison had a lot
to think about. This and the other two vessels she had seen must
be part of a fishing fleet that needed aerial reconnaissance to
direct them towards the shoals they trawled. The sails they used
for guidance and propulsion had to double as shelters in the
event of a storm or even a rain shower because, perhaps like cats
and Kelgians and certain other furred species in her experience,
it was physiologically dangerous for them to get wet.

These ships were manned, for want of a better word, by very brave sailors indeed.

Back in her room the ventilator had been closed to admit a narrow band of light and none of the heavy rain that was rattling against the hull. The spider pointed to a formerly empty shelf. During their absence someone, probably acting on its instructions, had left them a small stack of wide, pale yellow dried leaves, a thin, short-handled brush, and a small wooden container of what looked like ink.

Considering the spider-hostile weather outside, she thought again, this was a very good time to begin talking.

CHAPTER 25

Using its power-hungry tractor beams in reverse rather than the noisy thrusters, *Rhabwar* had come in low and quiet to transfer Prilicla and the Trolanni casualties to the station before returning as it had come, to orbit where the captain would be able to watch the spider ships without them seeing him, or if they did, they wouldn't know that the new star in their sky was watching them.

"There are three vessels," it reported simultaneously to the med station and the waiting courier vessel, "but all are stationary with their bows resting on the beach. Five gliders are flying around them at low altitude, too low for the med station to spot them. A number of ship's personnel have been moving about on the beach and under the nearby trees, but too few, I feel sure, for them to be mounting an attack. In any case, the personnel concerned and the gliders went back on board their ships about ten minutes ago and just before a rain cloud blotted out the area.

"Doctor," it added, "have you any medical or other developments that you want me to relay to Courier Two?"

"None, friend Fletcher," Prilicla replied.

"None?" the other said. "What about your missing pathologist? What's the shape-changer doing about finding her? With the increased number of casualties I should think her presence is desirable right now."

"It is . . ." he began, when Naydrad, who had been assisting him with Keet's treatment, answered for him in its usual tactless disregard for the fact that the listening patient was wearing a translator.

"It is not desirable, Captain," it broke in; "it is necessary. Physiologically the Trolanni are an unusually complex life-form. This one will survive but its mate will almost certainly not, unless Murchison, who is a specialist in other-species pathology, returns to us soon. We are all concerned for her safety and the possible loss of her unrivaled expertise."

Unlike the Kelgian, who could not help saying exactly what it was thinking at any time, the captain tried to be more circumspect.

"Your medical team is two members short," it said gently, "and Danalta would be of more use to you there than remaining in the vicinity of the bay. What I'm trying to say is that Pathologist Murchison may not be returning to you. Isn't that a strong possibility, Doctor?"

Prilicla felt a tremor shaking his limbs and body, the significance of which Naydrad, but not Keet, would understand. He controlled his emotions with difficulty and stilled his body before he was able to speak.

"It is a possibility, friend Fletcher," he said, "but I hope that it is a remote one. Danalta lost contact with Pathologist Murchison shortly after its capture and while it was still on the ground rescuing the communicator. The shape-changer has since been trying to discover the ship to which friend Murchison was taken and where within that ship it is being held, so far unsuccessfully.

"I shall not call off this search," he went on, "because I have known Pathologist Murchison for many years. I know its personality, its warmth, sympathy, humor, its sensitivity, and in particular the intensity of feeling it holds for its life-mate, and many other qualities that cannot be put into words. Of even more im-

portance, I know its emotional-radiation signature almost as well
as I know my own.

"The spider ships are at extreme range for my empathic
faculty," he concluded, "and while I cannot honestly say that
I sense its presence at any given moment, if friend Murchison was to terminate, I feel sure that I would know of it at
once."

The captain broke contact without speaking.

Murchison began with the approach long-hallowed by tradition, even in the days before mankind had learned how to leave
Earth, by drawing pictures of the people and things she wanted
to name. They were small and simple; small for the reason that
she didn't know whether or not the supply of broad leaves was
limited, and simple because the ink ran like water and she had
botched the first two attempts by overloading the brush. She held
the leaf horizontally sketch-upwards for the few seconds it took
the ink to dry, then showed it to the spider.

Pointing at herself and the body outline in the sketch, she
said, "Human." She repeated the gestures and the word several
times before pointing at the spider and its outline and deliberately said nothing.

The silent questioning seemed to work because one of her
captor's clawlike digits moved down to touch the spider outline.
It made a low, clicking and cheeping noise that sounded like,
"Kritkuk."

Ignoring the sketches, Murchison pointed at herself and
then the spider, and repeated, "Human. Kritkuk."

"Hukmaki," it replied; and, more loudly, "Kritickuk."

The emphasis on the second word, she thought, might be
due to irritation at her not pronouncing it correctly. But it wasn't
doing such a hot job of pronunciation on "human," either. She
tried a different approach, knowing that it couldn't understand
any of the words yet, but hoping that it would get the message.

"You are speaking too quickly for me," she said in her normal speaking tempo, then went on slowly, "Please . . . speak . . . in . . . a . . . slow . . . and . . . distinct . . . voice."

Plainly it had understood the message because this time, while the word didn't seem to be that much slower, she was able to detect additional syllables in it.

She started to say it but the word choked off into a cough. Taking a deep, calming breath she tried again.

"Krititkukik," she repeated.

"Krititkukik," it agreed.

Pleased at her first linguistic success, but not wanting to waste time trying to teach it better Earth-human pronunciation, she knelt down on the folded hammock and, with a new leaf spread flat on the deck before her, she thought hard and began sketching again.

Drawing two circles to indicate their different planets in space might be too confusing at this stage although, being a sailor, her spider would certainly use the stars for navigation between its world's many islands and might be well aware of the fact that its surface was round. Instead she drew a straight line to represent the horizon across the widest part of a new leaf, placed a small circle with wavy lines radiating from it to indicate that it was the sun and added the outline of the island. Around and below it she drew small, flat crescent shapes to denote waves, and on one side of it she drew three flat domes to depict the spider's ships and not to scale, a glider flying above them. She pointed to each of the symbols in turn.

"Sky," she said. "Sun. Sea. Island. Ship. Glider."

The spider supplied the equivalent word sounds, and a few of them she was even able to pronounce without being corrected, but the other began walking around her in a tight circle as if in agitation or impatience.

Suddenly it reached forward and took the brush from her hand and began slowly and carefully to add to her sketch. It drew three small, flat rectangles that had to be the buildings of the medical station on the other side of the island. It reversed the brush and used the dry end to point several times at the station.

She wasn't giving away information that the spiders did not already know from their aerial reconnaissance and they would have been stupid if they did not already know that she had come from there, so she took another leaf and filled it with a drawing of the medical-station buildings in greater detail. She showed the sand below them sloping to the wavy lines of the sea and, on a clear area of sand, four stylized figures: herself; the cylindrical shape with many short legs along its base that was Naydrad; a featureless cone that was Danalta when it wasn't being something else; and Prilicla. In outline the empath looked very much like Krititkukik except for the two sets of wings and the fact that it was a little distance above the ground.

The spider remained motionless for the few seconds, either in surprise or because it was waiting for the ink to dry, then it pointed the brush first at Murchison herself, then used the end of its thin handle to touch her image in the sketch, followed by those of the others, and finally the station. It repeated the process, but this time when it touched each of the four figures it followed by touching the buildings, and ended by tapping repeatedly at the med station alone. Then it looked at her and made a chittering, interrogative sound.

It was saying, she felt sure, that it knew all of them had come from the med station, but where had the med station come from?

One of the most important rules while opening first-contact proceedings with a less advanced species, was not to display a level of technology that would risk giving the other party a racial inferiority complex. Looking at this spider sea-captain, and considering the degree of bravery, resourcefulness, and all-around adaptability required for a profession that called for constant travel over a medium—water—that was an ever-present and probably deadly danger to them, she did not think that her spider would recognize an inferiority complex if it was to stand up and bite it in its hairy butt. This time she fetched the water container before selecting another, unmarked leaf.

The horizon line she placed low down, with the island, three ships, and med station sketched in less detail. Then she poured a little water into her cupped hand, added a few drops of ink to darken it, and then filled in the sky with a transparent grey wash which, she hoped, would indicate that it was a night picture. When it was dry, instead of a sun she painted in a few large and small dots at irregular intervals. A sailor was bound to know what they were.

"Stars," she said, pointing at each of the dots in turn.

"Preket," said the spider.

She pointed to one of the domelike ships and carefully pronounced the spider word for it, "Krisit." Then she drew another one of them, this time high in the night sky, pointed at it, then to herself and at the med station.

"Preket krisit," she said.

The spider's reaction was immediate. It backed away from her and began chittering loudly and continuously, but whether in surprise, excitement, fear, or some other emotion, she couldn't say because it was speaking far too fast for her to understand any of the words even if she had already learned some of them. It came closer and jabbed a claw at the picture so suddenly that one edge of the leaf split apart. Again and again it pointed at its three ships and the island, at the starship and the medical station and then at the starship again. With the claw it pushed at the starship so violently that the leaf was torn in two.

Plainly the other was trying to tell her that the three ships and the island belonged to the spiders and that it wanted the strangers to go away. Thinking about the kind of people they were, armed fisherfolk with the capability for long-range reconnaissance, it was possible that they preyed on others of their kind as well as their ocean's fish. The visiting starship, especially if they thought that it was manned by sea-raiders like themselves, had already established a base on their island. They would considerate it a threat that must be driven off, captured, or destroyed.

Somehow Murchison had to show them that neither the visiting ship nor the medical station were a threat and that they were, in fact, the opposite. She held up both her hands, palms outwards, for silence.

When it came, she lifted the brush again and held it close to the other's face, but this time she didn't use it to sketch. Instead she snapped off a couple of inches of the handle, at the end opposite the hairs so that it remained usable, and held them apart for a few seconds. Waiting until it seemed that she had all of the spider's attention, she brought the broken ends together and spat delicately on the join before handing both pieces back to the spider.

"Join it," she said slowly. "Fix it. Mend it."

While she was speaking, the other made sounds that seemed to have a questioning note, but immediately got the idea. Onto the join it spat a very small quantity of the sticky saliva it had used earlier to seal the knots of her restraining rope, and when it had hardened, handed the brush back to her. Apart from the small gob of hardened saliva where the repair had been made, the brush was a good as new. She began sketching with it again.

This time she didn't bother showing the island, ships, or sun. At the left of the picture she drew instead a vertical line of four figures to represent herself, a spider, Naydrad, and Prilicla. Slightly to the right of them she placed a similar line of figures, except that her figure was divided by a narrow space at the waist and one of her legs was separated by a short distance from her body. The figure of the spider showed three limbs detached from its body, and similar radical dismemberment to the forms of the Kelgian and her Cinrusskin chief. A little farther to the right she drew a larger picture of the med-station buildings, followed by another vertical line of figures that were whole again. To make her meaning even clearer she drew four short arrows linking the damaged figures to the station, and another four pointing from it to the whole figures.

Again she indicated the join in the brush handle and said slowly, "We mend people."

The spider didn't appear to understand her at all because it pushed the sketch away before retying the rope around her ankle and sealing the knot. It left quickly without speaking.

Murchison threw the brush angrily at the discarded sketch. The rain had stopped and sunlight was shining through the narrow opening in the ventilation wall. She moved to it, hoping that more light would lighten her spirits, and wound down the ratchet until it was fully open.

Noise as well as light was pouring in, but the excited chittering of crew members and the creaking of wooden mechanisms could not drown out the single, loud clicking voice that was almost certainly that of the captain using a speaking trumpet. On the beach outside she could see spiders swarming over the other ships, opening their sail seals and raising the boarding ramps.

Something important was happening, Murchison thought, something that would almost certainly involve this armed fishing-fleet opening hostilities against the medical station. Angrily she returned to sit on the folded hammock, knowing that her lamentable recent attempt at communication was certainly responsible for it and that she deserved everything that was going to happen to her.

It was while she was glowering despondently at the empty doorway that she noticed something amiss. Beside it there had been an unlit lamp with single containers of water and sand on each side of it, and now there were three containers there. Feeling greatly relieved but completely undeserving of her sudden change in fortune, she spoke quietly.

"Stop showing off, Danalta," she said, "which barrel of sand is you?"

CHAPTER 26

Throughout the ship the sound of spider voices and the loud creaking and rumbling of wooden mechanisms being operated reached a climax. The level of light coming from the corridor increased and with it came a steady flow of warm air that could only be blowing off the beach as the sail shields were opened fully and deployed. A moment later the rocking action of the waves intensified as the ship pulled free of the sand. The fleet had set sail and she knew its objective.

"They're going to attack the med station," said Murchison urgently above the ship noises. "We have to get back there to warn them. . . ."

"You already have warned them," said Danalta. Its sand-container shape, which had grown an eye, ear, and mouth, moved sideways to reveal her communicator lying on the floor with its TRANSMIT and RECORD lights blinking. "I was here during your conversation with the spider, and Captain Fletcher, with the help of Dr. Prilicla, who uses a similar form of language, says that it has almost enough to program a translator for spider talk when we get back. Prilicla needs you there, it needs all of the med team, as quickly as possible. One of the Trolanni casualties is giving cause for serious concern."

She picked up the active communicator and clipped it to

her equipment belt. Apologetically she said, "For a while I forgot what I do for a living. I must report to Prilicla at once."

"It will waste less time," said Danalta firmly, "if you report to it in person. Pathologist Murchison, we must return to the station, now."

Rarely had words been spoken with which she was in more complete agreement, Murchison thought fervently as she looked around her low, cramped, and highly uncomfortable prison, but returning to the station was not going to be easy, especially for her. She pointed at the ventilator opening.

"Those ships are moving fast," she said, "and we're already two hundred meters from the beach. Even if we left now, by the time I swam ashore and ran all the way back, we might not get there until after the fleet arrived."

The sand container slumped into a more organic shape and rolled up to her feet, growing a rudimentary jaw with very sharp teeth as it came.

"With my assistance we will both go by sea," said Danalta as it bit through the rope securing her ankle. "Will I enlarge the ventilator opening for you?"

"No," she replied sharply. "It will open widely enough to let me out. We don't want to damage their ship unnecessarily. I was trying to make friends with them."

"Then jump," said Danalta.

Instead of jumping she made a long, shallow dive that took her about twenty meters from the ship's side before she had to surface. She heard the splash of Danalta's less graceful entry into the water, the excited chittering of spiders as more and more of them spotted her, followed by the hissing plop of crossbow bolts striking the water all around her. She took a deep breath and dived again, then wondered if a few feet of water would make any difference to the penetration power of the crossbow bolts when she could swim faster and maybe be more difficult to hit on the surface. But the next time she came up for breath and looked back, she was in time to hear the spider with the speaking trumpet call out a few loud, sharp syllables after which the shooting stopped.

Relieved and grateful, she continued swimming. Then she wondered if her spider captain didn't want to hurt her, or if it believed that it would recapture her with the others at the station and simply wanted to save ammunition. A green, sharklike shape with a long, corrugated horn growing from the top of its head broke the surface beside her before she could make up her mind.

"Grasp the dorsal horn firmly in both hands," said Danalta, "and hold on tight."

She was glad of the extra grip afforded by the corrugations as the shape-changer picked up speed and its wide, triangular tail whipped rapidly from side to side, thrusting it faster and faster through the water. It was exhilarating and uncomfortable and a little like water-skiing without the skis. Danalta was cutting through rather than over the steep, breaking waves in the bay so that she had to twist her body and her head backwards every time she needed to breathe, but doing so showed that the distance between them and the pursuing ships was opening up. Laughing, she wondered what her spider captain would think about her moving so fast through the water that she was leaving a wake.

But she was beginning to feel very cold, and Danalta was moving even faster and the water was slapping and tugging and bursting in clouds of spray over her head, arms, and shoulders. In spite of the warm, morning sunshine reflecting off the waves and spray, her body temperature was dropping rapidly and the hands holding her to Danalta were losing feeling. She realized suddenly that while her equipment belt had stayed firmly in place, the swimsuit hadn't.

The spider ships were disappearing behind the curve of the coastline, and the wreck of *Terragar* and the medical station were coming into sight. Within a few minutes they were in the shallows in front of the buildings and the shape-changer was already turning its fins into legs.

Murchison stamped about on the sand and swung her arms

briefly to return some heat to her body, then, still shivering, she sprinted for the largest prefab structure that housed the recovery ward.

It was occupied by Naydrad and the three Earth-human casualties. With her teeth chattering, she said, "Charge Nurse, please throw me a set of my whites and . . ."

"You look fine the way you are, ma'am." said one of the *Terragar* officers, smiling broadly.

"The way I am," she said, beginning to pull on the tight, white coveralls, "is bad for your blood pressure. Naydrad, where's Prilicla?"

"In the comm room," said the Kelgian.

A faint tremor of pleasure and relief shook Prilicla as the pathologist joined him before the communicator screen where the face of the captain was staring out at them. He said, "Friend Murchison, I'm glad to have you back with us, and I feel that you are well but worried. Ease your mind. Friend Fletcher and *Rhabwar* will be with us several minutes before the spider fleet arrives, so that we are in no immediate danger from them."

"But, Doctor," said Murchison grimly, "they are in danger, deadly danger, from us."

"No, ma'am," the captain joined in. "I've never held with the adage that attack is the best form of defense. We will keep them away from the medical station until you people are ready to transfer to *Rhabwar*. Minimum force, if any, will be used."

Prilicla could feel the growing concern and impatience behind the words as Murchison went on. "Please listen, Captain. Unknown to me at the time, Danalta was making a record of my attempt at communication, but it didn't include the other things I saw the spiders do earlier, the way they have to live with and use their technology, or their behavior towards me and the, well, consideration one of them showed. They are intelligent, brave, and resourceful people, but terribly vulnerable."

"I understand," said the captain. "We'll try not to hurt them, but we do have to defend the station, remember?"

"You *don't* understand!" said Murchison. "The spiders use technology that is partially organic, something we've never met before. All of their fabricated structures large and small, their ships, gliders, tools, and, presumably, their living accommodations, are partly woven of web strands from their own bodies. I don't know how much they value this material, or how difficult or easy it would be to replace, but damaging anything they've made might mean damaging them, or a least a valuable piece of their personal property. You're on very sensitive ground here, Captain."

Before the other could reply, it went on quickly, "They use fire, but so far as I could see, only for heavily protected lighting, and they seem to be so afraid of it that their bodies as well as their structures must be highly flammable. And in spite of being sailors, they also have an intense aversion to contact with water. Their ships are designed so that the sails can be reconfigured to enclose the entire upperworks so as to shelter them from rain and spray.

"I'm sorry, Captain," it went on, and Prilicla could feel the apology backing up its words, "for adding these complications to whatever defensive strategy you've worked out. But if we are ever to establish friendly relations with these people, which from personal contact I consider to be a strong probability, you must not use any weapons against them that will generate heat. I'm thinking of signal flares, normally non-harmful pyrotechnics, or any form of radiant energy that would cause an electrical discharge. As well, you must not allow any of their sea or airborne personnel to fall in the water."

The captain was silent for a moment and, thankfully, still well beyond Prilicla's empathic range. When it spoke, its features and voice were calm and reflected none of what it must have been feeling.

"Thank you for the additional information, Pathologist Murchison," it said, glancing aside at another screen. "We should be closing with the spider fleet approximately one hundred and fifty meters off your beach in seventeen minutes. In that time I shall try to modify my defensive strategy accordingly. However, you will understand that operationally I do not do my best work with both hands tied behind my back. Off."

Murchison shook its head at the blank screen and moved to the room's big direct-vision panel. Prilicla followed to hover above its shoulder as they watched the three spider vessels that had rounded the curve of the island and were beginning to foreshorten as they turned in to approach the station. All six of their gliders had been launched and were making slow, tight circles in the sky above them. Distance had reduced the chittering of their crews to a low, insect buzzing. The pathologist's emotional radiation, he noted with approval, reflected wariness, concern, growing excitement, but no fear.

"Friend Murchison," he said gently, indicating the big diagnostic screen on the other side of the room, "this is a good opportunity for us to review the latest clinical material on the two Trolanni. Patient Keet's condition was not life-threatening and its treatment is progressing satisfactorily, but not so Patient Jasam's."

The pathologist dipped its head in affirmation and moved to the screen which was already displaying enlargements of the two patients' scanner images. For several minutes it studied them, magnifying and changing the viewpoint several times, while in the direct-vision panel the spider ships drew closer. But unlike Prilicla, it had no attention to spare for them.

Finally it said, "Danalta told me there was a problem with Patient Jasam, and it was right. But Patient Keet's condition, while not giving cause for immediate concern, is not good. There is a general impairment of blood flow, and organic degeneration in several areas that is not, I think, due to any recent trauma, and the indications would support a diagnosis of sterility caused by a long-term dietary deficiency. But Patient Jasam is in serious trouble. I advocate immediate surgical intervention. Would you agree, sir?"

"Fully, friend Murchison," he replied, gesturing towards the screen. "But there are three main areas of trauma, deep puncture-wounding whose effect on nearby organs is unknown. We should go in at once, certainly, but how, where and in what order? This is an entirely new life-form to my experience."

The Earth-human's feelings were predominantly those of concern, apology, and, strangely, an underlying but slowly growing feeling of certainty.

"There is nothing entirely new," it said, "under this or any other sun. Our Trolanni friend's CHLI physiology has a similarity—very slight I must admit—in its lack of supporting skeletal structure and the fine network of blood vessels and nerve linkages supplying the peripheral limbs and visual and aural sensors, to those found in the Kelgian DBLF classification. There are also similarities in its two fast-beating hearts to those of the light-gravity, LSVO and MSVK life-forms. The digestive system is very strange, but the waste-elimination process could belong to a scaled-down Melfan. If you believe the risk to be acceptable, I think I know what is going on, or what should be going on in there, but . . ."

It held up its hands with the fingers loosely spread.

". . . But I can't do it with clumsy digits like these," it went on. "It would need much more sensitive hands, yours, and the small, specialized members that the shape-changer can grow to get into and support the awkward corners. You and Danalta would perform the surgery. I could only assist and advise."

"Thank you, friend Murchison," said Prilicla, wishing that the other could feel its gratitude and relief. "We will prepare at once."

"Before we open Jasam up . . ." it began, and broke off because all around them the loose equipment in the room was vibrating to the increasing subsonic growl that indicated *Rhabwar* was making its low-level approach. Irritably, and without even looking at the ships closing on the beach, it raised its voice.

"I would like to make a closer, hands-on examination of both patients," it went on, "for purposes of comparison and to obtain physical confirmation of the scanner findings."

"Of course," said Prilicla. "But first give me a few minutes so that Naydrad can render them unconscious."

"But why?" it asked. "We're very short of time."

"I'm sorry, friend Murchison," he replied, "but unlike the *Terragar* officers, the Trolanni would take no pleasure in the sight of your body."

CHAPTER 27

From the deeply upholstered comfort of his control couch, which felt about as soft as a wooden plank due to the body tension required to make him appear relaxed to his subordinates, Captain Fletcher watched the image of the ships and aircraft of the spider landing force as it expanded in his forward vision screen.

Rhabwar was not a large vessel by Monitor Corps standards, but it was a little longer and its delta wing configuration gave it more width than the big, flattened, turtlelike ships of the opposition. The approach he had originally planned would certainly have caused maximum non-offensive confusion, if not utter havoc and demoralization, to the opposition. But he had remembered the words of Pathologist Murchison as she had been telling him how he should do his job.

His idea had been to go in low and fast and drag a sonic shockwave along the length of the beach. He didn't think that the ships would suffer or—except psychologically—their crews, but the thought of what the air turbulence created by a supersonic fly-past would do to those ridiculously flimsy gliders made it a bad idea. It wouldn't be like shooting ducks, he thought, but more like blasting butterflies out of the sky.

"Decelerate," he said, "and bring us to a halt one hundred

meters above the beach midway between the station and the waterline. Deploy three tractor beams in pressor mode at equal strength in stilt configuration and hold us there."

"Sir," said Haslam, "the slower approach is going to give them time to begin landing their people on the beach."

The captain didn't reply because he could see everything that was happening as well as the lieutenant could and had arrived at the same conclusion.

"Dodds," he said. "The opposition's ships are highly flammable. When we're in position, swing around so that our tail flare will be directed inland. Then put out one forward tractor to discourage the spider advance. Focus it to about ten meters' surface diameter and change the point of focus erratically for maximum turbulence as you play it back and forth along the beach across their path. The idea is to create a localized sandstorm down there."

"Understood, sir," said Dodds.

"Power room," he went on briskly. "We'll be supporting the ship's mass on pressor beams with no assist from the thrusters for a while. How long can you give us? A rough estimate will do."

"A moment, please," said the engineering officer; then, "Approximately seventy-three minutes on full power drain, reducing by one-point-three percent per minute until exhaustion and an enforced grounding seventeen-point-three minutes later."

"Thank you, Chen." said Fletcher, smiling to himself. The power-room lieutenant was a man who disliked giving rough approximations. "I'm putting this operation on your repeater screen. Enjoy the, ah, battle."

The misty-blue light given off by their three immaterial stilts as well as that of the forward tractor beam would be difficult for the spiders to see in the bright sunlight, so it would seem that the ship drifting to a stop above them was virtually weightless, or at least very lightly built like one of their own flying machines.

"A suggestion, sir," said Chen suddenly. "If your intention

is to make a blatant demonstration of power that will discourage, and probably scare hell out of the enemy without inflicting actual physical injury, this is the way to do it. . . ."

"The spiders aren't our enemy, Lieutenant," said Fletcher dryly, "they just act that way. But go on."

"But if they don't discourage easily," the other continued, "we could be faced with a siege situation so that balancing ourselves up here on power-hungry stilts would be a short-term activity as well as running down our power reserves. My suggestion is that we land and modify the meteorite shield to provide hemispherical protection widely enough to cover the station and ourselves. That way we can maintain the shield for a much longer period. Once we've made the point, which we have, that we are large, dangerous, and, if necessary, can float motionless in the air, there's no reason to continue doing so. With respect, sir, I think we should land sooner rather than later."

Exactly the same thoughts had been going through Fletcher's mind, but saying so to Lieutenant Chen would have made the captain sound petty-minded in the extreme. But a development that the other had not foreseen, at least not yet, was that if a spider aircraft should fly into one of the pressor beams supporting *Rhabwar*'s weight, it and its pilot would be smashed flat into the ground.

"Thank you, Chen," he said instead. "Your suggestion is approved. Haslam, take us down. Dodds, kill the pressors but maintain the forward tractor to keep that sandstorm going. Chen, how soon will the meteorite-shield modification be ready?"

"It's difficult to be precise," said Chen. "Fairly soon."

"Try to make it sooner than that," he said.

The gliders had sheared off at *Rhabwar*'s approach but now they were circling back again, possibly thinking that the grounding of the ship was a sign of weakness. All three of the spider vessels had run their prows up onto the beach and the nearest one had its landing-ramp lowered. The first few spiders were already crawling ashore with crossbows held at the ready. Dodds took a moment to check the focus of his tractor beam. The landing party now numbered close on twenty, with more of them coming down the ramps at intervals of a few seconds.

Directly in front of them a carpet of sand twenty meters in diameter and about three inches deep rose high into the air and exploded into a cloud as the tractor's point of focus was vibrated erratically in and out. A thick curtain of fine, powdery sand dropped in front of and a little on top of the spiders.

For a moment they milled about uncertainly. Then Fletcher saw a spider with a large speaking trumpet climb onto the superstructure of it ship to chitter loudly at them. At once they split into two groups that crawled rapidly along the beach in opposite directions. The sandstorm, its effect only slightly diminished by the fact that the line of targets was lengthening, followed them.

The other two ships were also disgorging spiders while the gliders were flying in tight circles above *Rhabwar* and the station, although fortunately not low enough for them to hit the meteorite shield when it came on.

"Sir," said Dodds worriedly, "the sand doesn't appear to bother them very much, especially now that all three landing parties are strung out along the beach. It looks as though they are trying move out of sight and circle round behind us. Shall I increase the power and area of focus, sir, to stir up more sand, or maybe try to box them in by—"

"Deploying another tractor would help," Haslam broke in. "I'm not doing anything else at the moment."

"—By pulling in some water instead of sand," Dodds continued, "and splashing it down in their path? That might stop them spreading out sideways. They'd be caught between the sea and a wet place."

Pleased with the lieutenant because this was an idea Fletcher had not already thought of himself, he said, "We're told that water has a very bad effect on them and we are, after all, trying to be friendly. Try it, but be very careful not to dowse them."

A few minutes later Dodds said jubilantly, "They certainly

are afraid of the water; they've stopped in their tracks. But now they're pushing inland again."

"Haslam," said the captain, "man another tractor beam unit—Dodds will give you the settings—and help him out. While he concentrates on the two farther parties, you take the nearest one. Keep moving up and down the line of spiders trying to advance on the station. Leave the waterplashing, if necessary, to Dodds. You shower them with sand only. Try to spoil their ability to see where they're going, and generally make them feel uncomfortable, but don't hurt them."

"Yes, sir," said Haslam.

More and more spiders were crawling down their ships' landing ramps, but not spreading out because of the threat from the containing splashes of water. If the positions were reversed, Fletcher thought, he would have been wondering why they were not being constantly drenched by water instead of dusted with harmless sand, but then, their minds might not share the same rules of logic.

Suddenly they were changing tactics.

"Look at this, sir," Dodds said urgently. "They're beginning to weave from side to side, then darting into the falling sand. And when I'm dealing with one flank the other one pushes forward and gains a meter or so of ground. I have to keep changing the point of focus, narrowing it or moving the tractor beam back to keep from hitting them. Chen, we're going to need that meteorite shield, like now."

"The same thing is happening here," Haslam said. "We'd need to drop a ton of sand on this lot to discourage them. They take turns at running in, zig-zagging at random, and . . . Hell, I hit one of them!"

It must have been the briefest of touches on one side of the spider's body, but the tractor beam lifted it two meters into the sand-filled air and flipped it onto it back. It lay with its six limbs waving. Haslam withdrew his beam without being told as a few of the others gathered round their injured companion to lift it back onto its feet. Through the air which was now free of sand, Fletcher had a clear view of the spiders further up and down the beach beginning to move purposefully towards the station again. Then high on the superstructure of the middle ship of the three, the spider with the speaking trumpet began chittering loudly at them.

The advance hesitated and slowed to a dead stop. Within a few seconds all three spider landing parties had turned around and were hurrying back to their ships, the injured one being half carried by two of its companions. The gliders were already coming in to land close to their boarding ramps.

"I'm sorry about hitting that one, sir," said Haslam, "and I don't think it was badly hurt. But it looks as though we've taught them a lesson because they've decided to pull out."

"Don't bet on that, Lieutenant," said Fletcher dryly. He was raising his hand to point at the scene in the forward viewscreen when the communicator chimed and its screen lit with the image of Dr. Prilicla.

"Friend Fletcher," said the Cinrusskin. "The traces of emotional radiation emanating from your crew have been characteristic of excitement, tension and concern, all of which feelings have suddenly diminished in strength. A long and tricky surgical procedure is about to be attempted—once, that is, we solve an associated non-medical problem. Can you tell me whether or not we can proceed without outside emotional interruptions or distractions?"

"Doctor," Fletcher said, laughing softly, "you will be free of distractions for the rest of the day. Judging by the look of that sky there is a heavy rainstorm, not just a squall, moving in. The spiders are returning to their ships as we speak."

They watched the dark grey clouds on the horizon expanding to fill the sky and the paler curtain of heavy rain rushing closer. The spiders and their aircraft were safely on board and the sail shields of the three ships were closed tight before the deluge arrived, but they could hear it rattling and bouncing off the flattened dome-like hulls which, he realized suddenly, looked very much like umbrellas.

"This must be the first time," Haslam said, "that a battle was called off because of rain."

CHAPTER 28

The patient had been prepped for surgery, the operating team of Danalta, Naydrad, and himself had been standing by the table for more than twenty minutes, and friend Murchison was still trying to solve Prilicla's associated non-medical problem. It was trying with such intensity to be patient and reasonable that its emotional radiation was making him tremble.

"Keet," it was saying, "your life-mate Jasam is unconscious and will not feel pain, either during or while recovering from this procedure. You, however, are feeling the non-material pains of concern, uncertainty, and the continuing emotional trauma over what you think will be the loss of a loved one. To be brutally honest, we may lose Jasam, but we would have a better chance of saving it if you would cooperate by moving out of visual range. Untutored as you are in medical matters, not seeing every incision, resection, and repair as they take place would be easier on you, too. Besides, would Jasam want you to suffer needlessly like this?"

Keet lay watching the towel-draped form of its life-mate from its litter, which it had insisted be moved into the operating room. It made no reply.

"In all my nursing experience," said Naydrad, its fur ruffling in disapproval, "never has the next of kin, or any other nonmedically-oriented relative, been allowed to witness a procedure of this complexity. On all the civilized worlds I know of, it is just not done. If this is the custom on Trolann, I think it is a misguided, unnecessarily painful, completely wrong, and barbaric custom."

Prilicla was about to apologize for Naydrad's forthright speech, but stopped himself because the reasons for the Kelgian species' lack of tact had already been explained to it, but Keet didn't give him a chance to talk.

"It is not the custom on Trolann," it said, radiating anger at the insult. "But neither is it the custom to have a druul present in our operating theaters working on us. Ever."

He could feel the pathologist beginning to lose its temper, but not completely, because the words it used were intended to achieve a precisely calculated effect.

Murchison said calmly, "The experiences you shared on your ship, your searchsuit as you call it, when Jasam was badly injured and you were unable to leave your control pod to help or comfort or even to be physically close to it, has made a deep impression on your mind. You don't want to be separated from Jasam—especially, as now, when you think that there is the danger of never seeing it alive again. I can understand and sympathize with that feeling.

"Perhaps this natural concern for your life-mate," it went on, "has temporarily clouded your intellect and memory, so I shall explain to you once again, that I, no matter how large or small my physical resemblance to one of them, am not a druul. Because of my greater knowledge in some areas I am here simply to advise on problems which may arise during this procedure. I shall not be working on Jasam directly or touching its body at any time. If you insist on being present during this operation, you have my permission to stay. However, seeing your life-mate under the knife will be distressing and psychologically damaging for you, so I suggest that you watch me closely rather than Jasam, just in case I should feel suddenly hungry and want to eat it."

"And they tell me Kelgians are without tact," said Danalta.

"Whatever that is," said Naydrad, its fur spiking in shock. "But the words were inappropriate."

Prilicla knew that Murchison was deliberately using shock tactics, and felt from Keet's emotional radiation that they were beginning to work.

"From your observation of Prilicla's work on your ship," the pathologist went on, "you know that it is capable of the most delicate and precise healing. You also know that it is hypersensitive to the emotions of those around it, and you must already have realized that your intense feelings of fear, concern, and other emotions can adversely affect its ability to perform the high level of surgery that is required here. For that reason you must at all times keep a tight control of your feelings, natural though they are, so as to avoid distracting Prilicla. Do you understand and agree?"

The Trolanni did not reply, but Prilicla could feel the intensity of Keet's emotional radiation begin to subside as it fought, successfully, to control its feelings and impose a measure of calm on itself. There was no need for it to speak to this frightful, druul-like creature because there was understanding and agreement and, he noted with pleasure, a feeling of apology.

"Thank you, friend Murchison," Prilicla said. "We will begin. . . ."

The high concentration of light around the patient, Prilicla thought, during the few times he glanced up to rest his eyes, when contrasted with the grey overcast outside the direct-vision panel, made it seem almost as if night had fallen, and the final time he looked up, the panel was black and it had. At intervals the quiet voice of the captain had been reporting no visible activity from the spider ships, and with the fall of darkness the infrared sensors were confirming its theory that the spiders were not nocturnal creatures.

"Or at least," Naydrad added, much too loudly for the captain to miss hearing, "they don't go out on rainy nights. Dr. Prilicla, I think you are in need of sleep."

"And I feel sure that you are, Doctor," said Murchison. "The patient's condition is still critical, but stable enough for us to seal off the lower thoracic area and suspend operations for a few hours. After all, the damage to the lungs where the deep air lines were jerked out by the onboard explosion has been repaired, and it is breathing pure oxygen with no mechanical assistance, as well as being fed intravenously. Repairs to the lesions caused by the traumatic withdrawal of the external feeding and waste-extraction systems can surely wait a little longer for attention?"

"You are probably right, friend Murchison," Prilicla replied, using the form of words that was the closest he could come to telling anyone they were wrong. "But there are still small traces of toxic material adhering to the ruptured bowel walls, and I would like to remedy that before any cessation. Friend Naydrad, stand by and apply suction where I indicate. Friend Danalta, be ready to follow me in and support the area under the first lesion while I am suturing. Friend Murchison, ease your mind. I promise not to fall asleep on the patient for at least an hour. Now, let us resume."

Naydrad's equipment made a low, derisive sound and its fur rippled in concern as it said, "This is the strangest stomach-and-bowel arrangement I've ever encountered. Dr. Prilicla, in coloration and structure, it resembles spaghetti, that Earth-human food you like to eat. Is it strange to you, Pathologist?"

"In the light of my earlier and non-serious remark about eating," said Murchison sharply, radiating disapproval, "it is unseemly to mention food in the presence of the next of kin. And no, the Dwerlans use a similar gastrointestinal tract, although, I admit, not two of them working in tandem. There is nothing new in multispecies medicine, just new combinations of the old. But this one is particularly complex."

Keet moved restively on its litter and said, "I don't seriously believe that any of you would want to eat the offal of my life-mate. Even a druul would think twice about doing that. But I can't see what is happening. Murchison, you're blocking my view."

"That was and remains my intention," said Murchison. "It is kinder to tell you what is happening after it has happened."

With Naydrad keeping the operative field clear of unwanted fluid, and Danalta extruding the fine digits that could insinuate themselves into the awkward crevices where no inflexible surgical instrument could go so as to hold open the site of the damage, Prilicla was able to see his way to perform the extremely delicate work of repair that was necessary, As the procedure continued, Keet radiated intense but—uncharacteristically for it—silent concern. Murchison was watchful but it did not have to speak at all, because the organic territory they were occupying was becoming increasingly familiar to them. But nearly half an hour later, it did speak.

"Keet," Murchison said, radiating an increasing level of pleasure and relief that the Trolanni could not feel, "this is going well."

"Thank you, Murchison," said Keet.

"You're welcome," said the pathologist. "But please remain quiet so as to avoid distracting the team. There is more to do."

Feeling happier than it had been since the start of the operation, Keet replied by not saying another word. But Murchison was radiating a growing level of concern that was being focused on Prilicla himself. Its words came as no surprise to him.

"You're tired, sir," it said, "and the way your legs are wobbling shows that you are badly in need of rest. The remaining work is simple tidying-up and can be completed by Danalta and Naydrad under my direction. But there is another complication which requires treatment. It isn't urgent or life-threatening, at least so far as the life of the patient itself is concerned, and it can wait, but I suggest we do it while we are in the area so as to avoid having to open up the patient at a later date."

"Do what, and why?" said Keet suddenly. "I don't want you cutting Jasam without a very good reason."

Murchison ignored the interruption but in its calm, lecturing voice managed to answer the questions anyway,

"The problem is principally medical and requires only minor surgery," it said, using its pencil light as a pointer, "involving as it does infusions into the patient's endocrine system, specifically the small gland in the area—just there—which is partially atrophied and inactive due to a build-up of toxic material that has been assimilated by the body over many years. With the removal from its toxic home environment and the introduction of the indicated specifics, the chances are that the gland in question can be restimulated to optimum activity in a very short time, and certainly within the period of the patient's recuperation."

"What are you talking about?" said Keet.

". . . Considering the fact that Trolann's population is dangerously close to the point of extinction," Murchison continued, "it would be advantageous after they are transferred to their new world for as many Trolanni couples as possible to be capable of reproducing their kind. With Patient Jasam's male reproductive system, the treatment is simple and straightforward with no complications foreseen. With Patient Keet, however, in common with the females of the other life-forms in my experience, the mechanism of reproduction and child-bearing is more complex. It would be better if you undertook that procedure yourself, after you have slept, of course. Do you agree?"

For a moment Prilicla was unable to speak. A sudden explosion of emotion from Keet, comprising as it did a mixture of excitement, relief, and pleasure that verged on the joyous, was sending a slow tremors along his body, wings and limbs. He was greatly pleased but not surprised at the way his assistant had handled the situation, and he knew for a fact that Murchison had made a Trolanni friend for life.

As the gale of pleasurable emotion diminished, he withdrew

from the table, stretched out his wings and limbs and refolded them tightly to his body before speaking.

"Well done, all of you," he said. "Friend Murchison, both of your suggestions are approved. Proceed at once with the work on Jasam, and explain to Keet that her life-mate will be rendered unconscious for a period of continuous sedation that will assist its healing, and that there will be nothing more constructive for it to do during that time than to undergo the procedure you suggested."

"Don't worry, all that will be explained to Keet," Murchison broke in. "But now, sir, will you please go to sleep?"

The figures of Murchison, Danalta, Naydrad, the two Trolanni, and the whole OR were beginning to fade around him.

Happily he murmured, "I *am* asleep."

CHAPTER 29

The bad weather continued with unbroken wind and heavy rain for the next six days, during which there was, as expected, no resumption of the spider attack. Keet had successfully undergone its minor surgery at Prilicla's hands and was waiting impatiently for Jasam to be released from its continuing sedation. In space, *Courier One* had returned with the latest news from the Federation, which consisted mainly of ranking Monitor Corps officers and senior administrators worrying aloud about what *Rhabwar*'s people were doing, or more accurately, what they were doing wrong regarding this unique double first contact situation. *Courier Two* was waiting impatiently to take back the latest situation report, and their excuses.

Captain Fletcher was trying to think of a few good ones, and asking for help.

"I've drafted a report on all this for the courier vessel," it said, radiating a mixture of embarrassment and uncertainty as a jerky gesture of its hand indicated the human and Trolanni casualties visible through the transparent wall of the communications room, "but I wanted to consult with you, Dr. Prilicla, with all of you, in fact, before sending it off. For reasons you will understand, and of which I am not very proud, I didn't want the discussion to be via communicator and be overheard by my officers. If this matter should come to an enquiry, or even a court martial, I'd prefer them not to know and so spare them the embarrassment of having to give evidence against me."

The captain had walked the distance from *Rhabwar* in the pouring rain to say these things. Prilicla used his projective empathy in an attempt to reassure the captain, but it wasn't working very well. Naydrad was the first to speak.

"I don't understand your problem, Captain," it said with a puzzled ruffle of fur. "With Kelgians this situation would not arise. We would either recount the facts accurately or, if we didn't want to disclose the information, not speak at all. Earthhumans!"

"Unlike the charge nurse whose species doesn't know how to lie," Danalta joined in, "I have a capability for verbal misdirection, diplomacy, politeness or therapeutic lying. But it is usually less complicated in the long run to tell the truth."

The captain radiated worry and impatience. It said, "But the truth *is* complicated, almost certainly too complicated for our superiors to believe. *Courier One* took back the news of the Trolanni first contact, which in the interim has gone fairly well, but the continued success of which may depend on whether or not they both survive the second contact with another intelligent species which includes Pathologist Murchison's capture by pirates . . ."

"That had a happy ending," Murchison broke in, glancing out at the three rain-shrouded vessels drawn up along the beach, and added, "so far."

". . . As a result of which," it continued, "the planet's indigenous species has virtually declared war on us. This is no way to conduct a first contact operation, and our temporal lords and masters will be gravely displeased with us, or with me, at least. *Courier One*'s captain said that there was serious talk about sending one of the dedicated first contact ships, probably *Descartes*, to take over our contact with the second species while advising us on how to conduct the first. He also said that unique-science investigation teams, which would, of course, take all the necessary precautions, were being assembled to unravel the Trolanni searchsuit technology and would be held back until an assessment could be made regarding the possibly harmful psychological effects of so much advanced space hardware appearing around the spiders' planet. But when Courier Two takes back my latest report, including the news that—despite the fact that the spiders are nowhere near achieving space flight, they might not be given a terminal inferiority complex by seeing a few unexplained lights in their sky—within a week near-space is likely to be filled with Monitor Corps ships."

The captain stopped and breathed heavily. That was due, Prilicla thought, to the fact that it had been exhaling air at a controlled rate while speaking for several minutes without inhaling. For Prilicla's sake it was trying to control its emotional radiation, which was anything but pleasant.

"Friend Fletcher," he said gently, "our areas of authority in this situation are overlapping, so it follows that the responsibility, or the blame for it going wrong, is also divided. However, it began as a medical problem with the transfer of the casualties from *Terragar*, and later the two injured Trolanni from their vessel to this station where, in order to protect both sets of patients, I had to force you into taking military action in their defense. This being so, the greater proportion of the blame must fall on me . . ."

The other's worry tensions were beginning to ease a little, but Prilicla could also feel an argument coming on. Unlike the Earth-human physiological classification, he could respire and speak at the same time so he left no time for an interruption.

". . . My advice would be to tell the truth," he went on, "but omit the incident of friend Murchison's capture and escape until a later time. Learning about it now would worry the pathologist's life-mate, and knowing Diagnostician Conway as I do, it would come out here and . . ."

"He certainly would," said Murchison softly.

". . . complicate matters," he went on. "While Conway has

more than enough rank to take one of the hospital's vessels out here, my thought is that there will be enough ships in the area as it is without another worried life-mate joining us. Keet worrying about Jasam produces enough sex-based emotional drama to go on with. I feel your agreement, friend Murchison.

"As for the rest of the report," he went on, "be complete and factual. No doubt you will renew your warning regarding the danger of making direct ship-to-ship contact with the Trolanni searchsuit. But also warn your superiors, politely if your service career is to progress as it deserves, of the danger of well-intentioned interference by people who will have much less knowledge and appreciation of the problem than we have.

"You should also relate in detail your concerns regarding the third and much more dangerous first-contact operation that is coming up," he went on, "the one involving the druul. As well as the opposing species being physically separated and disarmed, which will require military intervention, the Trolanni must be evacuated as a disaster-relief emergency. At a later time a similar exercise will be required for the druul as well, who, because of the bad reputation they have with the Trolanni, must be assessed for possible reeducation as candidates for membership of the Federation. You could also suggest that the advice of patients Jasam and Keet on the Trolann situation would be invaluable, providing we are let alone to continue treating Jasam's very serious injuries and building up their trust in us."

"But the Trolanni-druul situation isn't the immediate problem . . ." began the captain.

"Of course it isn't," said Prilicla. "But if you give the impression that it is—that you, personally, consider these future problems to be of more importance and difficulty than our present one—this should have a reassuring effect on your superiors. If you express deep concern for and an understanding of their future problems, they should feel that you are confident about solving this one and leave us alone to get on with it without interference. As well, if they try to help with our problem, I'm sure friend Keet will be able to furnish us with more information on the Trolann situation to worry them. They might decide that every time they try to help us with our troubles, you dump an even greater problem in their laps, and desist."

"And what do I tell them about the spider assault on the med station?" asked the captain. "Just how do I make that sound like a minor problem?"

"You tell the truth," Prilicla replied, "but not all of it. After an initial period of misunderstanding, tell them that the spider first contact is ongoing."

"Ongoing it is," said the captain, "but from bad to worse. Dr. Prilicla, for such a timid, inoffensive, and completely friendly entity, you have a nasty, devious, lying mind."

"Why, thank you, friend Fletcher," he replied, "for listing my most admirable personality characteristics."

Murchison and Danalta made amused sounds which did not translate while Naydrad ruffled its fur in puzzlement, but before any of them could speak, the communicator chimed and its screen lit with the features of Haslam.

"Sir," the lieutenant said briskly, "our weather sensors indicate that the present warm front will clear the island in five hours' time—just before nightfall, that is—and it will be followed by an extensive high-pressure system that could remain for the ensuing twelve to fifteen days. As well, there is another spider fleet of three ships closing on us. Judging by their present heading and speed, I'd say that they intend to pass south of us before morning for a landing on the other side of the island. Would you like to return to the ship?"

The question was, of course, rhetorical because the captain was already halfway to the entrance.

It came as no surprise that the attack from inland did not develop until the afternoon of the following day. By then the hot, high sun had dried off the rain-soaked vegetation, and the moment-to-moment situation as it developed on *Rhabwar*'s tactical screens was being relayed to the med station's communicator with a commentary by the captain.

Naydrad was with the Trolanni patients, talking to Keet. Jasam was still deeply sedated but giving no cause for concern while Danalta was doing tricks with itself in an attempt to amuse the *Terragar* casualties who were complaining because they were missing their daily dunk in the ocean. Only Murchison and himself were watching developments, and the pathologist was radiating a strange mixture of dissatisfaction and guilt.

The original three ships beached near them were showing a few ventilation openings but had not lowered their landing ramps. According to the captain this was an obvious attempt to lull them into a false sense of security while a surprise attack was made from the cover of the vegetation inland. The spider force could not know—because at their level of technology, the very idea of being able to see at a distance in darkness would not have occurred to them—that *Rhabwar* was fully aware of the arrival of the new fleet; or that a vessel that could detect life signs in space wreckage over thousands of miles' distance would have no trouble picking up the movements and body heat of beings crawling under a thin covering of overhanging branches.

"I hate it," said Murchison suddenly, "when I have to watch brave, intelligent, but undereducated people making fools of themselves like this. Are you feeling godlike, Captain Fletcher?"

They heard the captain inhale sharply and Prilicla felt the sudden surge of anger that was weakened only by distance. But its voice remained calm as it replied, "Yes, in a way. I see and know everything, and like a god I have to hide the truth from them for their own good. I'd rather we stopped them before they hit the meteorite shield. They've already seen us creating sand eddies and pulling water into their path, and gratuitous displays of superscience can have a bad effect on an emerging culture. Magic, apparent miracles, events which contravene natural law as they know it, can give rise to new religious or drastically change existing ones so that superstition can stultify scientific and technological progress. These people don't need that."

"Sorry, Captain," said Murchison, "I spoke without thinking."

The other nodded and went on. "The damage may already have been done. They've seen our ship fly, and the med-station buildings, and we checked their first attack by throwing sand at them and threatening to douse them with seawater, although neither stopped them trying to attack us because it was the rainstorm that did that. Maybe they think we were responsible for that, too. But allowing them to run into an invisible wall like the meteorite shield could be too much for a primitive species to take, brave and resourceful and adaptable though they are.

"The trouble is," it went on, "that we can't generate clouds of sand under the trees and neither can we drag water that far without it spilling on the way. We can use more power on the tractor to uproot trees and throw soil into the air, but not with enough accuracy to keep some of the spiders from getting squashed. Pathologist Murchison, didn't you mention earlier that they had a fear of fire as well as water?"

"I did," Murchison replied, "but I'd rather you didn't use it because I'm not sure whether the on-board fire precautions I saw were due to the material of their ships being flammable, or their bodies."

"My idea is to frighten them off without hurting them," said the captain. "Don't worry, I'll be careful. But I'd like them to come close enough for Dr. Prilicla to get an emotional reading from them. Specifically, why do they feel so strongly about us that they are willing to go up against a completely strange and obviously superior enemy?"

For nearly an hour they watched the enhanced images of the spider force as it moved slowly nearer, making use of all available cover and spreading out into line abreast formation as it came. The captain said complimentary things about the spider

238 · JAMES WHITE

commander's tactical know-how as the center of the line held back to enable the formation to form a crescent that would enclose the station and the grounded *Rhabwar*. They had closed to just under one hundred meters before the captain spoke directly to the station.

"Dr. Prilicla, are they close enough to give you an emotional reading?"

"Yes, friend Fletcher," he replied, "a strong but imprecise one. The strength as well as the lack of precision is due to the large number of sources sharing the same feelings. There is uncertainty and apprehension characteristic of fear that is under control, and a general feeling of antipathy towards the enemy . . ."

"Blind xenophobic hatred," the captain broke in. "I was afraid of that."

"As I've said, friend Fletcher," said Prilicla, "It is difficult to be precise, but my feeling is that they don't hate us so much as what we are doing."

"But we aren't doing anything wrong," the other protested, "at least that we know about. No matter, we have to stop them before they get any closer. Haslam, launch the chemical pyrotechnics. Spread them in front of their line at twenty-meter intervals. Dodds, use your tractor beam to pull off bunches of burning vegetation and drop them into any smoke-free gaps. I want our perimeter protected by a line of fire and smoke. Stand by to deploy the meteorite shield if that doesn't work."

Distress flares shot from *Rhabwar*'s launchers made low, fiery arcs in the sky before landing at the designated intervals among the trees.

"After three days' heavy rain," the captain added for Murchison's benefit, "the vegetation is still too damp for there to be any danger of us starting a conflagration. We will be producing mostly light, steam, and smoke."

The intense blue light and heat of the chemical flares, which had been designed to be seen across thousands of miles of space, caused the damp surrounding vegetation to fairly explode into flame. Dodds picked at the hottest spots with his tractor beam, moving clumps of burning branches into the intervening areas where the vegetation had been unaffected. A dense pall of steam and smoke rose into the sky so that the sun became a dark orange shape that wavered in and out of visibility. A few minutes later they could see through the dissipating smoke that the secondary fires were dying down, and those where the flares had landed were not looking too healthy, but they had done their work.

"A wind off the sea is blowing the smoke inland," said the captain. "The spider force is withdrawing and heading back to their ships. So far as we can see, no injuries have been sustained."

"Their emotional radiation confirms," said Prilicla, "but they are badly frightened and their dislike of us has increased."

"Sir," Lieutenant Haslam reported before the captain could reply, "the ships on the other side of the island must have seen the smoke. A glider has been launched. It is slope-soaring over the high ground and heading this way, obviously to find out what has been happening. I think we won this one."

"We won this battle, Lieutenant," said the captain, "but not the war. If we win the war that means we lose, because the only way to win this war is to stop it before anyone gets hurt.

"I'm open to suggestions."

CHAPTER 30

For the remainder of the day, between breaks for meals, checks on the patients, and a period of rest for himself, they watched the glider overhead because there was nothing else of interest happening. The spider aircraft was doing some very interesting things, like signaling to its mother ship on the other side of the island and the three vessels drawn up along the beach.

A large, circular panel close to one wing-root had opened and begun spinning in the slipstream about its two diametrically opposed attachment points. One face of the panel was bright yellow while the other matched the overall brownish-green color of the glider. The rotating disk was within easy reach of the pilot who used one of its forelimbs to check the spin at irregular intervals to show either the light or dark face to watchers below and on its more distant mother ship.

"Ingenious," said the captain admiringly. "It's using the visual equivalent of Earth's old-time Morse code. The spiders might not have radio but they can communicate over short to medium distances. The rotating panel would have minimum effect on the glider's flight characteristics, and any information being transmitted would be passed slowly, although if necessary the message could last for as long the glider remained aloft. Judging by the pauses in signaling, which last for anything up to fifteen minutes, I'd say that there is a similar device on the mother ship and they are talking about us."

"Sir," said Haslam. "It's not heading back to its ship. Why is it still climbing? I would have expected it to come down to take a closer look at us so that the pilot would have more to talk about."

The captain exercised the prerogative of a senior officer who did not know the answer by maintaining a commanding silence.

The litters bearing all of the patients were moved into the afternoon sunshine of the beach although, as it had been in the recovery ward, the druul-like Earth-human casualties and those from the Trolanni searchsuit were separated from visual contact by portable screens. There were a few spiders moving about the beach, but they stayed close to their ships and it was plain that another attack was not imminent. To conserve power the meteorite shield had not been deployed so that the patients could benefit from the sea breeze as well as the sunshine. They, too, lay watching and talking about the slowly ascending glider.

It was still climbing late in the afternoon when the patients were moved indoors and when the sun began to sink behind the high ground inland. When dusk fell at ground level it was still climbing, tiny with distance but clearly visible in the bright, orange light of the sun which for it had not yet gone down.

It began circling widely and performing slow, intricate aerobatics.

"Doctor," said the captain, "I'm beginning to worry about what our flyboy is doing up there. Its present altitude is close on five thousand meters and it must be cold up there. In the circumstances of the recent attack it doesn't seem appropriate for it to be showing off and selfishly enjoying itself like this. It's possible that it is performing some form of sunset religious ritual that the spiders, or maybe only their glider pilots, believe is important, but I don't think so."

"What do you think, friend Fletcher?" said Prilicla.

"The glider is far too high for its swiveling wing panel to be readable without a telescope," the captain replied, "and I can't imagine a species so afraid of fire as are the spiders being able to use it to process sand into glass and cast lenses. My theory is that the aerobatics are another form of signaling,"

It paused for a moment as if expecting an objection, then went on, "Of necessity the vocabulary would have to be restricted because there are only so many ways that a glider can move in the air, so its report would have to be simplified, couched in stock phrases that would be much less detailed than the visual Morse, and yet it is trying to describe happenings unique in its species' experience. But that high-flying aircraft and its message will be visible over a much greater distance than the shorter-range but more fluent swiveling wing-panel arrangement."

"Is there any support for your theory, friend Fletcher?" asked Prilicla, feeling that he already knew the answer. "Are there any spider vessels within visual range of this hypothetical signal?"

"I'm afraid so, Doctor," the captain replied. "Our radar isn't too accurate because their aircraft and ships are made from organic rather than metallic, reflective material. But it showed a fleet of six vessels, five of which changed course towards us within half an hour of the glider rising above their horizon. The other vessel headed in the opposite direction towards another fleet that is still too distant for us to resolve the number of units. My guess is that the sixth ship will launch a high-flying glider at first light tomorrow to relay the signal.

"Very soon all of the spiders on the surrounding ocean or on the land adjoining it will know we're here," it added, "and a lot of them will come to do something about it."

"But what will they do, friend Fletcher?" said Prilicla, the sudden intensity of his own anxiety overwhelming that of the captain. "We have not committed any hostile acts towards them, we did nothing wrong, and when they attacked us we did everything possible to avoid hurting them. If they would only stop and think about what we did and, more importantly, from our obvious position of strength what we did not do, this problem could be solved by—"

"We did nothing wrong that we know of," the other interrupted. "But don't forget that they're a new species. They may view our inaction as a sign of weakness or inability to hurt them, or maybe they just hate us for being here."

"If we could find a way of talking to them," said Prilicla. "If we could just tell them that we don't want to be here, either, that might help."

Fletcher shook its head. "Pathologist Murchison exchanged a few words, nouns, personal names, or whatever with what she called her spider captain, but not enough for the translation computer to do anything with them. And even if we were able to talk to them, that doesn't mean they would believe us.

"I can't help thinking about the bad old xenophobic days on Earth," it went on, "and how we would have reacted towards an apparent invasion from the stars. We would certainly not have tried to talk, or even to think about talking. We would have gathered our forces, as these people seem to be doing, and hit the horrible alien invaders with everything we had."

Prilicla thought for a moment, then said, "The Trolanni began by hating us, especially you druul-like DBDGs, but they got over their phobia after you projected the shortened Federation history lesson into space outside their searchsuit. Tonight why not do the same? The spider ships are sure to have watchkeepers on duty during the night to rouse their crews if anything happens. Make something happen, friend Fletcher."

The captain shook its head, in indecision rather than negation. It said, "The Trolanni had star travel and the advanced technology to support it and were half expecting to meet other star-traveling species. The spiders don't and weren't. They would not understand. We'd probably scare them even more, give them more cause to fear and hate us and, well, we could end up seriously damaging the future philosophical development of their

244 · James White

whole culture. Unless you can get an emotional reading from them to the contrary, first-contact protocol forbids us doing anything like that."

"They are too distant," said Prilicla regretfully, "and there are too many of them emoting at once for that kind of reading. All I can feel from here is a flood of hatred and aversion. If we could entice one or even a few of them closer, their subtler feelings could be analyzed. They will continue to stay away from us until the next attack. During an attack they will not be emoting subtle feelings.

"The ideal solution would be to find a way to make them talk to us," he ended, "and not fight."

"Yes," said the captain, and broke contact.

He joined the rest of the medical team as they were moving the patients' litters onto the beach for their daily supportive medication of fresh air and sunshine. A few minutes he spent hovering above and exchanging a few words with them in turn, beginning with the *Terragar* DBDG amputees before moving to the Trolanni CHLIs to join the quiet conversation they were holding. Keet was well recovered and fully capable of moving around without a litter and meeting the others, but the knowledge that the druul-like healer and patients would not hurt either of them had not yet penetrated to the deeper, emotional levels of its mind, so that it preferred to stay on its litter behind the screens knowing that the other patients could not leave theirs. Jasam was no longer in danger, but it would not help its condition if it was forced into premature visual contact with the other DBDGs. In any case, talking to the patients was not his primary reason for coming outside.

The person who had already spoken with the spiders, he had decided, was the logical one to reopen the conversation.

An hour later, with Prilicla hovering at its shoulder, the pathologist was walking slowly in the direction of the sea and radiating feelings of mild disappointment because it was unable for reasons of personal security to immerse itself. It was carrying a small sheet of plastic that had been rolled, speaking-trumpet–fashion, into a cone because they had agreed that using a mike and *Rhabwar*'s thunderous external loudspeaker would have been unnecessary vocal overkill. He was towing a small float containing the translation-computer terminal.

"I know I exchanged words with that spider captain, if that is what it is," said Murchison as they crossed the line of disturbed sand where the meteorite screen had briefly been switched on, "but only a few nouns and a verb, maybe two, and stopping the others from shooting crossbow bolts at me might not have been an act of friendship. It may not have wanted to waste ammunition in the sea because it was expecting to capture all of us later."

For a moment it radiated minor embarrassment, associated no doubt with a minor infringement of its Earth-human nudity taboo, then went on, "When it saw me I was wearing the only swimsuit I had with me, and this underwear is, well, differently styled and colored. It might not recognize me again. I think you're expecting too much of me, sir."

"Perhaps," he replied, "I'm expecting a miracle. When you are ready, friend Murchison."

They walked and flew for about thirty meters beyond the mark in the sand left by the meteorite shield. If it had been switched on they would have moved freely through it, for it was designed to stop only incoming objects, but they would not have been able to go back again. A few spiders were moving about close to their ships, and two of them were moving back along a ramp they had built between the beach and the wreck of *Terragar*, although what people who knew nothing of metal would think of such a hard, nonorganic structure, was anyone's guess. Prilicla could feel Murchison's irritation at being ignored as it lifted the speaking trumpet to its mouth.

"Krisit," it said, pointing at the nearest spider vessel, then turning to indicate *Rhabwar*. "Preket krisit." It repeated the words several times before pointing at itself and saying several times, "Hukmaki." Finally it pointed towards the spider vessel that had been first to arrive and so presumably contained her spider captain, and shouted, "Krititkukik."

There was no visible reaction, but he could feel the cloud of hostility that was emoting from the ships being laced with eddies of interest and curiosity. On the upperworks of the nearest vessel a spider appeared and began chittering loudly and continuously through its speaking trumpet, which was not directed at them. A party of five spiders assembled around the end of the boarding ramp. Suddenly they came scurrying towards them, unlimbering their crossbows as they came.

"Krititkukik," Murchison shouted again. "Humakik."

"They aren't coming to talk," said Prilicla.

"I don't have to be an empath to know that," Murchison said, radiating the anger of disappointment. "Captain, the shield!"

"Right," said Fletcher, "I'm powering it up for full repulsion in ten seconds from now. You've got that much time to get back across the line or you stay out there with your friends."

Prilicla banked sharply and flew back the way he had come, weaving from side to side as the crossbow bolts whispered past his slowly beating wings. Then he thought that evasive action might not be such a good idea because the spiders were shooting while on the move, which meant that their accuracy would suffer and he might dodge into one of the bolts. He decided to do as Murchison was doing and move straight and fast while giving them a steady target at which to aim and hopefully miss.

They crossed the disturbed line of sand with a full two seconds to spare before the meteorite shield stopped any more bolts from reaching them. The pathologist halted, turned, and for a moment watched the bolts that were heading straight at them bouncing off the shield and falling harmlessly onto the sand. The intensity of the spiders' emotional radiation was such that he was forced to land, shaking uncontrollably. The pathologist raised its speaking trumpet again.

"Don't waste your breath, friend Murchison," he said. "If you speak they will not listen. There are no calm, thinking minds among them. They feel only anger and disappointment, presumably at not being able to harm us, and an intensity of hatred and hostility so great that, that I haven't felt anything like it since the Trolanni reaction when they thought friend Fletcher was a druul. Let's return to our patients."

On their way back Prilicla was walking rather than flying beside Murchison. He saw it looking at his trembling limbs and felt its concern for the empathic pain he was feeling.

"Oh, well," it said, knowing that he knew its feelings and trying to move to a less painful subject, "at least we gave our bored, convalescent patients a little real-life drama to amuse them."

Before he could reply, Fletcher's voice sounded in their headsets.

"There'll be no shortage of drama around here," it said, in the calm voice it had been trained to use while reporting calamitous events. "The six spider vessels nearing the other side of the island will join the three already there within the next hour. An additional six units are hull-up on the horizon on this side, and there are two other three-unit fleets, which according to our wind-strength calculations, won't reach us until early tomorrow. All the indications are that the spiders are mounting a combined land, sea, and air assault. Your patients will have ringside seats."

CHAPTER 31

Neither the Earth-human DGDGs nor the Trolanni CHLIs were feeling worried by the impending attack because both species were star-travelers and were aware of the effectiveness of the meteorite shield. *Terragar's* officers were feeling concern over the fact that the ongoing first contact with the spiders was not going well, but they were not deeply concerned because the ultimate responsibility for its mismanagement was not theirs and in the meantime they were willing to enjoy the spectacle. The feelings of Keet and Jasam were more selfish, radiating as they did intense relief that they were both alive and likely to remain that way, as well as general confusion at the strange things that were happening to and around them. Murchison, Danalta, and Naydrad had their feelings under control. It was the captain, whose voice was being relayed from *Rhabwar's* control deck, who vocalized its worries by telling them not to worry.

"There is no immediate cause for concern," it said. "Our power pile will enable the life support and ship's thrusters to be operated indefinitely; but not so, the tractor-beam units and meteorite protection. In a planetary atmosphere they drain five times the power required for operation in a vacuum, and this ship was designed for speedy casualty retrieval rather than a duration flight."

"You mean," said Naydrad with an impatient ruffling of its fur, "that nobody expected us to be fighting an interspecies war with an ambulance ship. How long have we got?"

"Forty-six hours of full shield deployment," it replied, "after which we'll have to lift out of here, or remain unprotected until someone rescues us. I shall explain the tactical situation as it unfolds...."

But they didn't need the other's continuous evaluation and commentary because they could see everything that was happening for themselves.

The three ships from the other side of the island came into sight, hugging the shoreline and beaching themselves in the spaces between the first three. All six vessels dropped their landing ramps and opened the upper sail-shields where, Prilicla knew from previous observations, the gliders would be launched. There was no other visible activity and very little intership conversation. This was probably due, the captain thought, to all of the battle orders having already being issued so that they were awaiting only the signal to begin. The nearest six-unit fleet, all its sail-shields deployed to catch the wind off the sea, was approaching fast in line-abreast formation. Just above the horizon beyond them, at about fifty degrees lateral separation, two more high-flying gliders were performing signal aerobatics for three more fleets which totaled fifteen units. They were still below the horizon and would not, the captain estimated, arrive until early the next day.

The six latest arrivals found gaps in which to come aground and they, too, closed their sail-shields apart from a few ventilation openings, and lowered their landing ramps. The beach was becoming really crowded, Prilicla thought, so that *Terragar* had disappeared from sight behind a line of giant, greenish-brown molluscs. There came the sound of the senior spiders on each ship using their speaking trumpets, followed by a lengthening silence.

"I don't think we'll see any action today," said the captain.

"Plainly they are waiting for the other fifteen ships to arrive before attacking us. . . . Oops, I stand corrected."

Spiders were crawling down the landing ramps of every ship to begin forming into lines on the dry sand above the water's edge. All of them were armed with crossbows and, in addition, eight of them carried between them what looked like two heavy battering rams with sharply tapering points. Simultaneously gliders were being launched on the seaward side, two from each ship.

They climbed slowly and heavily into the wind off the sea, and only when they made slow, banking turns towards the beach to take advantage of the thermals rising from the hot sand was it possible to see that the gliders carried passengers as well as pilots and that both were armed with crossbows.

The aircraft continued to gain height slowly and steadily while the ground forces deployed three-deep into a crescent formation, with the battering rams placed front and center, before advancing on the med station and watching patients.

The captain's voice returned, giving orders rather than a commentary.

"Dodds," it said briskly, "shoot a couple of flares inland and drag them along the perimeter. The vegetation has dried out since last time so be careful not to start a major fire, just give me a line of burning bushes and smoke. There's no sign of an attack developing from that quarter but I want to put them off the idea in case they burn themselves."

"Sir," said Haslam, "shall I whip up another sandstorm on the beach?"

"Negative," it replied, "there's no point in wasting the power. Last time we didn't want them to hit the meteorite shield, but they found out about it when they were shooting at Murchison and Prilicla. But have your tractors ready just in case. Dr. Prilicla."

"Yes, friend Fletcher," he said.

"There is no risk to your patients out there," it went on, "because there is no way that the spiders can get through our shield, but I don't know what they might do to themselves while they're trying. It could be visually unpleasant, so I advise moving them indoors before . . ."

The captain's next few words were drowned by a wail of protest and accompanying emotional radiation.

"Thank you for the suggestion, friend Fletcher," said Prilicla, "but I am receiving strong vocal and emotional objections from my patients and staff, all of whom would prefer to see the action at first hand."

"Bloodthirsty savages," said the captain dryly, "and I'm not talking about the spiders."

There were twelve ships drawn up along the beach, each one carrying two gliders and a crew complement of anything up to two hundred. The bright yellow sand in front of the station was disappearing under the brownish-green bodies of over two thousand advancing spiders and, if it hadn't been for the knowledge that the meteorite shield made them invulnerable, it would have been a terrifying sight as the spiders halted about fifty meters from the shield and readied their crossbows. Apart from the faint whisper of glider slipstreams as they circled and climbed above the station, there was utter silence. Plainly, all the necessary orders had already been given and they were awaiting only the signal to attack.

"This is stupid," said Murchison from her position among the medical team grouped around and below him. "They aren't going to get anywhere with this attack so why don't they just forget it and go home? After all, we haven't hurt them in any way and we're trying hard not to, but if this foolishness goes on, someone is sure to come to grief."

"We have hurt them, friend Murchison," said Prilicla, "but not physically or in any other way we can understand at present. Maybe we are horrible creatures from the sky, the forerunners of more to come, who are invading their land. That is reason enough, but I have the feeling there is another one. A large number of their people are close enough to give me an emotional reading. For some reason they feel hatred, revulsion, and loathing for us. The feeling is intense and it is shared by all of them."

"I can't believe that, sir," Murchison protested. "When I was taken onto that ship there was physical contact with the spider captain who treated me well, considering the situation. It showed intelligence and intense curiosity. Maybe it was a scientist of some kind with its feelings under strict control. I don't have an empathic faculty like yours, but if it had been feeling hatred and revulsion as well as curiosity I'm sure I would have felt it. My feeling now is that since my escape, we may have done something to make them really hate us."

Before he could reply, Naydrad curved its body into a flat L so that its narrow head was pointing vertically upwards and said, "Even at the beginning of a battle their pilots like to show off. Look at that."

At an altitude of about three hundred meters the gliders that had been climbing singly or in small, random groups above the full width of the beach had come together into a wide, circular formation. For a few moments they circled nose-to-tail like the star performers in an aerial display, then they banked inwards in unison, tightening the circle until they were directly above the med-station buildings and the watchers. The captain's voice returned.

"Nice coordination," it said approvingly, "but I don't think they're showing off. The pilots and passengers are unlimbering their crossbows with the idea, I'd say, of shooting straight down at you. They probably figure that the bolts will have more penetration with the gravity assist of a three-hundred-meter fall. It's a sensible idea but, not knowing how our shield works, completely wrong. . . . Now what the hell are they doing?"

One of the gliders had rolled into a near-vertical bank, tightening its circle and descending, sideslipping off height as it came. It was followed quickly by another three and then suddenly all of the aircraft were spiraling down towards them.

"Oh, no!" said the captain, answering its own question. "Because their crossbow bolts were stopped at ground level, they think the shield is a wall surrounding us instead of a protective hemisphere. They're going to crash into an invisible wall at full . . . Haslam, Dodds, deploy your tractors, wide focus and low power in pressor node. Try not to wreck their gliders, just fend them off before they hit it."

"Sir," Haslam protested, "I need a few seconds to focus on every target. . . ."

"And there are too many targets," Dodds joined in.

"Do what you can—" the captain had time to say before the first glider crashed into the curving invisible surface of the shield.

It looked as if the aircraft had broken up and collapsed into a loose ball of wreckage in midair without any apparent cause. Both occupants were entangled in the structure as it tumbled along the frictionless surface of the shield towards the ground. The second pilot, guessing that some strange weapon was being used against them, banked sharply in an attempt to climb up and away. But one wing struck the shield, crumpled, and its main spar penetrated the fuselage. The aircraft spun heavily into the frictionless surface and the passenger was thrown free before its pilot and the crippled glider began to slip groundwards at an accelerating rate.

"Haslam, Dodds, grab them," said the captain sharply. "Ease them down gently. Right, Doctor?"

"You're reading our minds, friend Fletcher," said Prilicla; then, "Friend Naydrad, instruct . . ."

The fall of the first glider was checked about five meters from the ground and eased down so gently that it barely disturbed the sand, but the second one was caught two meters up so that its speed and impact were only slightly diminished.

". . . Instruct the robots to return all patients to recovery at once," Prilicla went on. For a moment he stared at the semicircle of waiting spiders that had begun to edge closer while he tried to maintain stable hovering flight in spite of the almost physical impact of their emotional hostility. He made a quick, mental calculation and spoke.

"Friend Fletcher," he said, "will you please increase the . . ."

"The diameter of the meteorite shield by, I would estimate, ten metres," the captain broke in. "Am I still reading your mind, Doctor?"

"You are, friend Fletcher," he replied, looking up.

The perfect, circular formation of the attacking gliders had broken up in disorder and the individual aircraft were scattering wildly and trying to regain height, all except two which had collided over an unshielded area of beach. They had each locked one of their wings together so that they were rotating around their common center of gravity and descending in an uncontrolled flat spin. Their rate of descent was fairly slow so that the spiders under them had time to scurry clear of the point of impact. They would hit too far away and there would be too many uninjured and angry spiders in the area between for him to risk extending the shield farther to try for a medical rescue. He hoped their friends would be able to take care of them and relieve his team of the responsibility.

"Prepare for incoming casualties," he said briskly. "Four patients, hostile and noncooperative requiring physical restraint. Physiological classification GKSD with no prior medical data on file. Impact trauma is expected with probable external and internal thoracic damage, extensive limb fracturing, and associated surface lesions. I will assess and assign the treatment priorities. Naydrad, send the antigravity litters and rescue equipment. The rest of you, let's go."

He flew towards the wreckage of the first glider but Murchison, sprinting across the sand on its long, shapely Earth-human legs, reached it seconds before he did. The litter with the rescue gear came a close third.

"Both casualties are deeply unconscious and pose no present danger," he said, "or future danger, provided you get rid of those weapons. Do you need Danalta to assist?"

Murchison shook its head. He could feel its concern for the casualties, its excitement at being presented with a new professional challenge and a flash of anger as it pulled the two crossbows and quivers from the wreckage and threw them with unnecessary force through the one-way protective shield at the surrounding spiders. It said angrily, "For you two bloody idiots the war is over. Sorry, sir, my mind was wandering. These two are badly entangled in wreckage with several limbs trapped, and one thorax has been transfixed by a wing spar. Rather than cut them free here and transfer them to litters, I feel sure that there would be less trauma involved if we lifted them, wreckage and all, with a tractor beam and placed them close to the treatment-bay entrance. That way we'll reduce the risk of compounding their injuries before treatment."

"Your feeling is correct, friend Murchison," he said, flying towards the second wreck. "Do that."

Only the pilot in the second wreck was unconscious while its passenger was radiating anger, fear, and hatred. Suddenly it burst out of the wreckage and aimed its crossbow at him while scurrying rapidly towards the station entrance. Prilicla flew high and took vigorous evasive action while Danalta interposed its virtually indestructible body to protect him, then extruded the limbs necessary to give chase and disarm the fast-moving spider. But even a shape-changer of Danalta's ability needed a few moments to change shape, and the spider was more than halfway to the open entrance of the treatment room where Murchison and Naydrad were attending to the casualties in the pile of wreckage that had been the first glider. Ignoring the DBDG and CHLI patients still waiting to be moved indoors, it was heading straight for the medical-team members, its crossbow cocked and aimed.

Suddenly it was rammed into the ground, skidding to a halt in the sand and lying motionless, as a tractor beam in pressor mode held it as if under a heavy glass plate to the ground.

"Sorry about that," said Haslam, "I had to be fast rather than gentle. Let me know when you want me to release it."

Murchison ran towards it and stopped just outside the pressor field and bent forward for a closer look as Danalta arrived.

"You damn near squashed it flat, Lieutenant," it said a moment later. "Release it now. There are no limb fractures that I can see, but there is evidence of overall pressure trauma, asphyxiation, and it may already be unconscious. . . ."

"It is," said Prilicla as he flew closer, "but not deeply."

"Right," Murchison went on. "Danalta, lose its weapon and help me transfer it to a litter, under restraint. Naydrad, help me untangle the other two from this wreckage."

A few minutes later Danalta and himself were back at the other wreck. The thoracic injuries caused by the penetration of the wing spar appeared to be life-threatening but its emotional radiation was not characteristic of an imminent termination. With very little help from Prilicla's fragile limbs and pitifully weak muscles, the shape-changer extricated the pilot and transferred it, also under precautionary restraint, to the waiting litter. By that time all of the other patients had been moved indoors.

". . . Based on the actions of your lone hero," the captain was saying on the treatment-room communicator as they entered, "their attack strategy is plain. Deciding that they couldn't get through what they thought was a protective wall, and knowing from previous reconnaissance flights that there weren't many of us, they decided to go over the wall and land an airborne force to kill us before destroying the controls for the wall, except that it wasn't a wall. Considering their incomplete information, it was a neat plan. . . ."

"Our hero is regaining consciousness," Murchison broke in. "Naydrad, hold its torso still so I can scan it."

Prilicla flew nearer and tried hard to project feelings of comfort and reassurance at the returning consciousness. But it was so terrified and confused by its surroundings, and emoting the dread characteristic of an entity expecting the worst of all possible fates, that he could not reach it.

He glanced back through one of the room's big windows at

the spider horde beyond the shield, then up at the circling gliders as he felt the waves of hatred beating in on him. If those feelings weren't rooted in pure xenophobia then something the med team was doing or perhaps not doing was being badly misunderstood because the spiders' hatred and loathing was mounting steadily in intensity. But how could he explain a misunderstanding in the middle of a battle when all he could do was feel but not speak?

War, he thought sadly as he looked down at the terrified casualty, was composed mostly of hatred and heroism, both of them misplaced.

CHAPTER 32

Apart from the glider pilot pierced by the wing spar," Murchison dictated into the recorders as it worked, "the spiders taken from the two wrecks are presenting with multiple limb fractures but, according to my scanner, few of the expected internal injuries. This is due to the fact that their bodies are encased in a tough but flexible exoskeleton which bends rather than breaks. Three of them display physical damage which, in a previously known physiological type, is a condition which would be considered serious but not critical. One of these, the spider who tried to attack the station singlehanded, if that's the right word, got squashed by the pressor beam and sustained anoxia and minor limb deformation. Both of these conditions are treatable by temporary supportive splinting and a period of rest, so by rights it should go to the end of the line. But these are new life-forms to us and that is the reason why, with Dr. Prilicla's permission, I propose using the fourth and least damaged casualty as a medical benchmark for its more seriously injured colleagues."

It broke off to look searchingly at Prilicla before going on. "The mental condition of the fourth casualty must be causing severe emotional distress to Dr. Prilicla, perhaps of an intensity that could affect its work. For that reason I propose to render the fourth casualty unconscious before proceeding with . . ."

"Can that be done safely?" Prilicla broke in.

"I believe so, sir," it replied. "We know from experience that the metabolism, brain structure, and associated nerve and sensory networks of insectoid life-forms have much in common, as has the painkilling and anesthetic medication used on them. Graduated and increasing doses will be administered to Spider Patient Four and the effects noted and calibrated for use on the others."

"Proceed, friend Murchison," he said, "and thank you."

Gradually the close-range source of hatred, fear, and revulsion that was Spider Patient Four died away to become the mild radiation signature characteristic of a mind that was no longer capable of a sentient or sapient response. Strangely, the emotional radiation emanating from the multitude of more distant sources was also diminishing. The voice of the captain on their communicator gave the reason.

"The sun is going down and the spider ground forces are withdrawing to their ships," it said, and Prilicla could feel its pleasure and relief, "as are all of the gliders. The attack is over for now. We'll remain alert for any hostile night activity and kill the meteorite shield to conserve power."

"Next," said Naydrad, ruffling its fur irritably, "it will want us to operate by candlelight."

"Spider Patient Four appears to be deeply unconscious," said Murchison, ignoring the remark, "and there are no indications suggesting a physiological rejection of the anesthetic. Do you detect any emotional radiation to the contrary, sir?"

"I do not, friend Murchison," said Prilicla. "Now let us proceed at once with the patient who is most grievously ill. Friend Naydrad, is Spider One ready for us?"

"As ready as it will ever be," the nurse replied with another impatient tufting of its fur. "I have immobilized the patient on its undamaged side but otherwise have done nothing. Carpentry was not included in my medical training."

Nor in mine, thought Prilicla. He led the way towards the

glider pilot's operating frame and projected reassurance as he said, "The accurate cutting, smoothing, and extraction of splintered wood from the deeply perforated carapace of the patient and the rebuilding of the damaged exoskeleton and limbs are, to my mind, a form of carpentry in that initially we shall be cutting wood. Let us begin."

The impact that had torn the wing spar loose at its fuselage attachment point had also driven it transversely into the pilot's underbelly and upwards until it had penetrated the inner surface of the being's thick, leathery carapace, where it emerged for a few inches beyond it. But that natural body-armor had resisted penetration to the extent that it had caused the structural member to bend and break in a classic example of a greenstick fracture inside the abdominal contents, and removing the broken-but-still-joined spar, including the splinters and pieces of binding cord, adhesive material, and tattered wing fabric still attached to it, could cause more damage than that inflicted by the original entry wound.

The few inches of spar projecting through the hole it had made in the carapace, they left until later. The earlier scanner examination had shown that the wooden member was pressed so tightly into the surrounding tissues that it had sealed off most of the damaged blood vessels and reduced the bleeding in the area. That section of spar could safely be left in place for the time being while the more urgent repair work in the abdominal area was attempted.

Prilicla began by surgically enlarging the entry wound to give Danalta and himself more space to work, since speed rather than minimal surgery was required here. Carefully he slid a fine laser knife with an angled blade focus along the spar to the point where it had fractured and bent. There was a brief puff of vapor as he cut it in two and the small quantity of wood, spider blood, and body fluid in the area dried up or boiled away.

"Naydrad," said Prilicla, "withdraw the spar smoothly along the original angle of entry and apply suction where I indicate.

Danalta, be ready to help me control the bleeding and subsequent repairs. Murchison, remove foreign material from the lost blood and retain it for possible reuse. . . ."

There were a large number of spiders around, he thought, but he was not in a position to ask for volunteer blood donors.

". . . We will ignore any loose splinters for now," he went on, "and tidy up later. But Murchison, keep track of them in case they find a way into the circulatory system. Gently, Naydrad, begin the withdrawal."

Before the section of spar had been pulled free of the wound, Murchison's scanner was showing copious bleeding from two of the major blood vessels that it had been compressing.

He said quickly, "Naydrad, suction, let's see what we're doing. Danalta, clamp off the bleeders while I go after the the torn section of bowel. Murchison, enlarge the image of the operative field by four, and hold it as steady as you can."

Danalta was waiting with a blocky hand resting against one of the operating-frame supports to steady it, and with two long, pencil-thin fingers already extruded. When the digits reached the severed blood vessels they divided in half and each one grew two wide, wafer-thin spatulate tips which wrapped themselves gently around two veins above and below the tears and tightened until the blood diminished to a trickle and stopped. Prilicla inserted his own long, featherlike digits into the wound and isolated and tied off the torn length of bowel in a more orthodox fashion with running sutures.

"The tearing is too irregular and widespread for us to attempt a dependable, long-term repair," he said, "so we'll have to do a resection after completely removing the affected length. But not too much of it. The digestive and waste-elimination system in this species has a lesser redundancy of internal tubing than have our Earth-human and Kelgian friends. Naydrad, be ready with a sterile biodegradable sleeve with a fifty-day dissolution period. By that time, judging by our patient's basal metabolism, healing should be complete. Friend Murchison?"

"I agree," it said, radiating controlled concern. "But, sir, can I make a suggestion? Two, in fact. One is that we don't spend too much time on the tidiness of the work. The patient's vital signs, when compared with those of the spiders with minimal injures, are not good. Taking into consideration the severe trauma caused by it being transfixed by that wing spar, the other suggestion is that you do the remaining repair work from your present operating site rather than cutting open a flap of carapace, which would certainly increase the amount and duration of the trauma."

"Very well," he replied and felt her relief, "we'll do it that way."

Even though it was being performed for the first time on a member of a hitherto-unknown species, the procedure was in most respects routine. That was because the other-species Educator tapes that had been impressed on his Cinrusskin mind contained physiological and medical data as well as the surgical knowledge of five other intelligent life-forms—Kelgians, Melfans, Earth-humans, Tralthans, and the light-gravity Eurils—as well as his own. There were only so many ways, in spite of the wide variety of outward physical differences, that the internal plumbing of a warm-blooded oxygen breather could be put right, and he had good second-hand surgical knowledge of most of them. He was relieved to find that the spider physiology shared a few minor similarities with the Kelgian caterpillars and his own Cinrusskin species, but he had to keep searching for others.

Prilicla cringed mentally as he shuffled through the welter of other-species thoughts and impressions that filled his mind with apparently warring alien entities. Without the Educator tape system the practice of all but the simplest forms of other-species surgery and medicine would have been impossible, but the tapes had one serious, psychological disadvantage that barred their use to all but the most stable, adaptable, and, he suspected in his own case, the most cowardly and non-resistant of minds. That was because the tapes did not transfer only the clinical information possessed by the donor minds but their entire personalities, which included all of their pet peeves, phobias, short tempers, and greater or lesser psychological faults as well.

Many times the hospital's diagnosticians as well as his fellow senior physicians had described the process as an experience of multiple schizophrenia viewed from the inside, as the donor entities apparently struggled with the tape recipient for possession of its mind. The effect was purely subjective, naturally, but where mental or physical discomfort was concerned there was no real difference so far as he was concerned. His own method of dealing with the problem, a solution which had sorely perplexed the hospital's department of other-species psychology because most intelligent beings were incapable of acting in such cowardly fashion, had been to offer no resistance at all to the donor mind and to use its information no matter which of them thought they were boss of their mental world.

But in the physical world, while an other-species entity was occupying most of his mind, he had to remember to behave like a weak and incredibly fragile Cinrusskin and, if his donor entity should be a heavy-gravity Hudlar or Tralthan with a body-weight measured in tons, not to throw his non-existent weight around.

Like himself the spiders possessed six legs, but they were much more heavily muscled and he doubted if "cowardice" was in common usage in their vocabularies.

Even with Naydrad pressing down on the remainder of the spar where it projected through the carapace while Danalta and himself drew it out from underneath, the second half of the procedure took longer because the repair work to the lacerated blood vessels in the area, while operationally similar, was both more delicate and more awkwardly situated. But finally it was done, the operative field was cleared of foreign debris and the abdominal wound sutured and a small, sterile plate placed over the exit wound in the carapace. The repair work that remained was urgent and necessary but not life-threatening.

The glider impact had broken three of the patient's limbs,

with one of them sustaining a double fracture that had come close to being a traumatic amputation.

"We have already ascertained," he said with a glance towards Murchison, "that the limbs on this species are exoskeletal and are composed of hardened, organic cylinders with no external sensors or muscle system apart from those serving the digits at the extremities. They use a proprioceptor system which enables the brain to know the exact, three-dimensional position of a limb with respect to the body at any given time, and movement is controlled hydraulically by the increase or reduction of internal fluid. Much of this fluid has been lost because of its injuries, but the supply should be replaced artificially with sterile fluid until it is replaced naturally in the manner of other species who automatically restore blood or other body fluids to the required volume.

"With this patient," he went on, "we will use the accepted procedure for joining exoskeletal fractures and encase them in a rigid collar of the required length. We will begin with the left forward member and ... I'm tired, Murchison, but still operational. Control your feelings, you are emoting like a nagging lifemate!"

The other was radiating concern rather than irritation but it did not reply.

"I'm sorry, friend Murchison," he apologized a moment later, "for my lack of concentration and mental confusion. Certain aspects of the procedure brought my Earth-human and Kelgian tape-donor personalities to the forefront of my mind, and that is not a polite combination."

Murchison laughed quietly and said, "I guessed as much. But look out of the window, it's morning already. This has been a long op and you must be close to the limits of your endurance. With the experience we've already gained on this one, treating its limb fractures and the superficial injuries of the other spider casualties will be simple by comparison. The rest of the cases are non-urgent so that if we do encounter problems, they can wait until you waken. But I'm sure the rest of us can handle them."

"I'm sure you can," said Prilicla, looking at it through a thickening fog of fatigue that was becoming opaque to coherent thought. "But there is something about this one that concerns me, subtle differences in the external and internal body structure from that of your benchmark patient in recovery. This is a new species to us. The pilot may have sustained impact injuries that at first were not as obvious as physical trauma, deformation, and internal-organ displacement, perhaps, which . . ."

He broke off as Murchison laughed, louder this time, and there was an explosion of amusement from it and the other members of the team that momentarily hid their feelings of concern for himself.

"Perhaps you were concentrating so much on the surgical details," Murchison said, "that you were too busy to notice or identify the differences you mentioned. They are due to the fact that our benchmark patient is a female and this one isn't."

"You are right, I must be tired," he said, joining and adding to their waves of amusement as he flew unsteadily to the large, flat top of an instrument cabinet in a corner of the room and settled onto it. "But I shall observe and try to stay awake until all of our spiders are treated."

He surprised himself by doing just that before his increasing physical and mental fatigue rendered sentience and sapience next to impossible. With all of the spider patients treated and transferred to the recovery room, his last conscious impression was of Murchison standing before the communicator and speaking to the captain.

"I've already tried to talk to one of them," it was saying, "and I'd like to try again using simplified first contact procedure. These people aren't space-travelers so I won't need the complicated Federation historical material used during the Trolanni contact. There's nothing else to do here at the moment except brood about the nasty things that could happen to us. So I want to try talking to them again. What do you think?"

"I think yes, ma'am," Fletcher replied. "Give me half an hour to modify the program, then I'll stand by to advise on its usage. There are eight more spider ships hull-up on the horizon and another twenty on the radar screens but still no activity on the beach. That situation will certainly change before long and the result will be a lot of people, possibly including ourselves, being killed.

"Talking our way out of this trouble," it ended, "is the preferred option."

CHAPTER 33

Prilicla wakened suddenly with the feeling that he had been caught up in a riot. Many strident, other-species word sounds and waves of angry emotional radiation were beating into his mind. Suddenly terrified and still befuddled with sleep, he wondered if the meteorite shield had failed and the spiders were overrunning the station. But then his slowly clearing mind and empathic faculty made him aware that the loudest sounds and strongest feelings were emanating from two principle sources, one of which was long-familiar to him, and both of them were in the adjoining recovery ward.

Not trusting his trembling wings to fly, he walked unsteadily into the other room to find out what was happening.

With the exception of the recently treated and still-unconscious spider pilot and Captain Fletcher, who was staring at the proceedings from the ward communicator screen, everyone in the ward was trying to talk at the same time, so much so that parts of the conversations were lost in the derisive beeping of the ward translator going into overload. Farther down the ward the *Terragar* casualties and Keet were arguing, heatedly but in tones low enough for them to hear the quiet voice of Jasam, who was postoperatively debilitated but recovering well, making a contribution. But most of the vocal and emotional noise was coming from the argument between Murchison and the glider pilot's uninjured passenger.

The spider passenger was *arguing* . . . ?

Surprised but not yet knowing if he should be pleased, he turned up the output volume of his own translator unit and, borrowing a phrase from his Earth-human mind partner that seemed appropriate in the circumstances, said, "Will everyone please shut the hell up?" When the arguments tapered off into silence, he added, "Except you, friend Murchison. The spider passenger's words are being translated. We can talk to and understand each other now, and make peace before anyone else is hurt. This should be the best possible news, but instead it feels as if a war is starting. Explain."

The pathologist inhaled and exhaled slowly as it strove to regain its customary emotional equilibrium before speaking; then it said, "As you know, I'd already learned a few words of their language when I was captured, and with the help of the captain's first-contact material and a lot of sign language, we were able to make ourselves understood to the point where the translation computer could take over and finish the job. We can now talk to each other, and that includes talking with the other patients and staff, but we aren't communicating. It won't believe a damn thing I or anyone else says to it." Murchison spread her arms out horizontally to full extension with the palms of its hands facing each other. "There's a credibility gap this wide."

"I understand," said Prilicla. He began walking towards the disbelieving spider, slowly in case his appearance might frighten it, to stop beside its litter. It was capable of ambulation but was being firmly restrained by webbing for its own as well as for the other patients' protection. Then spreading his wings he took off to maintain a stable hover close to the ceiling where he was sure of getting everyone's attention.

"What the hell are you," said the spider, its chittering speech serving as a background to the accurately translated words, "some kind of performing bloody pet?"

He ignored Naydrad's agitated fur and the choking sounds Murchison was making and replied, "No, I am the entity in charge of the people here." Because the members of his medical team already knew what was required, it was to the Trolanni and Earth-human patients that he went on. "Everyone, please be quiet and, so far as you are able, stop emoting for the next few minutes. I must be free of extraneous emotional interference if I am to obtain an accurate reading of this patient's feelings and the reasons for the hostility the spiders show towards us. . . ."

"I'm not a spider," the patient broke in, "I am Irisik, a Crextic, and a free and intelligent member of the floating clan Sitikis, who will shortly join the other clans in wiping you off the face of our world. And if you don't know the reason for our hostility, then in spite of the strange and wondrous magic you have used against us, you are very stupid."

"Not stupid, just ignorant," said Prilicla, trying to maintain his stable hover in spite of the gale of strong emotion blowing up at him; "but ignorance is a temporary condition that can be relieved by the acquisition of knowledge. You have feelings of fear, anger, intense hatred, and loathing towards us. If you will tell me why you feel this way, I will tell you why there is no reason for the Sitikis to have these feelings. A simple exchange of knowledge about ourselves will solve the problem."

"Your problem, not ours," said Irisik, looking towards the injured glider pilot. "You will satisfy your curiosity regarding your victims as well as your hunger. In the end we will be eaten with the rest of your catch."

"I've told it over and over again that we don't eat people. . . ." Murchison began angrily, then stopped as Prilicla made the Cinrusskin gesture for silence.

"Please," he said. "I want to hear this patient speaking to

me and no one else. Irisik, what makes you think that we eat people?"

Irisik inclined its head, the only part of its body free of the litter restraints, towards Murchison. "This other stupid one," it said, "has been telling me many things, including the lie that it wants us to go on living. That, a sane, adult, reasoning person cannot and will not believe. Don't waste time telling me new and even more fantastic lies. You know the answer to your question, so don't pretend that either one of us is stupid."

Prilicla was silent for a moment. Considering the other's emotional state, and in particular its behavior and verbal coherency in a situation that was unique in its experience and which it fully believed would have only a lethal outcome, he found Irisik's behavior admirable. But not the feelings of solid self-certainty and disbelief that surrounded the creature's mind like a stone wall.

Murchison, he knew, would already have given it a simplified version of the work of the Federation, the Monitor Corps, the hospital, and the special ambulance ship nearby and the duties its crew performed, clearly without success. He thought of explaining that he himself felt only sympathy for its fears which would in a short time be proved groundless. But he felt sure, and his feelings were rarely wrong, that the wall of certainty surrounding the other's beliefs and disbeliefs was impervious to anything he could do or say.

Perhaps the wall could only be demolished from within.

"To the contrary," he continued, "pretend that I and everyone else here is stupid. You are an intelligent, logical being who has good reasons for feeling and believing as you do, so share these reasons with us. Whether you believe what I am telling you now or not, we do not intend to do anything to anyone here, apart from feeding them, for the rest of the day. So if you were to talk about yourself, your world and your people and why you believe the things you do, the day or days will pass for us in an interesting manner. If what you tell us is particularly interesting, it may be that so much time will pass that . . ."

"Shades of Scheherazade," said Murchison quietly.

No doubt it was an obscure reference from something in the pathologist's Earth-human past, but this was not the time to go off on historical tangents. He went on. ". . . that your friends will be able to find a way of rescuing you. There is a saying among our people, Irisik, that while there is life there is hope."

"We have a similar saying," the other said.

"Then talk to us, Irisik," said Prilicla. "Tell us the things you think we already know, and with them the many things that you know we don't know. Is there anything we can do to make you feel more comfortable, apart from letting you go free, before you begin?"

"No," said Irisik. "But how do you know I won't tell you lies, or exaggerate the truth?"

"We won't," Prilicla replied, settling to the ground beside the other's litter. "As strangers we might not be able to tell the difference, but the lies or exaggerated truth will be equally interesting to us. Please go on, and begin with the reason why you think we will eat you."

Irisik was radiating fear, anger, and impatience, but it spent a few moments getting these feelings under control before it spoke.

"You will eat us," it began, "because your actions from the start made it clear that that is why you are here. Piracy and food-gathering raids are well known to us, unfortunately, but they are by other sea clans who are too uncivilized, or too lazy, to fish or practice the arts of plant and animal husbandry and find it easier, like you, to steal rather than to cultivate. We don't know where you came from except that it was somewhere in the sky, but from the first time you were observed by the Crextic who walk the clouds, your intentions were clear. As a precaution they maintained a height too great for them to view your activities in detail, or to see you take our growing food into your great white ship. In fact, many of us could not believe that you could be so short-sighted, stupid, and criminal as to take immature livestock that would rob us not only of the animals, but of the many generations of food beasts that would have followed, but we were shown to be wrong. . . ."

. . . While the living food and fruit was still too immature and small to be seen by the cloud-walkers, Irisik went on to explain, the other strange animals that the strangers used for food had been clearly visible to them. They had observed how these creatures had been tethered to litters, how they had had their walking limbs removed to prevent them from escaping, how they had been exposed to sunlight and been periodically washed in the sea in order to remove wastes and harmful parasites and render them more fit for consumption.

While it had been speaking, Prilicla felt Murchison trying very hard to control its feelings of shock and abhorrence and its vain attempts to maintain silence. He didn't try to stop it speaking because it was wanting to ask the questions that he badly wanted answered himself.

"Some of these are members of our own species," Murchison said, gesturing towards the *Terragar* casualties. "Do you think we would eat them? Would Kritik—I mean Krititkukik—have eaten me?"

"Yes, to both questions," Irisik replied without hesitation. "It is stupid to waste a supply of edible food, regardless of the emotional connections, if any, that one may have with the source. It is not pleasant for the immediate family or friends of the deceased, and many choose to eat only the smallest of morsels and pass the remainder to hungry or needy strangers who have no memories of or emotional ties with the meal. But it must be done if the essence of a beloved parent or siblings is to continue into the future. Plainly it is the same with you people."

Murchison's emotional radiation was so confused that it was

unable to speak. Irisik went on. "Knowing your intentions and reason for being here, we spread the word about you and set about assembling all of the sea clans in this ocean. Some of them are little more than pirates and food robbers like you, and normally we would prefer to shoot our crossbows at them as sky-talk to their ships to ask for their cooperation, but everyone agreed to forget our differences for the present in order to kill the strangers.

"You may think me guilty of exaggeration," it went on, "but I assure you that the Crextic ships already assembled around this island are only a small fraction of those which will arrive within the next few days. In spite of your fire throwers, your invisible weapons that hurl sand and water at us, and your magic shield, we will smother and crush you with our cloud-walkers and surface fighters. The cost to us will be extreme, but we must ensure that no more of your kind are tempted to raid our world.

"And I must correct your mistake," it continued into the shocked silence. "Krititkukik is not a name, it is the title of the leader of our sea clan. It would have eaten your most desirable parts, as is its right, before sharing you with the rest of the crew. Being a sensitive person as well as one who was filled with scientific curiosity, and knowing that you were a strange but intelligent source of food with feelings, it would have concealed from you as long as possible the fact that you were to be eaten. Sometimes I think the Krititkukik lacks the quality of ruthlessness necessary to a leader."

Prilicla caught a brief, complex burst of emotion whose meaning was unmistakable, composed as it was of the strange combination of yearning, tenderness, and a feeling of grief over the impending loss of someone with whom one was deeply and emotionally involved. They were the feelings, he felt sure, of and for a life-mate.

"Believe me," said Prilicla, "you will be together again soon."

"I don't believe you," said Irisik, "or anything else that you or the other meat gatherers say to me."

"I understand," said Prilicla, "so I shall instruct my meat gatherers, as you insist on calling them, not to speak to you at all. You and the other sources of meat may talk to each other if and when either of you wish. The charge nurse will continue to administer food, medication, and to periodically check on your condition and that of the others, but without speaking to you . . ."

"Good," said Naydrad, rippling its fur. "I hate being called a liar, especially when my people don't even know what a lie is."

". . . until, that is," he ended, "you ask to speak to us. All other members of the medical staff including myself will leave you now."

Irisik was radiating surprise, confusion, and uncertainty. It said, "I know you aren't telling the truth, but your lies are interesting and I want to listen to more of them before I am killed. Please stay."

"No," said Prilicla firmly. "Until you believe that you are being told the truth, including the truth that we mean no harm to you, your people, or your world and the animal life here, we will not speak again. And remember, I know exactly how you are feeling about everything from moment to moment, and it is impossible to lie with the emotions. When I feel that you are ready to believe me, I shall speak with you again."

He led Murchison and Danalta into the communications room where Fletcher, displaying the symptoms of Earth-human elevated blood pressure, was glaring at them from the viewscreen. His two assistants were bursting to speak, but the captain got its question in first.

"Doctor," it said, "this is an unnecessary waste of time. I know the feelings of a person of your medical seniority and emotional sensitivity must be hurt at being treated as a liar. You wouldn't be human—I'm sorry, I mean Cinrusskin—if you didn't feel angry about that six-legged doubting Thomas. But I'm sure that with a little more patience and forbearance on your part you will be able to convince it that . . ."

"I know its present feelings, friend Fletcher," Prilicla broke in, "well enough to know that I won't be able to change them. It is a strong-minded, stubborn entity who considers itself to be one of the many victims around it who are shortly to be terminated and eaten. It won't believe us, but hopefully our other so-called victims will be able to disabuse it and the other spider patients of that idea."

"Very quickly, I hope," Fletcher said, its features losing some of their high color. "If there is a sustained attack lasting more than thirty-six hours, the screen will go down. Before then we will have to make a main-drive takeoff and crisp a few hundred spiders. That is not the Federation's idea of making friendly contact with another intelligent, if temporarily misguided, species. All our careers are on the line here, apart from the psychological trauma we'll suffer if things go that badly wrong."

"Yes, friend Fletcher," said Prilicla, feeling the other's tortured, emotional radiation all the way from the ship and trying to do something about it. "But there is a precedent. This is on a smaller, less bloody scale, but remember what happened when Sector General was caught in the middle of the Federation-Etlan War. Due to massive overcrowding the casualties from both sides were treated in the same ward. There is a close similarity to our present situation."

"Is there," said the captain, its mind obviously contemplating a future where all was desolation. Irritably it added, "I wasn't there, Doctor, and it wasn't a war. It was a large-scale police action."

Prilicla well remembered that vicious and incredibly violent battle which had been waged around Sector General, when six of the Federation's sector subfleets including three of its capital ships had opposed a much heavier force from the Etlan Empire, whose ruler had fed his people totally wrong information about the other side. He didn't want to argue with the captain who, like the rest of its Monitor Corps colleagues, were touchy about the fact that their organization comprised the greatest assemblage of military might that the galaxy had ever known.

But Prilicla had been there and it had certainly felt like a war.

CHAPTER 34

The sun shone down on the golden beach, the white, lacy edge of the deep-blue sea, and on the many ships assembling around the island that were continually launching their gliders. Apart from a small working party of spiders who were engaged in transferring odd pieces of *Terragar*'s equipment to the beach, there was no ground activity visible, but the aerial bombardment was unceasing.

Instead of carrying an armed passenger as payload, the gliders were loading up with the equivalent weight in rocks, climbing to an altitude of about two thousand meters and dropping them on the med station. More often than not, their aim was wide of the mark, but on the off-chance that some of those ridiculously unsophisticated missiles would pierce the flimsy structures, injuring or killing the patients or team members inside, the meteorite shield had had to be deployed. Everyone was safe for the time being, but that time was limited.

Another battle, verbal rather than physical, was raging between the spider patients and the other occupants of the recovery ward. Apart from Naydrad, that was, who had turned off its translator and whose fur was moving in gentle, restful waves while it watched the medical monitors in case the various blood pressures rose above acceptable safety limits. And in the communications room yet another and more polite war of words was raging between the other members of the medical team and Captain Fletcher and his crew.

"We can't understand why you're waiting, Doctor," the captain said as it restated the position in unnecessarily simple language for the recorders. "Plainly your idea isn't working. We now have shield power for less than twenty-one hours' duration. With no power to spare for pressor beams to lift us to an area of sea that is clear of ships, it will have to be an environmentally unfriendly takeoff on main thrusters. The vegetation on this half of the island, not to mention the spiders and their ships, will be toast. Go in and explain the scientific facts of life to Irisik and the spider pilot, now that it has regained consciousness. I know this is a hard decision for both of us to make, Doctor, but we can't sacrifice *Rhabwar*'s crew and the Trolanni patients by letting a bunch of misguided spiders overrun and kill us."

It softened its tone, and in spite of the distance separating them, Prilicla could feel the other's determination overriding its reluctance to cause emotional distress to an empathic friend as it went on. "You have the medical rank in the present situation, Doctor, but in this instance I am disputing it. So tell your spider patients, as gently but firmly as you can, that they are not to be eaten but they must leave us and return to their vessels at once before they, and the crews of the ships along the beach, die in the fires we will light during our takeoff. You can move the injured glider pilot in one of your litters, with the power unit and circuitry set for a non-catastrophic self-destruct shortly after they reach their ships. For a pre–space age species they've already been contaminated with too much advanced technology as it is."

"Friend Fletcher," said Prilicla gently, "please don't be feeling so uncomfortable about your threat to depose the senior medical officer during a medical emergency, and do nothing hasty. Irisik is one cynical spider and I have a strong feeling, amounting to a virtual certainty that it wouldn't believe anything I told it, which is why I shall tell it nothing and allow what it thinks are the other sources of food to do the talking. Please wait, watch the ward vision pickup, and listen. . . ."

Naydrad had just finished its round of patient observations and had curled its caterpillar-like body into its relaxer frame in front of the monitor screens when the silence was broken by one of the *Terragar* casualties.

"Charge Nurse," it said, "I'm starving to death."

"Your self-diagnosis is not confirmed by the monitor readings," Naydrad replied. "Considering the fact that your lower ambulatory limbs are missing and your food requirements are proportionately reduced, terminal malnutrition would only occur if fluids as well as food were to be withheld for twenty-plus standard days. Lunch will be in three hours. Until then, compose yourself and try to think beautiful thoughts."

"He can't think beautiful thoughts," another one of the *Terragar* casualties joined in, "and neither can I, because Pathologist Murchison hasn't been in for nearly three days. I like her around even if the spiders are keeping her from dunking us in the ocean . . ."

The other Earth-human patients radiated feelings of approval and minor disappointment while making whistling sounds that did not translate.

". . . but why," it ended, "won't she come in and talk to us?"

Unable to lie, Naydrad elected to remain silent.

"Among my people," said Irisik, speaking for the first time that day, "it is considered socially indelicate, unless the entity concerned is a close family relation or a loved one, to hold a lengthy conversation with what is in effect one's next meal. To do such a thing would unsettle the emotions as well as the digestion, and this one is delicate in its handling of your feelings. After all, your two walking limbs are missing and yet you feel no hostility towards it, the person who ate them. Or is it a religious thing with you, and you know that the food you contribute in this way enables part of your being to survive into the indefinite future?"

"No!" said the *Terragar* casualty, radiating irritation and impatience. "It isn't religious. She doesn't eat intelligent entities. . . ."

"But all living creatures have intelligence," Irisik broke in. "Are you saying that it eats only vegetation?"

"No," said the other. "Meat is eaten, not frequently, and only when it originates from beings of very low intelligence."

"Like you?" asked Irisik in a disparaging voice. After a moment, it went on. "But who sets the level of intelligence for edibility? You yourself do not appear to be of very low intelligence, so I suspect that a process of mental persuasion, perhaps reinforced by the use of mind-altering poisons rather than a spiritual belief in survival after death, is used to hide from you your status as a food animal. The mental persuasion must be both subtle and strong if it can make you, an apparently young and healthy person whose body has already been partially eaten, argue on behalf of your eater.

"My own mind," it added, "would not be so easily influenced, especially by another member of my own species."

"But my legs weren't eaten, dammit," the other replied. "They were cooked, maybe, but definitely not eaten. I was there and remember exactly what happened to them."

"They might look like outsized druuls," said Keet, joining the conversation, "but we know that they don't eat people, they repair them."

"Or perhaps you only believe that you know what happened," Irisik went on, "because mental influence or chemicals have been used to influence you into thinking that way. It is natural among civilized beings to conceal the true facts from their prey so that they will not dwell unnecessarily on their fate, and remain content until the ultimate moment." It swiveled its head towards the Trolanni patient. "Food appearance and presentation are important. Repairing its wounds, so as to avoid the possibility of a premature death, is a sensible course if the food is to live and remain fresh until the time for consumption arrives.

There is no reason why living food should be made to suffer unnecessarily."

Prilicla felt a brief eruption of fear and uncertainty from the two Trolanni which they controlled and negated within a few seconds. From its litter, Jasam said weakly, "When a bunch of outsized druuls tried to tether and board our searchsuit, we had the same idea. But the others who came along later placed themselves in great personal danger while retrieving the first group and learning to communicate with us and repairing our injuries. Plainly they were taking far too much trouble, when we had time to think about it, for a very meager addition to their food supply. As a species we are deeply frightened about our future survival, and these druul-like creatures and the others from their two ships have promised to help us to solve your problems, but we have no fears regarding our survival as individuals. Neither should you."

Irisik paused before replying. "You say that you and your captors have walked the web between the stars, in ships with structures so hard that they have been neither woven nor grown, and that you have the knowledge to make and use many wondrous tools to build and repair these vessels and the sailors who fly in them. By your standards we Crextic are not educated. But I know the difference between education and intelligence and, with respect, an educated person can also be gullible."

Keet lost its patience. "I know that skepticism is supposed to be a sign of intelligence, but this is ridiculous. You are a seagoing spider who disbelieves people who have sailed among the stars. It's a waste of time trying to make you see sense because you probably haven't got any. Your mind is tightly closed."

The growing irritation and impatience from both Trolanni did not quite blot out the quieter, more complex emotional radiation coming from Irisik. The Crextic's mind was beginning to suffer from the first stirrings of self-doubt.

For an instant Prilicla wondered if he should go in and join the conversation, then decided against it. A phrase used by Chief

Dietitian Gurronsevas back at the hospital came to him, regarding the preparation of food. He would let Irisik stew in its own juices for a while. He could feel growing uncertainty and a need to ask questions, but decided to wait for Irisik to voice them.

Keet left its litter and and moved quickly to the row of the *Terragar* casualties.

"There is something that Jasam and I must say to you," it began. "It is an apology for the way that our searchsuit defense systems caused you to be burned and lose limbs. We could not believe that anyone who looked like a druul could want only to help us, but we were wrong. We ask your forgiveness and, if and when we return to Trolann, we offer help with the replacement of the burned limbs. Our technology on the interfacing of organic and inorganic materials is advanced. Your metal limbs would be linked to the relevant nerve connections to produce the sensations of pressure, touch, and temperature you knew in the past, although possibly not with the former degree of sensitivity, and be visually indistinguishable from the missing ones. Your fellow officers on *Rhabwar*, who have had firsthand experience of our searchsuit technology, will confirm this. Unless you have psychological or religious objections to . . ."

"We haven't," said one of the casualties.

"Could they be made four or five inches longer than the old ones?" asked another, and explained, "I've always wanted to be tall as well as handsome."

The third made a derogatory sound that did not translate, and gradually the conversation became increasingly general, serious, and animated as Keet, Jasam, and the *Terragar* casualties talked about their respective futures.

When Irisik tried to join in, it was pointedly ignored. Its emotional radiation, Prilicla noted with satisfaction, was revealing a strange mixture of growing indecision and increasing certainty.

". . . I know that the druul are not nice people," one of the *Terragar* casualties was saying, "but the Federation won't . . ."

"Not nice?" Keet broke in. "They are vicious, cunning, implacable, depraved vermin who want only to kill and, if possible, eat, everyone and everything who is not a druul. And they have been known to eat their own casualties rather than waste time and resources in treating them. They should be wiped out, exterminated down to the last member of their merciless and murderous species."

". . . As I was saying," the Earth-human went on, "the Federation will not instruct its Monitor Corps to exterminate a whole species just on your say-so, and they know that we wouldn't do it if they did. That would make us as uncivilized and savage as you say they are. Instead they will investigate the druul and—"

"Maybe you have sympathy, a fellow feeling towards them," Jasam broke in, radiating sudden suspicion, "because they look so very much like you. People can give sympathy, kindness, and even affection towards pets or dolls or smaller editions of themselves. Until they turn vicious which, believe me, they will."

"I do believe you," said the other, "but we're talking about an intelligent species here. We have no right to destroy them. The Federation will subject them to a covert sociological and psychological assessment. If they are as blindly antisocial as you say, they will almost certainly be isolated on their home planet to survive as best they can, fight each other to mutual extinction, or demonstrate to us over a lengthy period that they have learned sense and are on the way to true civilization, in which case we would help them as we are planning to help you."

The two Trolanni were silent, angry, and disappointed, but their more subtle feelings were rendered unreadable because of the buildup of emotional radiation coming from Irisik. But it, too, remained silent as the Monitor Corps officer continued speaking.

"Your people will also be assessed," it went on, "but as a technologically advanced star-traveling species, that will be a formality. Over the past century we have discovered several planets, as fresh and clean and unpolluted as this one and without indigenous intelligent life, that would suit your requirements. Considering the relatively few Trolanni remaining on your dying home world, transportation for yourselves, and your personal possessions and technical support hardware, would be no problem. . . ."

Feelings of pride and enthusiasm suffused the words like a bright, emotional fog as it went on. ". . . We have Emperor-class capital ships—technically, vessels of war although they haven't been used as such since the Etlan police action. Their beam weapons will clear large areas of ground for building and cultivation, and colonization transports and specialist officers to advise on moving your population to a new, clean world. We will help you while you are getting established, but not too much because taking over the responsibility completely would be psychologically undesirable. You might become overly dependent on us rather than independent. That's an important part of the Federation's first-contact philosophy. And you can forget about the druul. Unless they begin to show evidence of civilized behavior they won't be going anywhere."

"But wait," said Jasam, radiating sudden worry. "You're talking about moving a planetary population. You will need very big ships."

"Don't worry," said the other, "we have big ships."

While they had been speaking, the pressure of Irisik's emotional radiation had been building up to the point where angry words would be its only release. Prilicla knew to the split second when it would speak.

"You are talking and behaving as if I am not here," it said furiously. "It is not easy for me to say this, for I am a person of rank and influence among my fishing clan, but there is a possibility that I have misunderstood the situation and I wish to speak to all of you about that."

"They may not wish to speak to you," said Naydrad, breaking its long silence, "or even listen to you."

The Crextic glider pilot, who was still post-operatively debilitated from its recent major surgery but was otherwise recovering well, spoke for the first time.

Slowly and weakly it said, "Irisik is the mate of our clan's Krititkukik, our senior captain and fleet commodore. As such she is rarely placed in a position where it is necessary for her to apologize for anything, but she is trying to do so now. She is an independent, strong-willed, intelligent, and abrasive person who must be finding the process of apologizing very difficult."

"Cloud-walker," said Irisik sharply, "your tone lacks respect. Be quiet or, or I'll bite your head off."

"Promises," said the pilot softly.

Prilicla concurred. Judging by Irisik's emotional radiation it was finding it very difficult to apologize, but not impossible. Now was the time for him to rejoin them and, so far as the Crextic patients were concerned, start laying down Federation law and telling them the unpleasant truth—possibly more unpleasant than their earlier personal fear of being eaten—about their present situation. But the spider had come to a crucial decision, and from the dialogue that was developing and the accompanying emotional radiation, Prilicla knew what it was. He was flying slowly and happily into the recovery ward when the captain spoke urgently from the communicator.

"Doctor," it said, "the heavies have arrived. Three Monitor Corps cruisers, the cultural contact vessel *Descartes* and Sector Marshal Dermod's flagship *Vespasian*, no less. He has been appraised of our situation but says, regrettable as it is, that we must not risk jeopardizing the successful Trolanni contact by allowing them and our other casualties to be killed due to our bungled contact with the Crextic. The sector marshal says we must on no account sacrifice our own people and two members of an intelligent, star-traveling species. It says that it was a difficult decision but he had to make it. We are ordered to move all casualties to *Rhabwar*, warn off the spiders, and take off forthwith."

Prilicla's flight path wavered for a moment, then steadied as

286 · James White

he said, "Right now that would be very inconvenient, friend Fletcher. Please tell the sector marshal that our second contact with the Crextic is ongoing and at a delicate stage which must not be interrupted by a hasty evacuation, and remind it that this is predominantly a medical emergency, with all that implies."

"But, but you can't say that, dammit," the captain burst out. "Not to a sector marshal!"

"Be diplomatic," said Prilicla, resuming his flight.

CHAPTER 35

Prilicla flew into the recovery ward and hovered above and between the lines of patients. He was noticed but ignored. Considering the conversation that was taking place between Irisik and Keet he could live with the delay, for a while.

"... It seems that I have been completely wrong in my assessment of this situation," Irisik was saying, "and when they learn about it the Crextic will be grateful for the healing that was done for us here. But these healers are strange creatures, not unfriendly but still frightening. I don't know how long it would take, if ever, for us to come to like them...."

"Dr. Prilicla," the captain broke in. "The sector marshal rejects your suggestion and orders an immediate return of the medical team and casualties to *Rhabwar*. We can warn the Crextic to move clear before taking off, and hope they heed the warning. I'm sorry, Doctor. Start evacuating your casualties at once."

"Friend Fletcher," said Prilicla, "please ask the ..." At that point one of his Educator tape donors, a straight-talking Kelgian, slipped suddenly to the forefront of his mind and he ended, "We've begun to make good progress here, so tell Sector Marshal Dermod to stay the hell out of my fur!"

"... You've said that your home world is poisoned and dying and that there aren't many Trolanni left on it," Irisik was saying. "Here there are many islands, particularly those close to the polar continents where high seas and treacherous currents make them dangerous for plant and animal cultivation but which you, with your greater knowledge and machines, could use. So why go to another and perhaps less suitable world when you would be welcomed here?

"You bear a closer physical resemblance to the Crextic than these others," it went on, "so that even the most intellectually timid among us would have no difficulty in accepting you as strange but helpful neighbors. You Trolanni would be too few in numbers to threaten us and your knowledge is too valuable for us to waste it by hurting you. . . ."

"That," said one of the *Terragar* casualties, using one of its obscure Earth-human sayings, "would be like killing the geese that lay golden eggs."

Prilicla was well pleased at the way things were going, but it was a time to be tough and, to use another Earth-human expression, tell the Crextic a few home truths.

". . . If you have an ethical problem with this," Irisik continued, "as we would have if the positions were reversed, think of it as paying ground rent, or a simple exchange of knowledge for a peaceful and pleasant living space. In time we would learn fully to understand and trust each other, and in more time you could show us how to harvest the metals that you have said lie deep beneath our surface, and work them into machines which will enable the Crextic one day, as these others do, to walk the web between the stars. . . ."

"Doctor!" the captain's voice broke in urgently. "Look at your ward repeater screen. All the Crextic vessels are launching their gliders and ground forces. Get your med team and casualties back to to *Rhabwar*. Now, Doctor."

Prilicla looked at the repeater screen which showed spiders pouring out of the nearer ships and forming up on the beach while their gliders were moving in thermal-seeking circles above the hot sand as they strove for height. He felt sure, but not very sure, that the Crextic would wait until more force arrived and that an attack wasn't imminent.

"Friend Fletcher," he said, "if you've been listening you'll know that we are making good progress . . ."

"Not to all of it," the captain broke in. "We're too busy here readying the ship for a hot blastoff. But everything said was and is being relayed to *Vespasian*. We've no time to retrieve the buildings and non-portable equipment, so just get your people out of there."

". . . and it would be a major crime to throw it away," Prilicla continued, as if the other had not spoken. "Neither, I feel sure, would it favorably impress our Trolanni friends if we were to burn all the nearby Crextic ships and many hundreds of sailors just to save the lives of a few patients and medical staff."

"So we *are* to be killed—" Irisik began, its anger and disappointment outweighing its personal fear. "You lied to us."

". . . You will now have realized, friend Fletcher, that the ward translator is on and our conversation is open," he said, then continued briskly. "Naydrad, use the robots to help you move the Trolanni and Earth-human casualties to *Rhabwar*. Please link my translator to the ship's external speaker system. The Crextic patients and I are going out and will try to talk some sense into their Krititkukik. Murchison, Danalta, set the other Crextic litters and restraints for remote control and quick release on my command, then assist Naydrad with the other patient transfers."

"No, sir," said Murchison, radiating feelings that were a strange combination of affection, respect, and downright mutiny. It glanced towards the shape-changer who twitched its upper body in assent, and added, "We are staying with you."

"As will I," said Keet.

He knew from the intensity of their emotional radiation that he could not make them change their minds. There were occasions, he thought gratefully, when insubordination had its place. It was obvious that the captain thought otherwise and was voicing its feelings without the usual verbal niceties.

"Are you losing your mind entirely, Doctor?" it said angrily. "And have you no control at all over your medical staff? Explain our situation to your spider patients, urge them to pass it on to their friends, and tell them that they will all die if they don't move away fast. And don't dare go outside. The meteorite shield has been withdrawn to support the launch system. . . ."

Prilicla turned down the volume on his headset and addressed the Crextics.

"We have no intention of eating or harming any of you," he said while the irate voice of the captain muttered in the background, "and you have a choice. You are free to go with the other casualties to the safety of our ship. Or leave here now with me, to rejoin your friends and help me convince them that I am telling the truth. If we can't do that, then we and many hundreds of them will be burned to death.

"The next attack is about to begin so there isn't much time to stop it," he went on as he took control of the spider pilot's litter. "I am asking for an immediate meeting with your Krititkukik and will explain the situation to you as we move outside. . . ."

Although the preparations for the attack were continuing, the Krititkukik came out to meet them without hesitation. It was a responsible commander, Irisik insisted, who preferred to win a battle with the minimum possible butcher's bill. But it was still at a distance when the pathologist drew his attention to a difference in its appearance. A tubular collar into which variously-colored twigs and vegetation had been woven was encircling its long, thin neck.

"It wasn't wearing that when I met it on its ship," said Murchison. "Is it an insignia of rank?"

"No," said Irisik.

The spider's emotional radiation was far from unpleasant but it was so intense, poignant, and deeply personal that it made Prilicla waver in flight. Similar feelings were reaching him from the approaching Krititkukik. Considering the intimate nature of those feelings, he did not expect Irisik to elaborate, but it did.

"It is the Collar of First Mating," it said through a surge of emotion, "worn by the male as self-protection and as a compliment to his partner's sexual ardor which could and might be aroused to the point where the female loses control and bites off her mate's head. There have been no cases reported for many centuries, and now it is worn only twice. On the night of first mating as a promise of the life of loving to come, and when the life of one aged partner or the other is about to end in gratitude for the life and loving that has gone before."

The effect of its words on the females Murchison and Keet, and on the male subject of the discussion, Krititkukik, forced Prilicla to drop to the sand before he was forced to make an undignified crash-landing. Again, as he had done in the ward, he allowed Irisik and Keet, with a little help from the recuperating glider pilot and the other two Crextic casualties, to make the conversation run while he monitored the emotional radiation of all concerned.

The Krititkukik was a highly intelligent being whose credence was not won easily, but when it was an equally intelligent and much-loved life-mate who was leading the attack on the basis of all its hard-held beliefs, the battle, although lengthy, was lost from the start.

Finally it said, "Suppose I believe you, Irisik, which is what I would like to do; the sailors of the other Krititkukikii assembled on and around this island may not. They want to kill the strangers, no matter what the cost, to keep more of them from coming and eating our people. . . ."

"You saw what happened to me when I crashed into their invisible shield," the glider pilot broke in. "They don't eat people, they make them well again. Look at what they did for me."

"We made the same mistake at first," Keet joined in, "when the strangers tried to help rescue us from our wrecked ship. But they healed my life-mate, who was in a much worse condition than your glider pilot, and now both of them will live. And we certainly don't want to eat spiders. Irisik has invited the few of my species who are left to join you on your beautiful, unspoiled world, and in return we will teach you, in the years or the centuries to come, how to leave it and walk the star web that connects it to the other worlds, in peace and prosperity. . . ."

"Yes, yes," said the Krititkukik, its level of resistance dropping but not quite to zero. "Irisik and you and the tall, soft, lumpy one who escaped from my ship have already told me all of this, many times. But it is like a story told to please young children, full of good things that are not real. And like children you have tried to frighten us with threats of a great fire when your ship lifts into the sky if we do not behave. Why should we believe you? You have helped a few of my people, including my life-mate, and promised great things for the future, and threatened much death and devastation now when your great ship with its invisible shields rises into the sky, but the strangers face no punishment for not telling us the truth and risk nothing and . . ."

"We risk our lives," said Prilicla, breaking in gently. He indicated the disturbance in the sand that had shown the surface limits of the meteorite shield and went on, "We no longer have protection. You can kill us now and we could do nothing to stop you. But if you don't call off your attack we will be burned to death with all of your people on this beach. Think about that, Krititkukik, and about the reasons we have given you for this risk we are taking, and believe what we say."

Prilicla could feel the other's growing uncertainty, but there was no indication of immediate hostile action being planned. He went on. "Why don't you test the truth of what I'm saying with your weapon?"

"Doctor, this is madness!" Fletcher's broke in. The other must have been shouting for its voice to sound so loud, considering the reduced gain on Prilicla's headset. "I'm going to pull you in with tractor beams before you get everyone killed. I mean all of you, including the Crextic casualties—that way we can save a few of them though they probably won't love us for it. . . ." Its tone, although still loud, softened a little. ". . . The transfer will be sudden, and will be very rough on you physically, Doctor, but you are, after all, heading back to the best hospital in the galaxy for treatment. . . ."

It broke off again as a more authoritative but quieter voice— too quiet for Prilicla to distinguish the individual words—broke in, then the captain went on. "Sir? But, but you can see that an attack is developing as we speak. I understand, sir. No action on my part unless expressly ordered by you."

Prilicla didn't ask for clarification because the situation around him was at too delicate a stage. He felt the sudden agitation of Keet and the medical-team members as the Krititkukik unlimbered its crossbow and loosed a single bolt, which flew through the intervening space unhindered until it clattered against the wall of the med station and fell onto the sand. The crossbow was replaced and it raised its speaking trumpet. First it spoke to the gliders circling above them, then to the sailors assembling on the beach. But this time their translators were online so that they could understand as well as hear everything it was saying.

All of the Crextic ground forces and gliders were being ordered to cease offensive actions and return without delay to their ships, with the exception of one aircraft which was instructed to gain altitude so that it could perform the signal aerobatic that would transmit the same message to the more distant ships and aircraft. The relief of the people all around bathed Prilicla in a bonfire glow of friendship and warmth, but again there was one exception.

"There is disagreement," the Krititkukik said. "More than a quarter of the Crextic assembled here are little more than pirates, violent, unsubtle people with whom we normally would have no dealings. But they are influencing the others. In an effort to convince them of your good feelings for all of the Crextic, I told them that your ship was defenseless, but that if they attacked and forced it to leave, it would kill many hundreds of us as it went. The cloud-walkers' signals are of necessity short, simple, and incapable of carrying closely reasoned arguments. This uncivilized element disbelieves me and they intend to press home their attack, very soon."

With its words the bright, warm emotional cloud of pleasure and relief coming from the people surrounding him congealed suddenly into a dark, icy cloud of fear and angry disappointment. For the first time in his life, Prilicla could think of nothing that he could say that would help relieve their emotional distress. Even though it must have heard the Kritikukik's words on *Rhabwar's* aural sensors, friend Fletcher, too, was silent or at a loss for words.

But the silence was not complete. There was a faint growling sound, so deep that was felt in the bones as well as being heard through the ears, that seemed to be coming from everywhere and nowhere. From the top of its shapeless body Danalta extruded an ear that resembled a fleshy dish-antenna, and shortly afterwards grew a hand with one upwardly-pointing digit. They followed its direction and looked up.

Vespasian was making a slow and increasingly thunderous approach.

The Monitor Corps' Emperor-class battleships were unable to land on a planetary surface because of the complex antennae, weapon mounts, and other structural projections sprouting from a hull so vast that, even at an altitude of several miles it looked like another shining metal island, except this island was floating on its four ravening underjets. Looking tiny beside the vast capital ship, its escort of three cruisers traced wide, fiery circles around it, their thunder sounding falsetto by comparison.

Ponderously avoiding the spider ships in the area, *Vespasian* closed on the bay and dropped to less than one thousand meters' altitude, its underjets exploding the surface of the sea into dazzling white clouds of steam that boiled upwards to almost obscure its vast underside and making it seem that it was riding on self-generated clouds.

For a few moments it hung there, the incredibly loud, hissing thunder making it impossible for anyone to hear themselves or anyone else speak. Then it withdrew, again avoiding the spider ships in the area as it began a rapid ascent spacewards, accompanied by its cruiser escorts. When the noise reduced to something less than deafening, a new voice sounded over *Rhabwar*'s external speakers.

It said, "Dr. Prilicla, Sector Marshal Dermod. I have found that a prior show of police force can often avert a riot by forcing the rioters to calm down and see sense. I am now returning my ships to orbit and withdrawing their sound pollution so as to give everyone down there a chance to talk together which, with your help and a little more of your creative insubordination, I'm sure they will.

"You have done very well, Dr. Prilicla," it ended. "Very well indeed."

CHAPTER 36

By the evening of the following day, the majority of the Crextic vessels had withdrawn from the island to return to their various homelands, the exceptions being the flagships of the Krititkukikii from every clan fleet, and their advisors. During the days and weeks that followed, many gliders were continually airborne, flying at the cold, upper limits of their operational capability as they signaled the results of the talks that were going on in what had been the medical station, to the other relay gliders farther afield.

There was plenty going on, although the negotiations between the Federation's cultural-contact specialists from *Descartes* and the Crextic representatives—but strangely, not with the Trolanni, whom the spiders considered their new friends—as often as not, resembled non-violent riots. But one of Sector Marshal Dermod's cruisers kept station on the island, maintaining a distance and altitude that would not inconvenience the signaling gliders.

Only once, when it seemed that the negotiations might degenerate into physical violence, did the sector marshal order it to make a low pass over the medical station, to remind anyone who might be thinking of using muscle instead of mind, where the real strength lay. Apart from the horrendous noise of its passage, no spider injuries were sustained, and the Monitor Corps negotiators pointedly ignored the incident, but thereafter the talking continued more peaceably.

For the ensuing three weeks Prilicla spent his every waking moment with them, including the times when he had to eat, a process which startled but did not disgust the spiders. When the cultural-contact specialists from *Descartes* expertly plied their tridi projections to illustrate and explain in detail the organization and political ramifications of the Galactic Federation to the Crextic—the two Trolanni present had already seen most of it—the spiders' feelings reflected in turn incredulity, wonder, fear, and distrust. By pinpointing the individual emotional radiation of the person concerned, he was able to subtly guide the contact specialist into a conversational area that the other found more reassuring.

Captain Fletcher was also content because a cargo shuttle, too small to do more than scorch an insignificant area of sand on the beach, was plying between the orbiting *Vespasian* and *Rhabwar*, carrying with the relays of cultural-contact specialists the fuel cells and organic and engineering consumables that would shortly result in a virtual refit and resupply of its beloved ambulance ship so that it could again take off with a pressor-beam assist and not burn up half the island as it left.

Then the day came when Prilicla knew that their work on the spider planet was complete, because the supply shuttle touched down with no supplies on board since it carried instead no less a personage than Sector Marshal Dermod.

The dark green Monitor Corps uniform with its insignia of rank and quietly impressive ribbons meant nothing to the Trolanni and Crextic gathered in what had been the station's recovery ward, but the habit of command in its manner said all that was necessary about it as a person—a person who meant exactly what it said.

"My warmest compliments to everyone here who has been involved in successfully concluding this epoch-making agreement between three different intelligent species," it said. "Not only has there been it a first contact between the Federation and the Trolanni, but a second contact with ourselves and the Crextic, and another possible future contact with the druul. . . ."

It looked along the line of joined litters which served as a conference table and raised a hand to quell an outburst from Keet and Jasam, then went on. ". . . I know that you have already discussed this matter with my subordinate officers and members of the medical team, but I am required to restate our position officially. Federation law forbids us to exterminate any intelligent species, regardless of the past and present evidence of their concerted violence and antisocial behavior towards others. Instead, a rigorous and lengthy psychological and sociological assessment will be conducted regarding the possibility of their reeducation. Should the findings go against them and, as our Trolanni friends have insisted, they turn out to be nothing but intelligent and amoral animals, they will not be exterminated. Instead their world will be placed under Federation Interdict until they either become civilized, which seems improbable, or they exterminate themselves.

"The Trolanni currently living among them," it went one, "will be evacuated and transferred, at the invitation of the Crextic, to this planet to share a part of it with them, and to cooperate in the future to the benefit of both species.

"Such an event as this has no precedent in the history of the Federation," Dermod continued, glancing up at the hovering Prilicla, "and we were worried in case it did not succeed and we had the druul-Trolanni conflict repeat itself here. But my empathic advisor assures me that the Crextic and Trolanni feelings, based as they are on mutual help and future scientific and commercial advantages, are honest and will be more long-lasting than any agreement based on empty diplomacies. As a precaution we will observe the situation from orbit. If the cultural contact fails, we will move the Trolanni to another planet which has no sapient life-forms to oppose their resettlement, but I do not foresee that happening because this is a contact that the Crextic and the Tro-lanni both want and need. At no time will we interfere in disputes which you are plainly capable of solving yourselves, nor will we give unwanted technical help, because psychologically that would be bad for both species. In time, perhaps not too long a time as progressing cultures go, I can foresee the Trolanni and the Crex-tic being welcomed into the Galactic Federation.

"But our more immediate plan," it went on briskly, "is to take Jasam and its searchsuit back to Trolann to explain the sit-uation to its people, advise them regarding the evacuation, and begin instructing our scientists regarding the organic-cybernetic interface and the lifesuit technology they use for self-defense. This will have important applications far beyond their use as fully-sensitive limbs for amputees. Meanwhile Keet has elected to re-main here with Irisik to prepare everyone concerned for the arrival of the first Trolanni evacuees. The medical station will be left here for their use as will the remains of *Terragar*. Both will be a constant reminder of the future that lies ahead for both species.

"*Rhabwar*," it added, looking at Prilicla and then Captain Fletcher, "will return to Sector General when convenient."

"Thank you, friend Dermod," said Prilicla.

"Doctor!" the captain said, its face deepening in color and its emotional radiation reflecting shock and embarrassment. "You don't talk that way to a, to a sector marshal!" To its superior officer, it went on quickly, "Please excuse Dr. Prilicla, sir, it some-times takes friendly informality to excess. And yes, sir, we can leave within the hour."

"A degree of informality is acceptable," said the sector mar-shal, its eyes turning towards Prilicla, "especially from someone who has achieved so much here. I feel no insult at your mode of address, little friend, and your empathic faculty is already telling you that, among other things. . . ."

There was an unusual feeling of warmth and expectancy emanating from the sector marshal that was characteristic of a pleasure soon to be shared. It showed its teeth in the grimace Earth-humans called a smile.

". . . Besides," it went on, "just before leaving for this meeting I received a signal from Administrator Braithwaite at the hospital to say that you have been appointed, or, more precisely, you have been elected unanimously to the rank of Diagnostician. My warmest congratulations, friend Prilicla."

To Captain Fletcher it added dryly, "As I recall them, my words were 'when convenient,' not 'as soon as possible.' One does not give orders to a Sector General Diagnostician."